The Candle Is a Fool

A Forty-Day Journey through the Passion of Jesus

David Andrew Thomas

Printed in the United States of America

ISBN 978-1-7330809-4-1

The Candle Is a Fool

For more information about the author please visit
https://agmd.org/u/ThomasEcuador

Published by

JCK

Fort Gratiot, MI

To honor the memory of my father, John R. Thomas,
who first taught me the wisdom of God's folly

For the foolishness of God is wiser than human wisdom, and the weakness of God is stronger than human strength.

~the Apostle Paul, 1 Corinthians 1:25

FOREWORD

When I was a boy, we always had a banner of some sort hanging in our dining room. Handmade by my mother or one of her friends, they displayed spiritual messages and symbols and served as a constant reminder of our Christian heritage. The one that stands out the most in my memory, however, was one made by my father. It simply read, "The Candle Is a Fool." The summary judgment was accompanied by the image of an enormous candle with a dramatic, multi-colored flame. It was beautifully done, and though I knew Dad to be something of a Jack of all trades when it came to knowledge both arcane and practical, the banner introduced me in a new way to his artistic abilities. Along with the banner Dad wrote a short story, no more than a page or so, that was simultaneously whimsical and deeply serious. Set in the Roman barracks in Jerusalem on Good Friday night, the story is narrated not by a person but by a common sponge kept by the soldiers for cleaning. The sponge is the consummate observer and critic, noting that among all the characters it watched from its bucket, none displayed so great a folly as the candle that it saw burning on the table a few feet away. "The candle is a fool," the sponge remarks, because its very purpose is to give itself for others and in so doing to fully expend its very being. Absently, the sponge draws an inference between the candle and the young carpenter that these same soldiers, now enjoying the last of the candle's light and substance, crucified that very day. If only the candle were more like the sponge, the story concludes, absorbing until all it had consumed was squeezed from it perforce, then it would have been so much wiser and happier. Truly, what other life strategy could there be?

Inspired by my father's tale, I began to write this story during the end of my first term as field missionary in Ecuador. Over time, and with the encouragement of good people, I have polished it and expanded it. Obviously, it is a different kind of tale than the one Dad wrote, but at its kernel the message is ultimately the same.

The Candle Is a Fool is different from other biblical fictions in two ways. First, following a long-standing Christian tradition of using imaginative stories to stir Christian faith and practice, I have deliberately written the story to challenge and encourage the reader's personal devotion to Christ. It isn't just a romantic yarn that transports us back to Jesus' day to pass the time or pique our fancy. To better serve its devotional purpose, I have framed the story as a forty-day spiritual pilgrimage, broken into daily readings so that you can walk the journey, step by step, pondering and praying as you go. These forty days symbolically correspond to the forty days of devotion between Ash Wednesday and Resurrection Sunday. The story is, after all, about Jesus' ultimate sacrifice and victory for our redemption. But the book's forty days can, of course, be played out at any time of the year, or read all at once for that matter. The program of daily readings is a suggestion for those interested in following the plot that way.

The second item the reader will almost immediately note is that *The Candle Is a Fool* is filled with details of the biblical world. These are intentionally woven into the narrative, as I want the story to speak for itself. A major goal of the story is to transport you, the reader, in a sort of "you are there" fashion back to the time and perspective of those who experienced these powerful events. I focus heavily but not exclusively on some lesser-known personalities of the Passion story to draw this aspect out. My desire is to relate the drama of Jesus and His disciples in modern storytelling form, but also be as accurate as possible to both the Scriptures and history as we can know it. *The Candle Is a Fool* is carefully researched, even as it appeals to artistic license on those plot gaps and natural human matters that cannot be known about the people Jesus touched, but that we might plausibly imagine. I explain a great deal about these things in the Afterword, which is not included in the forty-day program of readings, but may be read between characters as you go along, or at the end, whichever you might prefer. (For those following the book for Lent, the corresponding character explanations in the Afterword might be read on Sundays, which according to tradition are not numbered among the forty fast days.) This "academic" aspect may serve to enrich your study of the Scriptures even as the flow of the story is intended to enrich your faith.

I should offer a word of preparation to you, the reader, regarding the nature of the story itself. You must know that what the New Testament tells us about Christ's sufferings is a drama neither sentimental nor cheery. While the Gospels and Acts themselves do not revel in violence for its own sake, they are forthright about what happened and, perhaps more accurately, assume a knowledge of these matters in the mind of the reader; the ancient world was often a brutal one and the ancients experienced that brutality firsthand. Consequently, what we find when we read about Jesus' final days and hours is a dark saga filled with betrayal, manipulation, fear, disillusionment, heartbreak, shocking cruelty, and death by public torture. It is also a story of true heroism and, on the part of some, unexpected virtue. It has rightly been called "the greatest story ever told." This legacy carries over into the history of the early church. The tale is finally redeemed as bright and hopeful not by the conclusion that things weren't really as bad as all that, but rather that as horrific as they were Christ nevertheless endured it all for our sake and rose from the dead to bring us eternal life. For these reasons the writer J.R.R. Tolkien calls Jesus' Passion-and-Resurrection a "eucatastrophe"—a "good disaster"—because of how God uses it to redeem us.

Before I conclude this foreword, I would offer thanks and recognition to those who have helped me along the way as I developed the story. More than I can remember commented and encouraged me during various draft stages, and these will forgive me if they remain unnamed due to my faulty memory. But I do wish to thank especially my brother, Roger Thomas, a skilled writer and published author himself, who has always encouraged me in this project. Roger's role in proofing, formatting, and facilitating the publishing of the book cannot be overstated; he is my brother in both senses of the word. Ted Terry was the first professional voice to express serious interest in the story and prompted its first significant expansion. Dr. Joseph Castleberry of Northwest University was particularly helpful, and his thoughtful suggestions regarding style and content at a crucial juncture made a significant difference in the final version. Dr.

Jeremiah Webster, also of Northwest, was a great help, as was my good friend, the widely published Dr. Wayde Goodall, who read the manuscript early and always spurred me on towards the book's realization. Frank Breeden of Premiere Authors also encouraged me to further develop and strengthen the story. A special thanks to Rav Yitzchok Adlerstein of the Simon Wiesenthal Center, who corrected me on Jewish customs and saved me significant embarrassment. Wilson López of Guayaquil, Ecuador provided the photographic skills upon which my son, Joseph, elaborated for the cover art. Writing the final stages of the story coincided with my daughter Eden's childhood, the two deeply intertwined in my memories. Most of all, I thank my very patient wife, Patti, who has provided vital pointers as she read and re-read the manuscript over the years. She and my entire family have continually offered invaluable moral support and guidance on polish and presentation. Any errors or flaws found herein are, of course, my own.

"Why?" is perhaps the most sensible question we can ask about the Passion, and we might direct it toward any number of details associated with those fateful hours and days. *The Candle Is a Fool* is my attempt to ask and answer that question through the experiences of biblical personalities both unknown and under-known. More specifically, why, on Jesus' darkest day, did witnesses to His death agonies—people who up to that hour had not known or even met Him—inexplicably and incredibly come to see Him as the righteous, innocent, sovereign Son of God? And why, in the days and weeks and years following His resurrection, did His disciples choose the path of sacrifice that they knew must end for them as it had ended for Him.

> *And the light in the darkness shines, but the darkness*
> *has not comprehended it. ~ John 1:5*

David Andrew Thomas
Louisville, Kentucky
March 25, 2020

Part I

Mary of Bethany and Judas Iscariot

I Am who probes mind and heart…
~Revelation 2:23

THE WASTE

Mary of Bethany

John 12:1-8, Luke 10:38-42, Mark 14:3-8, Matthew 26:6-11

Day One

She had just finished kneading the last of the dough when Martha hurried in, bringing more water from the cistern, and an air of something more.

"The Teacher comes," she announced with a mixture of elation, anxiety, and the particular tone that trims the voice of a hostess who knows important folk will soon taste her cooking. Mary gave her an accepting look, but kept her own counsel as she finished the loaves and set them to baking on the hearth.

The Teacher comes. As he had before, now he came again. Mary and her brother and sister knew him, and he knew and loved them. Bethany, their village, lay about fifteen stadia east of Jerusalem on the lee slope of the Mount of Olives. For a couple of years now their house had served him as a home away from home, a convenient hostel while he ministered in the Holy City. Nobody would have called this reception their first. And yet, though fully expected, her sister's announcement went through Mary with a thrill that surpassed Martha's nervous joy as the autumn gust surpasses a summer breeze. The Teacher came to see them, as he had before. And they would welcome him as they had, offering their best—even as they knew that things had changed and would never feel as they had at the beginning.

Mary and Martha worked together with practiced urgency, bustling between the kitchen and the courtyard, their individual labors in the cramped spaces resembling something of an agreed upon discord as they strove to finish their work. The Lord would soon arrive. Just as pressing, though, was the fading of the light. The afternoon waned, and Sabbath eve would soon be upon them. They had already prepared rooms for the Lord and a few of his disciples (the others would lodge in nearby homes), but the final touches of the Sabbath meal remained.

Mary paused for a moment now, unwilling to let some other task distract her and lead to the ruin of her bread. Her sister, always in control, did not.

"I will check on the goat," Martha said absently and a bit short of breath, and went out.

Mary looked about her. The plain walls of her home looked back at her, tinged with the warm color of late afternoon. Though the current atmosphere in the house was gladsome, its very stones whispered memories of pain and sorrow. Indeed, it seemed they spoke suffering as their native language.

The youngest of the three, Mary could not recall the days when her then-prosperous family left their comfortable home in Jerusalem for this village. She was too small at the time. But Martha, and Lazarus (though not as clearly), remembered, and they had told her. Their father, Simon, once respected and well-connected, fell leprous. The disease first came upon his arms as a pronounced dry blush. Simon was too pious a man to try to hide something the Law required him to reveal, but denial besets the pure of speech as surely as deceit the profane, so he wore his clothes carefully and he hoped. When it spread to his left hand, however, and began to scale, he did his duty. Thus began a tumultuous and exhausting season during which the priests repeatedly declared him unclean, then clean again, then once again unclean, and so on. The affliction would not be still. Only Martha remembered her father's grave tone and her mother's fearful, drawn expression the day when the decision finally came down, with no more turning. He must go and dwell outside the camp. He must leave the Holy City.

Simon's wife would never have left him even had she other options to consider; she had none. But it were better to be lepers than a widow and her orphans, and without Simon, though he yet lived, such would be the essence of their lot without him. In the eyes of their fellow Jews, they would all live as the unclean. The family trade could continue, albeit greatly humbled, with them under one roof. They would suffer together, but they would eat and they would have each other. And as stern and juristic as the priests were in their pronouncements, the one mite they threw Simon through indirect hints and artful silence was their tacit tolerance of this arrangement. They knew the leprosy afflicted

Simon alone and would not touch his kin (it never did), but the Law was the Law. God had smitten the man, and go he must; if his family wanted to share his banishment, no one would stop them.

And so they had removed to Bethany—the House of Affliction. The Essenes, Israel's strictest sect, had founded the city in an act born of mercy and their fierce devotion to the codes of ritual purity. The unclean must keep their distance, and the Sanctuary must not behold them. But here in this little village for the destitute they might be as close to the Holy as the rules would allow, and could gather the scraps that fell from the banquet table that was Jerusalem. It made for a bitter draught. Her parents' grief during their first days in this dismal village, though not living memory for Mary, folded itself into the very fabric of her young personality, as unhappy chapters in one's primal childhood are wont to. The chronic nature of her father's illness continued, and they lived through one season of heartbreaking hope after another during which its uncleanness seemed to have left him for good. But just as the discussions grew serious, and arrangements for their return took on life, it would come back upon him. This cycle happened time and again—Simon could never rid himself of the leprosy until the day of his death—till joy grew rarer than silver. Though the rash never spread beyond his arms and hands, his new name among acquaintances and strangers alike was a moniker of shame: Simon the Leper. Those people, after all, acted their own roles in how these things must play out, and that meant to shun. Lepers had spoken something they shouldn't have, and that is why this had befallen them. If the words of the Law read thus of kings and prophets, how much more a common man? Simon, always careful, always circumspect, fell silent and turned in on himself, wondering what he had said or done that had brought this exile upon his family. Brooding and confused, and increasingly afraid to touch his children, he became a different man.

Bethany, truly.

But, with his wife, he somehow managed to make a home there. They raised their little ones, and although self-respect wouldn't be the word for it, in the course of time Simon achieved a certain stature in the place. His neighbors, after all, shared misfortunes akin to his, else they wouldn't have lived there. Even an ash heap has its princes. Bethany also served as a last stop of sorts for those travelers (mostly Galileans) who, avoiding Samaria, walked the valley of the Jordan then pilgrimaged up the road from Jericho to Jerusalem. Tired and in need of food and drink at the crest of a steep, long climb, they would buy what his wife and children set before them. So by the time their parents passed away, Martha and Mary—still young—knew how to receive and refresh the weary, and the House of Simon the Leper had a modest reputation all its own.

Martha touched her arm.

"The Teacher is here."

Prayer: *Lord Jesus, even in my uncleanness You have chosen to come to me again and again. Fill me with holy hope and wonder in anticipation of Your visitation. I know that whatever I prepare for You, in the end, incredibly, it is I myself that You desire. Give me the grace of humility to believe that great truth, and to receive You through surrender. Amen.*

Day Two

They received him together—Martha, Lazarus, and Mary—at their door. He appeared as he had on previous visits, beaming, gracious, and humbly accepting their hospitality as if he were any common traveler in need, grateful for the unexpected welcome. Indeed, he looked genuinely footsore and ready for a rest. But as through a cheap cloth poorly veiling its wearer, Mary perceived his lordship gleaming past the dust of the road. Though his disciples seemed more concerned with arrangements and the Master's dignity than he himself ever did, there shone that intangible in the posture, the movements, the expression that bespoke the power her family had already seen gloriously revealed. How could this moment be real? How should she act? How could they welcome Jesus of Nazareth as if this were any other visit, week of the Feast though it be? Mary gazed at him in the midst of the general hubbub, feeling disconnected from it all while Lazarus fairly glowed and Martha tried to maintain her composure. Well, Mary thought, the Lord is weary, and he shall have his rest. The Sabbath is nearly upon him, and the Sabbath meal would be given in his honor. Martha had seen to it, with Mary's help. They would give him that, anyway. She shook inside for her other thoughts, but Martha's urgings dispelled them.

"The basins, sister, the basins! And the water!"

Of course, of course. They must wash and ready themselves first. Mary got to it while Martha was off to the kitchen. Soon enough the men were refreshed and fully received into their lodgings. The Teacher and his inner circle of disciples had found their rooms and unburdened themselves of their (very limited) belongings. Lazarus hovered joyfully, eager to receive the Lord at the table set for him, but not wanting to hurry his guest unduly. The sun dipped low. Mary heard Simon Peter murmuring something to his Master and the Lord's low reply, then they emerged and made their way to the place where all had assembled. Mary stood just outside the room, listening to their voices and especially bending her ear for *his* voice—*the* voice— but for the moment all remained indistinguishable to her. The men talked on, loudly here, softly there, now laughing a bit. A festive expectation mingled with solemnity filled the air. Lazarus invited, urged; Jesus reclined, and the others followed suit.

Martha stood there now, holding a flagon of wine. She inquired of her sister with her eyes, and Mary stepped briefly into the doorway, surveying the room, then stepped aside with a nod. All reclined at table and the holy feast could begin. Mary watched as Martha filled the cups while the men around the table gave themselves to their conversation. The Teacher reclined on the near side, next to Lazarus. Martha poured his wine now, looking serious for the responsibility, almost grave, but the Teacher smiled up at her and softly spoke a few words. That earned him a self-conscious smile in return, and Martha moved on to her brother. By the time she had finished, Mary had fetched the bread and now placed it on the table before the Lord. She, too, heard him thank her kindly, but all she could manage was a quick bow of her head before she turned and hurried out, her belly aflutter. She glanced over her shoulder as the lamps were lit and the prayers began, and the last thing her eyes saw were the feet of the Master crossed behind him as he rocked slowly with the voices raised in song around the room.

The feet of the Lord. Yes, and how could she forget? He arrived that first time, a couple years ago now, and Martha welcomed him into their home. His Galilean fame had spread even unto Judea, and they were honored to receive him. But while Martha had fulfilled her role as the lady of the house, Mary had defaulted. She tried, truly, to behave as if her chores weighed most heavily on her mind and as if the Teacher spoke and behaved as any other rabbi might. But she could not because he did not. She caught bits of what he spoke to his disciples, and she had never heard such things—the most beautiful words as had ever sounded in her ears. She couldn't help but eavesdrop, lingering more and more while she labored, and the Teacher finally caught her eye. She started, expecting a stern look; surely he meant his words for the men who followed him, and not a gawking young woman who'd do better to mind her chores. But no, there she saw the approval in his eyes—a look that reminded her a little bit (and oddly, from a man so young) of her father. Soon she found her place on the floor by his feet, leaning on one hand with face upturned, rapt, her scullery cloth forgotten in her lap. The benevolent consent that came from his face stilled the last of her qualms, and if his disciples had had any objections, it quieted them, too. Only Martha found the situation unacceptable. When she had turned to give her sister an order, Mary was nowhere to be found. Upon discovering the truant at the Master's feet, Martha promptly enlisted the Teacher's righteousness to aid in the chastisement of her sister.

"Lord, don't you give a care that my sister has left me to do all the work by myself?" she fussed, glaring indignantly down at her. "Well, tell her to help me!"

Ah, that small matter of naming him *Lord*, only to take issue with his ways and order him about.

"Martha, Martha…" he began, with no less affection—or authority—than he had bestowed upon his newest disciple.

No, Mary would not be the only woman that Jesus of Nazareth schooled that day in the gospel of the Kingdom. He brought a minor revolution in the House of Simon the Leper, or so they both thought. Little did they realize the import of that exchange, and the true meaning this holy man invested in his upheaval of their domestic order. Martha harbored no rancor afterward, and the two sisters wondered together about the young rabbi and his peculiarities. But they had only begun to learn from him.

Prayer: Lord Jesus, I confess that I have been busy and distracted by many things. Grant me the wisdom and the grace to be drawn in by Your words, to sit at Your feet, and to commune with You. And as I dare to enjoy You in a world that cannot even bring itself to respect You, grant me the strength to endure the ill-conceived chastisement of those who do not understand. Amen.

Day Three

Now both sisters worked to lay the table with the fruit of their labor. More bread, figs, and the roast meat went by Martha's hand while Mary nervously filled the plates for her to take to the men. Her hands shook as she filled a bowl with fruit, and for a moment a tender, quizzical expression overtook Martha's businesslike demeanor.

"Come see, my sister, all is going quite well."

And so she came. Yes, they enjoyed themselves, eating and gesturing and amiably interrupting each other. Two of the disciples at the far side of the table were telling a story while the others chuckled. Mary wanted to see what the Lord did, how he would respond, but she couldn't see his face. She looked at her brother's profile, his visage shining in the lamplight, and if his joy told her anything the Master was indeed content.

The crowds had been growing over the last several days, seeking a glimpse of Lazarus. He had been raised from the dead. The Lord Jesus had raised him. Her brother had been dead—*dead*. And the Lord Jesus had raised him up, from the grave, from the dead. Of course they wanted a glimpse of Lazarus. Mary herself still wanted glimpses of him. She wanted to stare at him, and found herself doing exactly that. She did it now. After her eyes had drunk in enough for the moment, Lazarus' own laughter broke the spell and she turned away, more shaken than any faltering labor might show.

It had descended upon them in a matter of a day, indeed, almost within an hour. His stomach went sour, and then the stabbing pain ripped into his side; the fever and cottonmouth came next. Mary and Martha took turns laving his brow and administering drops of water to the tongue because his belly wouldn't take anything else. The fever broke in the darkness before the dawn, but came raging back with the rising of the sun. When the delirium started and he began to mumble nonsense, the sisters knew it was no passing thing. Martha's motherly concern and Mary's tenderness united to overcome their mutual fears, and together they decided they needed to send for the Lord, and now. Though the religious leaders had recently threatened him grievously, prompting his withdrawal across the Jordan, the women were desperate.

Catastrophe has a way of revealing what lies in the heart, and had the sisters' familiarity with the Master resembled that of so many others who sought his favor in crisis, they might have pondered a more elaborate plea. But they knew him indeed, or thought they did, and the message they sent said as much in its economy as it did by its content: *Lord, he whom you love ails.* They enlisted a dependable, hardy friend, told him where he would likely find Jesus—a full day's journey an earnest man might make by sundown—and sent him running down the Jericho Road. With Martha back at Lazarus' side, Mary stood and watched the messenger go. She stared him out of sight as if her longing gaze could speed him towards his destination and return with the Healer before she had to turn away and go back to her sick brother and her own fevered hopes.

But by the time she drew more water and found her place by the bedside, a gurgling rasp sounded in Lazarus' throat. For all their efforts and prayers, he breathed his last before the sun was high.

Martha, standing with her head bowed, wept quietly; she would keep herself together, and she would think of what must be done next when she could overcome her shock and sorrow. Mary, though, could not bring herself to leave Lazarus' side. They had shared a tender, unique bond with their brother, and the grief of his departure cut and numbed them all at once. And that was not all. Those ancient stories of Simeon and Levi defending Dinah's honor, of Laban bartering with Eleazar for Rebekah's sake, well, they were more than mere legend. A brother played a central role in arranging a woman's marriage, even while their father lived. With him gone, as things stood in their case, Lazarus had become more important still. Both Martha (though older) and Mary still had hopes for security and a family. In this patriarchal world those hopes had suffered a devastating and perhaps irreparable blow.

The Teacher's coming was at least a day and a half away. If she could have, Mary would have begged to delay the entombment. Death lay fresh on Lazarus, and life might yet be lingering nearby. They had heard the stories, the amazement in the disciples' voices as they described the miracle of the little girl, and of the widow's son. The Lord Jesus had called these ones back before they were too far gone; surely he could do this for them, too. He could do it for Lazarus. But the reality of death, and the force of customary respect for the dead, led to the inevitable. They washed and anointed the corpse, wrapped it in linen cloths, and buried their brother before dark.

Martha held Mary like a child that night and they wept themselves to sleep. How could this be? Their childhoods had been destroyed by an ugly rash that nowadays must flee powerless at the Master's touch—nay, at his *bidding*. Simon their father had died before the name *Jesus of Nazareth* meant anything to any of them. Grievous as it pained them, this they did not question. Today's sorrow, however, cut the deeper and the bitterer. Now they *did* know Jesus, loved him for himself, welcomed him, even at risk. They had given themselves to him. And he had known and loved them. Not only had his name meant much to them, their names meant something to him (didn't they?). But in the end it had made no difference. The son had died as the father had died, prayers unanswered. Lazarus had been the friend of a healer who could tame the deadliest ills by his glance, but now lay in the ground as cold as the next corpse. What good had it done him to love and serve the miracle worker? Lying there in the gloom, Mary did not understand, could not understand, and her darkness of mind tormented her as nothing she could remember. The Lord might have been there, but he was not. He could have healed before death came and claimed her brother, but his mysterious comings and goings had made that impossible. It seemed to Mary that while her father's death had been a tragedy, her brother's had been a waste. How could the Master heal strangers—mere anybodies who took hold of him as he passed them by—and not come and touch the one he loved and spare them wave upon wave of grief? Why hadn't he come? Hers was not a reasonable question, and she knew it. Lazarus succumbed before the Master could have even received their call. But her complaint sounded all the louder within her for its lack of reason, because it birthed from the hurricane chaos of her despair rather than her ordered thoughts. And so it persisted, like a millstone grinding in her tortured brain: Jesus could do anything. Why hadn't he done this?

The sun rose the next day like Mary knew it would. And with it began the mourning, a lament that would exhaust them as much as their brother's mortal illness had. But their grief was all they had left of him, truly, so they did not begrudge it. The last thing a loved one does to you is wound you—the deeper the love, the deeper the wound. That parting stab would have sufficed to keep Mary weeping over her brother for days on end. But she also grieved another. When the sun set that second day, a new sorrow deepened; when it set the third the sorrow grew deeper still. The Lord had heard, the Lord had received the message; but even knowing, the Lord had not come. Now she grieved not just her brother. In a way, she lamented her Lord as well. And by her side, her sister shared her laments.

Prayer: *Lord Jesus, Your ways are not my ways, and Your thoughts are not my thoughts. I rarely understand You, and many of those times I thought I did, I was mistaken. Help me in my weakness not to become bitter when You act like God and not like a good luck charm. Have mercy on my untamed emotions. Help me trust You to work things out according to Your perfect will for me, sight unseen, which is always best. Amen.*

Day Four

Jesus' voice made her start and she realized she had been gazing into their midst at nothing in particular, and she refocused in time to see him in the lamplight, smiling and nodding at someone's remark. Martha fluttered past her, busy but content and seeming happy for the moment to leave Mary to her thoughts.

He came in the late afternoon on the fourth day of Lazarus' death. Four days. Though the sisters didn't know the exalted theology mooted by the scribes, they very much felt what those sages universally concluded: after the third day, no hope remained. Death had been death and no swoon, and their brother would not be coming back to them. The numbness began to subside, leaving only the pain. So when the rumor of the Lord's arrival filtered through the crowd of keening mourners, Martha chose not to disturb her sister. She left Mary where she grieved, sitting on the unswept floor of the house where, years ago, she had first listened to Jesus' teachings. It fell to her as the eldest anyway, so she slipped out as discretely as she could and made her way to the place Jesus awaited her.

Mary was so overwhelmed by her emotions, and those of her guests, that she had only barely become aware of her sister's absence by the time she returned. But now Martha crouched and whispered something in her ear while the other women milled about. Mary started at first, but immediately inclined her ear to the message, then turned to look Martha in the eye. Rising suddenly, she was out and off down the path to the main road. She didn't notice the gaggle of women that followed her, so singular was her intent and determined her gait.

The Lord was seated upon a rock, surrounded on either side by his disciples when she saw him. Straight towards him she went. He rose to meet her, but running at the end she collapsed before him, sobbing from a reservoir she didn't know she still held within her. Through her blinding tears she made her complaint known, lifting her face only enough to behold his sandaled feet. Over the weeping of the others, Mary heard the Teacher's voice ask where they had laid Lazarus. Oh, that voice. It was compassionate, it was tender to her plight, but as warmly as it spoke to her sorrow, something altogether deeper than natural human grief moved it. In it rang a profounder lament, a more sorrowful resignation, and another love than Mary's mortal ears had known.

Mary arose and gathered herself as best she could at the invitation. With the crowd following behind, she led the Lord, now weeping himself, to where her brother lay.

The details, the sequence of what happened next, Mary could never forget. Her mind, then, did not rehearse these things for posterity's sake, as if to ensure for her children an accurate retelling of what Jesus of Nazareth, the young rabbi from Galilee, did that afternoon. No, she went over and over them in her mind as a bride runs her hands over her wedding jewels. She deliberately remembered them as a mother strokes the head of her babe, once and again, because those curls were already unforgettable. There came the order, Martha's ever-present concern for domestic decency, and Jesus' direct but tenderly instructive retort. They rolled the stone back as he had said. He stood before the opening and spoke to the heavens while Mary covered her mouth—not for the stench, but for the something she felt coming.

Then sounded the Master's booming voice, commanding Lazarus from the tomb, calling him by name.

And Lazarus came forth.

In the hours and days that followed, the sisters' wonder over how to receive their brother again was exceeded only by the dilemma of how to receive the one who had restored him to them. Had King David himself arisen, warm and ruddy, and asked for lodging in their home, their amazement could not have been greater. Just who was this man, this Jesus? Who *was* he? Even those things Martha had spoken to him that day—those names and titles—had she understood any of it, really? Thinking back, she flushed to remember her cheek in ordering the Lord to command her sister to get up off the floor when he later showed the stuff of his authority by commanding her brother to get up out of the grave. A compliant teacher you might draft to do your bidding, but when you find one who proves he will indeed raise you up on the Last Day, you realize you may not have them both.

As for Mary, whatever envious thoughts she had harbored towards the others who seemingly could come and go with the Lord as they pleased—Magdalene, Joanna, and the others—those thoughts died when Lazarus came to life. And now as she stood in the doorway of the feasting room, trembling again, she knew what she had to do. She turned and made her way to the place where she slept.

****

If the disciples who walked with him had responded with fear when their Teacher had calmed the storm, what of a simple woman who saw him raise the dead—*her* dead? And her fear, her awestruck wonder, was the beginning of wisdom for her. She understood more by each passing day that *miracle* was not a strong enough word to describe what had been done for her. Surely, at first, she saw things that way. Others had been given their cleanness, their legs, their sight, and now she had been given a wonder as well—just greater according to her need. Here was why she no longer felt jealous of the others; the Master had noticed her, too, as when her father had given her a gift to match that which he had given Martha when they were girls. But it gradually came to her, and grew in her, that life from death is no mere miracle, and that Jesus of Nazareth was no common miracle worker, if there was such a thing.

With an understanding she did not fully understand, with the eyes behind her eyes, she began to behold him. Her fear grew, but it was a loving fear, a holy fascination that drew her in instead of repelling her. It wrapped its arms around her inner self and called her its own. Who was Jesus of Nazareth? How easily "messiah" had rolled off her tongue—as it did everyone's tongue—as a voiced longing for whatever kind of utopic change one hoped and wished for. *If only I would come into wealth; if only a friend would come to power; if only the Messiah would come.* Now she realized she could not have been more wrong. Messiah was no champion, not even in the sense of a Samson or a Jephthah. This messiah—surely *the* Messiah—came entirely for his own purposes, acted according to those purposes, and did nothing to satisfy human whims or win another cheering follower. *Joy* was his quest, and he would not allow mere happiness—or sentiment, even less—to frustrate his victory. Something deeper than her instincts told her that with every miracle and every word, whether apparently small or breathtakingly mighty, this Messiah answered not just momentary griefs but the everyman trial that comes of being a sinner in a broken world. He answered not just questions but life itself, and as he did, he laid claim to all and expected all to obey as surely as her brother's dead body had obeyed, bound hand and foot though it was. The glorious weight of what had happened in the House of Simon the Leper, the immeasurable greatness of the Master's work for her and in her now compelled Mary. To admit him to be who the miracles proclaimed he must be could mean only one course of action for her; to refuse that surrender would mean turning her back on both miracle and man, because the meaning of the one led inevitably to the identity of the other.

Tucked away in a small cubby in the wall near the head of her pallet lay the trove of her secret things. Her siblings knew about it, just as she knew of theirs. Many of the baubles she kept hidden there held value only for her and her memories; no robber would have given them a second look. But behind it all, and disguised with a stone and bit of loose mortar, Mary guarded her most cherished possession. Ever the conscientious patriarch, even in his destitution the Leper had cached wealth from more prosperous days to ease his children's path forward after he had gone. This beautiful thing looked back to her father and forward to the one who would take his place in her life, for Simon had gifted it to his daughter to keep for the occasion of her betrothal. The alabaster flask—itself very precious—held within a treasure that made it costly far beyond Mary's own ability to redeem. The *litra* of spikenard unguent would serve her as a handsome dowry, a powerful inducement in the hand of her brother to seal the marriage contract and secure her future. Mary pulled the stone out and laid it aside, then dug a little with her fingers, pulling the flask from its place. Unwrapping it carefully—a cloth protected the satiny smooth surface from harm—she looked at it, shining softly in the lamplight. Its cool globe filled her unsteady hands, a dense and weighty prize. After contemplating it for a moment, pondering all this priceless thing meant to her, she stood, turned on her heel, and walked out, carrying her secret with her.

Prayer: *Lord Jesus, forgive me for having tried to bend Your power to accomplish my will. I turn away from having trivialized Your lordship in my life, and I seek to embrace You on Your terms alone. Guide me by Your truth to that place where my search for happiness gives way to the joy You have for me, and through You in me, joy for others. Whom have I in heaven but You? And earth has nothing I desire besides You. Amen.*

Day Five

Martha served on the far side of the table when Mary entered the room, while the men busied themselves with their food and their small talk. Lazarus did not notice his younger sister. She hadn't told her siblings of her plan, of course. In former days they surely would have stopped her had they known, but given all that had happened, who could know what they would say now? No matter. Keeping it to herself had nothing to do with their approval one way or the other. Her own heart, now pounding in her breast, gave her more than enough to deal with. Besides, devotion of the kind that drove her always proceeds from a place within that does not readily explain itself to others. She had agreed to something and that covenant constrained her, revealed to her that gestures weren't enough anymore.

Mary held the alabaster in one hand and grasped its narrow neck through the cloth with the other. This was the point of no return; the flask and its contents were by design intended as a rare luxury—once broken the nard could no longer be preserved, and so its user must pour it out all at once in a single, ostentatious binge. She pursed her lips and felt rather than heard the fragile carved stone of the flask half-crack, half-crumble in her hand. For all the times she had taken it out to admire it and daydream how it might fulfill its purpose for her, she was amazed at how easily it yielded to her fingers. She wasn't breathing now, it seemed, but she was moving toward the Lord. *Courage*, she whispered to herself. Now she stood behind him. The talking went on but the room might have been dead silent for her consciousness of it, and for the blood singing in her ears. She felt Lazarus aware of her, and Martha had stopped going from guest to guest. But these things her eyes saw dimly, and in the background. What truly filled them was the vision of the ointment flowing out onto her Master's hair, dripping down the locks in all directions, as if it were a living thing doing what it had been born to do. She had done it. The King, the Son of David, had been anointed. No one moved or spoke, though Jesus seemed to bow his head slightly, and turn a bit to the right, toward her, as the ointment coursed down his brow.

There was too much for his head, but Mary's inner voice urged her on. *Pour it all out. Give him everything or you haven't given him anything.* Yet in truth Mary had already moved beyond giving—she responded, rather, answering as best she could to the King's unspoken but deafening declaration: he was her rightful sovereign and she his handmaiden. And she gave the only proper answer. By her yielding she acknowledged him, declared who he was.

Now Mary turned and knelt, almost collapsing as she had when she had quite nearly accused the Lord that day, the day he revealed his glory. The initial shock of her own action had given way to super-awareness, and she knew the murmurs and rustlings going on around her were directed at the spectacle she had made of herself. Well did a leper's daughter know the burn of shaming eyes. The Lord's bare feet, in front of her again, lay together behind him on the couch as he reclined at table.

How does one touch the Passover lamb? Does one roughly shove it aside because it is doomed? Do you coddle it as if it were a pet or absently feed it dainties as if it would see the morrow? No, if you touch it at all you do so after a fashion befitting its place and what it will suffer on your behalf. Mary intuited these things, but she did not fathom what she felt. Something beyond her mind's ability to grasp moved her, and she merely yielded. No one else besides Jesus of Nazareth knew he was that Lamb; Mary was the only one besides him in that room who sensed it, and even she couldn't know that she knew. What she did understand was that the only proper response for the young rabbi who raised her dead brother was to give up her own life—was, in a way, to die herself. It was one thing to prove oneself deserving of a noble demonstration by saving another from disaster. Had the Master come and healed, what gift could repay him? But Jesus had taught her that wisdom abides not in the vain attempt to avoid tragedy, but rather in the mysterious power to redeem life through it. This truth bound itself up in every incomprehensible decision he made, in every riddle he spoke, indeed, in his very person. Truly, he applied it above all else to himself. The Teacher therefore had shown himself worthy not just of his disciple's honor, but also of her folly; not only must she bless his royalty, but also his humility.

She upended the alabaster, emptying its last drops onto the motionless feet before her. Someone gasped. Mary dropped the useless flask onto the floor, forgotten. Now she would finish her worship. Bending low, she reached up and stripped her tresses of their dignity, cast aside their covering, and, like a sable curtain, she let her glory fall. She made herself the slave and her hair her Lord's rag, that he might enjoy the richness due his majesty and not be burdened by its excesses. And as for that divine fragrance that filled the place, did it not proceed from his very bosom? Jesus himself was the Balm of Gilead.

Mary completed her servitude and, overwhelmed, bowed still, with a tremor of shame running through her—shame not for her extravagance or impropriety, but for the realization that all this might not be enough, surely could never be enough. Any pretense of strength, pretense of leverage, pretense of self-ownership—all this had abandoned her. She had exerted power by surrendering all power in the company of the strong. But God offers his gift publicly, in the presence of strangers, inviting the mockery of fools. He does so because the solitary soul who responds gratefully is worth the price he pays in abuse from the many. Mary, instinctively, had followed that lead, had told that story by her prodigal self-abasement.

And as if on cue, the next lines in the drama came. But they did not come from the Lord Jesus.

"Why this waste?" the incensed voice called out. The room stirred. Mary could not raise her head; her forehead remained inappropriately close to Jesus' heel. But she recognized by the Judean accent that this must be Judas Iscariot, the only non-Galilean among the Twelve.

31

"Why, why," he sputtered in theatrical outrage, "this surely could have been sold for three hundred denarii—a full year's wages! It—it could have been given to the poor!"

Murmurs of approval for his words rose here and there about the room; Judas seemed to have sympathizers for his sentiments, and they joined in his rebuke. As obvious as the sky above, Bethany's poverty lay all about them, and Mary had squandered that which could have brought relief to a great many of her neighbors. Her own family had so very little, and this the key to lift the burden of herself from them was no more. If she had a thought to spend her only reserves, where was her sense for their need?

Mary hid herself behind her Lord in that moment, feeling very small. For an instant, her mind saw double. Perhaps she had erred, perhaps she had done wrong. But the center of her heart that had decided the matter days ago—that did not quail. A unique confidence always accompanies reckless abdication to a clear conscience. Tears filled her eyes. Who were they to speak of *waste*? The gift must needs transcend questions of poverty and wealth because *we* are the payment, *we* are the toll, *we* are the price for his glory in our midst. As for the worshiper, nothing can be taken from her who gives all she is and has away. And nothing will be denied her who offers her poverty to him for whom wealth is an afterthought. If death cannot resist him, what is lack? What is the future? With her soul answered, she could afford to give not just wealth but herself—her very life and her fears.

"Leave her alone."

The Teacher spoke with half, nay, a *fraction* of Judas' volume, but somehow the thunder of his indignation filled that place and silenced all else. Mary lifted her face and saw Jesus looking to her rather than her detractors. In his eyes burned an admiration that made Mary feel smaller still, but in a wonderful way, a way that made her feel safe forever. Jesus knew her, and in that knowing he made her to know his amazement that *she had known him*. His regard was her reward. Once again, her Lord proclaimed that the better thing that Mary had chosen would not be taken from her.

"Why do you bother her? She has done a beautiful thing to me—she has anointed me for my burial beforehand. The poor you will ever have with you, but you will not always have me. Truly, what she has done for me will be proclaimed wherever the good news is told, in all the world, as a testimony."

Prayer: Lord Jesus, I choose to break the alabaster of my life and pour out the poverty of my person upon Your feet, as if it were wealth. I choose, but I lack the ability to carry out my choice. Lord, turn my weakness into strength. I trust in Your love for me, that You will look upon this that I offer with eyes of mercy, You will defend my heart against the voices that would shame me, and You will cause Your acceptance to enter my inmost being and change who I am so that I might rest in Your presence. Amen.

NIGHT

Judas Iscariot

Matthew 26:14-16; Mark 14:10-11; Luke 22:3-6; John 13:2-30

Day Six

Judas stared into the olive groves of the Kidron Valley. Though he watched the pilgrims streaming down the hillside, he might have been looking into a wasteland for all that he really took in as he sat and seethed. Yes, Judas was angry. But Judas' fuming was cold and deep, not the flushed, hot variety that some of his more impetuous brothers tended to display. Had Simon felt this angry he might have sworn an oath or raged, only to whimper like a dog about the whole affair an hour later. No, Judas prided himself on a more calculating temperament, a temperament that saw things clearly and made cool-headed decisions he wouldn't regret later. And as his gaze idled upon the monotonous progress of the devout, the decision of his life rolled over and over in his chest.

He had a right to his offense. Yes, he did. The Teacher had upbraided him in front of the others, demeaned him for a woman's sake. Why entrust him with the treasury if he could not speak plain truth about the proper use of treasure? Judas Iscariot was no mere beast of burden. He had his dignity, and he had lofty regard for his abilities. Even the Teacher, in his better moments, would have admitted as much. And yet other words and actions had thus repaid his loyal service—Judas scolded and silenced in the presence of his brothers, all for the flattery of a woman. As usual, the Teacher went on with things as if he had immediately forgotten the entire affair, all lessons and benevolence. But Judas would not forget. Not this time.

"Do you see them yet, Judas?"

He started slightly, as if his pitched thoughts might speak aloud to those who drew near. Here with guileless smiles came Philip and Andrew.

"Ah, no, not yet," he feigned, returning their greeting as if he had been on the sharp lookout. "But…"

"Look! There!"

Emerging from behind some shrubs, and going decidedly against the flow, appeared Simon and John. They led a small donkey by a rope. Andrew raised his voice and received a response. He and Philip started down, but thought the better of it and ran the other way, back towards the others. Judas got to his feet.

Yes, came the thought, go back to your master. They bring the mount, after all, for *him*. The men with the colt stepped free of the crowded road now, making their way to the crest, towards him. But Judas stood a solitary man. The anger, momentarily suppressed by the need for decorum, resurged. Under normal human circumstances that emotion rarely listens to reason, but his crouched within him, a brute beast beyond taming. All but over was the struggle between the sincere conviction that he spent these years with a great man (yea, the greatest of men), the clarion vision of that man's selfless love—and the opposite suspicion that all the messiah talk had finally gone to the Teacher's head. The latter voice had never debated with the former, for surely it could never have won the argument; it had merely spoken first and last and loudest. Now all that remained on the battlefield of his soul were questions that ran to and fro like pillaging mercenaries: *Who does he think he is? To what end has he led you? What will you have to show for all this? What is your next step? What will become of you?*

This inner cloud did not vaguely resemble anything like a careful mulling; the questions did not put themselves to their host as if to seek real answers. No parsing of the past or the present turned within Judas. His thinking reflected the final contrary shift that happened within him that Sabbath's eve meal as the rebuke sounded in his ears. Naturally, he felt insulted. But underneath the umbrage, and in fact the true root of it, rose the shapeless realization that the Teacher's words went far beyond the defense of an overly emotional female. Their Galilean rabbi had admitted something. No, that was not right. He had *declared* it, rather, and taught it with the full weight of intention. Yes. The others might not have understood the instruction's import, but Judas had. Here now, after all they had been through, after all they had suffered together, there would be but one figure, one focus, one adored luminary—and hence only one beneficiary—among them. That conclusion collided with Judas' most fundamental motives and made him very, very angry, and, like all angry men, his brooding thoughts about it all did little to illuminate his own heart.

And so it came about, a little over an hour later, that Judas found himself amongst the cheering babes with nothing whatever to cheer about. Before, the throng would have been his element, being part of something bigger than himself that could take him someplace, a movement with possibilities and a future. Now he weathered the hosannas, wearing a smile that might have been carved into his face by the backward thrust of a dagger, while the evil questions continued their rampage within him.

But it hadn't always been so.

****

Like the others, Judas began the journey with a flourish of bright idealism and hope. It happened that while on a purchasing venture in Galilee he heard the young Nazarene rabbi, and soon followed him faithfully. A Judean, he possessed a more cosmopolitan character than the other disciples, having more experience with the cities of the south (especially Jerusalem) than the others, though not stuffily so. He enjoyed company and knew how to handle money, which he had learned from his father's dealings. As for his being selected, no one could ever fully discern the Teacher's motives. But as Judas showed good faith and zeal from the outset, the rest showed no more surprise at his inclusion among the Twelve than they did for the Zealot, the tax collector, or any of the other unlikelies who made up their troupe. In practice, that acceptance had played itself out. He witnessed the teaching, the miracles, and the increasing public of the Teacher's ministry. Judas believed that the Kingdom had come—or would come quickly—and that he had been chosen to witness it and preach it firsthand. Soon enough he assumed the role of keeping the moneybag, receiving gifts, paying for collective expenses, and, under certain circumstances, doling to the poor. When the Teacher had sent them out, two by two, he had gone, done the work, and ministered with authority and power. Judas was an apostle indeed.

No one will ever know when things began to change for him. He certainly loved the attention of the multitudes, but didn't they all? As one of the Twelve in the midst of hundreds and sometimes thousands, the fame vaulted him to a prominence that took his breath away; Judas had never imagined being so recognizable among complete strangers. Yet in the course of time his joy at seeing the people's delight in the Teacher—the simple and wholesome satisfaction over bringing others to him—underwent a subtle change. People would look at him with pleading eyes, begging for access to the Healer, then they would thank him graciously, over and over, for anything he did that could get them closer. And Judas enjoyed it. Yes, he enjoyed it, this intoxicating toll, this tithe of honor they gladly paid him so that they might see the Lord face to face. The Teacher's popularity had made *him* popular. And the poor? Truly, Judas never felt so well of himself as when it came to distributing those gifts. What importance, what power he felt, making sure all was fair and proper, what approbation over their relieved expressions and lightened steps as they went their way. Surely, his service to the rest, both their own number and outsiders, justified his borrowing a few coins now and again. Such was the power of the purse.

And so, to the naked eye, Judas appeared as any of the other disciples. He suffered difficulties with the others, he rejoiced at the triumphs, and he wondered with the others over the Teacher's odd turns and predictions. His behavior and reactions matched those of his brothers. Yet even as the multitudes feasted on miraculous manna, Judas' soul hungered. Yes, on the outside he looked like the other eleven, but inside he had fallen to an ever restless weighing, assaying, and previsioning. Simon had submitted easily enough when rebuked, and all furrowed their brows at the Teacher's words about carrying their own cross, but Judas' fear took another form. What, precisely, was all this coming to? By the time they reached Jerusalem that week, all the fevered talk of danger and the events at Bethany had conspired to create an atmosphere of anticipation that felt unique even for the disciples, who thought they had seen it all. Judas, now possessed of a strict winner-take-all mindset, also felt the change. And he wondered how he would live through it.

Prayer: Lord Jesus, grant me the very power of Your Holy Spirit that I may take warning. You became human like me, but You are also the One and Only Son of God. Help me resist the temptation of becoming overly familiar with You, to treat your glory like a common thing, and to slip into the subtle trap of profiting selfishly from the stunning truth that You have redeemed me entirely by Your grace. May I never, ever lose my awe of You. Amen.

Day Seven

It was the afternoon of the third day of the week, two days after the Teacher had made his grand entrance into the city to the cries of "Son of David!" The leaders hadn't liked that, but the Teacher continued with his grand delusions, as foolhardy as ever. Yesterday he wrecked the booths of the money changers and those who sold the sacrifices. All of those merchants, truth be told, worked for the priests every bit as much as they occupied the courts by their leave. And it continued today. Now he had gathered a crowd and before them all had humiliated his rivals with parable after parable. He left nothing unsaid this time, and Judas wondered, truly, what he hoped to accomplish by his show. After a particularly effective dressing down of the Sadducees, the hawk-eyed Judas noticed something.

While the other disciples tended the crowd, which pressed in ever closer after seeing the priests stymied, Judas stepped away to watch the vanquished from the corner of his eye. They took counsel together in a small circle, and though Judas could not hear their words he could certainly read their faces. Absent were the huffings and puffings, the furious gesticulations, and the almost comical after-arguments about the words that should have been spoken and who should have spoken them. Judas had seen them all many times from the Pharisees. Not now. In their place he saw icy, determined hate. These were men who understood that to lose to an upstart country rabbi meant to lose it all. And the priests did not lose—ever.

Something clicked inside of Judas just then. What an odd feeling, to suddenly understand those men so well. As he had from Judas, this young preacher had come and taken something from the priests and claimed it for his own. His preeminence, his gain meant their loss, no doubt about it. And like Judas, the priests could not rest with that being the way of things. Being of the city as they, he knew they would not leave it alone. Quickly he glanced from the whispering priests to the Teacher, and back again. Their impromptu concluded, with one more glare— almost thoughtful, that look at their foe—they turned to go. In a blink or two, Judas did the math, like a lad counting a few coins in his palm. Yes, Judas' moment of clarity had come.

Who would win this war? Who would emerge victorious? Would it be the priests, with the full power of the nation behind them, and their collusion with the might of Rome? Or would it be this itinerate Galilean preacher with his fishermen, his widows, and his street urchins tagging along behind him? Judas looked past the pillars, across the vast, crowded courtyard, and up at the Temple's towering façade, gleaming in the sun and blinding his eyes for its brilliance. Summing it all, he had his answer.

Now, what to do? Well, Judas was no man's fool. The time for a change had obviously come. To survive he must distance himself from that which would surely come to ruin, and by the feel of things likely sooner rather than later. He had had a good run, but the thing had finished its course. No use wasting precious minutes waxing philosophical about life's ups and downs, though. Time was of the essence. True, he could walk away before things took their ugly turn. Anticipating and acting accordingly for the sake of one's own life—this he called common sense. Who could fault him?

The question was whether he could go one better.

Ah, the priests. Yes, the noose tightened, and inevitably so. They would have their prize; they would reclaim their honor. But they yet lacked something they needed. Judas looked hard at the multitude; he could barely see the Teacher now for all the people around him. Oh yes, those nettlesome, frustrating crowds; they formed a veritable shield about the man. The priests were almost out of sight now, but as if he spoke with them face to face he felt sure he had something they wanted, something they needed, something no one but an insider could give them. An exchange, a quid pro quo. Yes, Judas might walk away with more than his freedom, more than his good name when all this came crashing down, as surely it would. While he still had something to barter with he would not just cut his losses, but might also garner a bit of severance for his trouble. Why shouldn't he redeem the situation—a bit of security for that which must surely fall of its own weight anyway? This he called shrewd.

So when the others made for the Mount of Olives late that afternoon, Judas avoided the Teacher, made an excuse to the others in respect to his purse-keeping duties, and slipped into the masses. An inquiry, a solicitation, and a knock later and he soon found himself in hallways that few eyes ever saw. His escorts led him to a room where he stood and waited while they went on. When the high priest himself came out, flanked by other important holy men, his nerves almost betrayed him. Judas knew they wanted what he had to offer; he hadn't realized they wanted it this badly. But he remembered from his father that successful dealings depended on a steady hand, so he swallowed hard as Caiaphas sat, arranged himself, and looked up with guarded interest. Stammering a bit, Judas began.

In the end it didn't take nearly as much explanation as he thought. It turned out the priests understood Judas every bit as much as he had come to understand them. They almost seemed to have been awaiting him. Surely he hadn't missed the opportunity? No, no fear for that. The timing was just right. Rendezvous points and agents for the Temple were set in motion. Oh, the intrigue. It felt rather exhilarating, having these powerful, untouchable men ask his opinion and consult with each other about his answers, right there in front of him. The transaction lacked a minor detail: no one mentioned what they might do with their prisoner once his cleverest disciple had handed him over. But then, who negotiates how a buyer might use the goods once he acquires them? What vendor sets such terms? Besides, his wage—a tempting bounty at a tithe of that which had been wasted on the Teacher's feet—told more than the story of Judas' greed: the Torah priced the ransom of a slave at thirty pieces of silver. The scalding metal was cool to his touch as he counted it out, the priests waiting patiently with nothing but the dull plinking of coins sounding in the room. All there. Done and done.

Judas left them, his own man again for the first time in years. How could they all Twelve have judged Israel, anyway? Absurd, he thought euphorically, as the heavy purse jangled against his hip. Only one man rules at a time. Now he must envision a more realistic future. Thirty pieces, yes. Plenty enough for a fresh start. But first he must…no…yes…he must deliver…A tunnel closed about him as he made his way out of the city gates. He felt he could see its end, the completion of his task, the fulfillment of his agreement for which he had been paid well, and in advance. He could see little else.

****

Judas Iscariot, like every person, thought well of himself. He imagined himself a person whose company others would desire, a man whose esteem worthy people would surely seek. The flattery of the crowds, pressing his hand to win his favor, the poor learning he was their source, well, these things made perfect sense to him. He was a fellow worth knowing. And even on those rare occasions when he didn't think well of himself, underneath it all he still did. In any case, this was not such an occasion. He felt confident about his plan, even if he saw his actions as an unfortunate necessity. His astute thinking and prescience had set him apart; his subtlety of character had elevated him above the uncouth, two-dimensional Galilean peasants he'd kept company with these last few years. No, they hadn't known him—the Teacher hadn't known him. He transcended their understanding, of that he proudly assured himself. Yes, Judas cut a complicated, enigmatic character. He mystified like Esau forsaking his birthright for a crock of pottage; he rang as cryptic as a crude word in a strange tongue; he was profound and complex like the twisted roots of a weed sprouting in a dung heap. By doing what would only baffle and grieve his brothers as incomprehensible, Judas had yielded, not to the intriguing and impenetrable, but to the bland and wholly predictable. What he did was about self-importance and cowardice, and money. What he did was about Judas.

Prayer: Lord Jesus, deliver me from the darkest enemies of my soul, my own devices and clever designs. Such "wisdom" clouds my heart, distorts my thinking, and masks Your glory from my eyes. Help me not to settle for the dullness of pride, and grant me Your heartbeat that I might not rest until I attain, by your grace, the loftiness of a modest opinion of myself. May I never betray you, my Lord. Amen.

Day Eight

Why did Judas bother to sup with his fellow apostles one last time? To see the deed through, of course. He must stay close to the Teacher as long as possible, to assure his patrons of their quarry. The money in hand, he couldn't afford to botch things. But in truth he already felt reasonably sure of where they would all go when they finished their meal; the Teacher had his habits, and Judas had already told the priests everything they'd need to know. Perhaps the simplest explanation for Judas' attendance was that duplicity had become for him a way of life. He did all he did and perceived all he perceived with a tangled heart. Tonight would just complete a performance he'd already perfected by long practice.

They had celebrated the Passover together before, of course. The rituals began as they always had, although, remarkably, the Teacher had arranged for him to recline in a place of high honor—next to himself. Except for his nervousness about the timing of things, he took this in stride and trusted his instincts. *Perhaps the Teacher seeks to make amends for the dishonor done me at the Bethany dinner*, thought Judas. The Teacher made his opening remarks with particular feeling, exhorting them dramatically. All listened carefully, while Judas observed these goings on with another eye. Then things took a turn.

The Teacher got up from the table and stripped. Fashioning himself a slave with towel and basin, he began to wash their feet, one after another. Simon made a fuss, always the dramatist, and the Teacher made his answer, ever the sage. The betrayer's thoughts wandered in dark places, and the double-entendre instruction that brought the fisherman into submission didn't make it far past Judas' hearing. Soon it was his turn. When his rabbi knelt bare-kneed on the floor behind him as he had for the others, the stony thing that once was his heart stirred with a tremor, began a futile entreaty, then lay still. Yes, Judas had mastered himself. He had trained his ear to that calculating malevolence whose voice was neither living nor dead. So he acted his part, as the others had, not saying a word while the selfless, true king bathed the heels of the crass, the treacherous, the utterly false. Judas swore that he could still smell the perfumed oil lingering on his bowed head, nearly a week later. As for the Teacher, he treated Judas as he had the others, carefully washing, even caressing his dusty feet until they were refreshed and ready to walk their chosen path.

The Teacher dressed and took his place again, and again began to teach. *Do you know what I have done to you?* Judas looked as focused and thoughtful as he could while the Teacher went on about their brotherhood. How would this end? He thought of the priests and their henchmen, and where they awaited him, even now. *I refer not to all of you...I know those whom I have chosen.* Judas' ears perked up. *But this...to fulfill the Scripture...*Ah, more messiah foolishness. *He who eats my bread has lifted his heel against me...*

"I tell you the truth, one of you eating here will betray me."

This was unexpected. The remark threw the room into a chaos, with the disciples looking about and muttering among themselves. Then one by one, each in their turn, they asked him, *Is it I, Lord?* Judas breathed hard while the questions flew, and thought he saw Simon mouthing to John, who reclined on the other side of the Teacher. More murmuring, now by John, though for all the chatter even Judas couldn't hear it.

"That one to whom I give the bread dipped in the dish," this said half to John, half-openly. "The Son of Man goes away just as it is written of him, but woe to that man by whom he is handed over. It were better for that one if he hadn't been born."

The sorrow in that voice had no bottom to it. As thoroughly as Judas had hearkened to another master, yet a part of him felt compelled by the one who had taught him so much. And he alone of the Twelve had not exonerated himself with a question, which only made him stand out all the more.

"Surely not I, Rabbi?" he belatedly affected.

To the very end, playacting. He might have stood on a stage reciting a script for the way it came out—wooden, obligatory, bloodless. Had more contemptuous words ever been spoken? Verily, Judas had come to despise the Teacher, and his disciples. Truly he despised them, though not as the priests did—powerful men who hated a rival and a threat—but rather as a haughty man who disregards an inconsequential passerby. His scorn was that of a soldier who slew an enemy while he slept; it was the disdain the thief felt for his unwary mark. But as highly as he had come to regard his schemes, for all the cunning he credited himself with, he still could not see that he was no better than a weevil turning circles on the open table in a futile effort to evade detection. No, the Teacher did not know him, that much was certain. And the calamitous day rushed upon him when the Son of Man would declare that with finality before the only court that mattered.

"So say you," came the soft, injured reply.

Now the Teacher reached over, took the bread, and, dipping it into the dish, proffered it to Judas, son of Simon Iscariot. It was a singular honor.

Judas had been a fine man in his day, named for the patriarch and the hero both, and once given to goodness. He had been granted a gift, indeed, the gift above all gifts, to be envied by many, even in his day. He had seen what many prophets and holy men had hoped and dreamed for, but had not. Yet he stumbled with the stumblers over the scandalous stone. Like them, he vainly believed all that transpired, the whole of his conspiracy, had come about by his own wits. But it was not so. By listening to and becoming a lie, he had made himself a puppet, not just of his own cravings, not just of Caiaphas' lust for power, not even of that insatiable darkness poised to engulf and indwell him, but of the Wisdom that saw through and would finally subject them all to its own purposes. And in no man did that Wisdom dwell so undiluted as in the Nazarene, whose presence reduces and reveals everyone for who they really are.

Before him now, in the Teacher's hand but inches from his face, awaited Judas' choice. Or, had he already moved beyond that last gateway? Oh, to be so honored before his brothers. The undead blackness urged him get on with it; it had places to go and things to do.

Taking the morsel, Judas's fingers touched the Teacher's. By the bye, like Uzzah, like Nabal, he touched without a second thought. Something smothered his senses as he ate the sop; the last remnants of his conscience fell silent.

"What you do, do quickly," the sternest tone the Teacher had used that evening, and usually reserved for...

Judas rose out of obedience. Truly, he obeyed now more speedily than he ever had. That which held him in its grip had no power to resist that voice. As the others puzzled, Judas collected his things, clutched his purse, and hurried out.

And it was night.

Prayer: *Lord Jesus, You kneel before me still, stripped to the waist and towel in hand to wash my dirty feet. As I look upon You, remove from me the stony heart and put in me the heart of flesh. Work in me Your true nature so that pretense, vanity, and disdain would find no place in me. I know that in the end I must obey one voice or another. Let that not be any voice but Yours, laying another blessed command upon me. Amen.*

Part II

Procula Pilate's Wife, Petronius the Centurion, and Demas the Criminal

Worthy is the Lamb who was slain…

~Revelation 5:12

THE DREAM

Procula, Wife of Pontius Pilate

Matthew 27:19

Day Nine

Procula wandered restlessly along the colonnade, idling in the rose shafts that the westering sun sent across the plaza. Though errant servants or soldiers occasionally broke the stillness, bustling to finish their work before day's end, she still sought a comforting solitude as she took in the enormity of her surroundings. The plaza, adorned with lawns and trees and graced by magnificent statues and fountains, accentuated the two great houses that stood opposite each other on its northern and southern extremes. Groves and pool-dotted gardens stretched interminably along the marble pavement that pampered her sandals, their dark greens and dusky olives blurring to a haze against the grays of the masonry that hemmed in the whole. This, the palace of Herod the Great, stood as a magnificent testament to the grandeur and genius of its architect and builder. So speaks wealth, she thought, and so speaks rank and status. It showcased what she and any Roman noblewoman aspired to. The difference between her and the others was that she had attained it. So pondered the prefect's wife that spring afternoon.

These thoughts did not typically occupy the forefront of her mind, at least not anymore. Instead, they had come to form the backdrop of her very existence, like a theater stage upon which actors played their sundry roles. Part of her reverie, naturally, proceeded from the fact that her husband had been laurelled and sent out as the very voice of Rome, where they had toiled with the striving so innate to all political existence there. In Rome she died her deaths with every setback and gloated tenuously with every advance that accompanied her husband's political ascent. While in a way that could never be and would never be over (when she felt her sharpest, she actually hoped not), she fashioned it her glory that she had graduated to *this* place now, and repeatedly told herself that she had achieved security in her exalted position. This confidence, of course, gave her another reason to feel complacent: Procula had come to believe her own lines in the play, assuming her proper place as if she had ever and always been cast in that enviable role.

Nevertheless, of late, and inexplicably in a particularly nettlesome way on this very journey, certain thinking had elbowed its way into her consciousness. It was an uneasiness, a wondering that unnerved her with the breadth of the questions it persistently put to her. Why here and now she could not explain to herself. Perhaps she missed her son, left behind in Caesarea on this trip, now less a child and more a companion to her than ever before. Perhaps the surging masses of Jews, whose din she could still faintly hear in the city beyond, collectively hoping for a divine visitation during the Passover, created an air of expectation that infected all who came to this exotic place. Procula noted an especially fervent sense of anticipation this year, and several days ago had witnessed the raucous cheering of the crowd as one of their local prophets entered the city. When she glimpsed him at a distance, tottering along upon a small beast amid clouds of dust and waving palm branches, the spectacle strangely, even fearfully fascinated her. What power drew the people to such a one? What might dwell there that she couldn't know but yet might mean the undoing of men like her husband and *his* power? Pilate's power—perhaps that was it. Let the gods forbid it, but maybe the prefecture *itself* was beginning to bore her, its novelty now gone and its drudgery realer than its promise had ever glittered for her. This fleeting suspicion terrified her most of all. Whatever the reasons, what had been complicated and uneven in her mind was becoming even more disquieting, so that on this lovely afternoon (now she rested on a seat of sculpted white marble) she began to think about her thinking—always a sign to her that something must be wrestled into submission within her.

Procula lifted her eyes and regarded the walls nearest her, then frowned. The Holy City did not help her frame of mind. The gardens were spectacular, the palace beyond princely, and the light heavenly, but no amount of Herod's genius at staging could delude a guest that his Jerusalem residence served any practical end other than as a fortress designed for militant defense. He built its perimeter with one motive: to protect its inhabitants from the subjects without. Though Herod was long dead and gone, that purpose remained; these high walls guarded against the ever-present threat that gave them birth. Procula recalled that even as Pilate took control a little over three years earlier, the Jews in Jerusalem clashed with his policies and caused an uproar for him. And the situation hadn't improved with time. Just yesterday some rebels failed in an attempted uprising at the Temple. So in spite of all the sumptuousness and the intended honor and comfort, here in this strange city she couldn't help but feel the pressure of her situation. Beyond these realities, she had utterly failed to convince herself that she belonged merely because of her station. There was something intransigently *oriental* about Jerusalem, and even if she flattered herself that, given the opportunity, she might be able to adapt to it, she knew she would never get that chance. Her stays here never lasted more than a matter of days and always served as the handmaiden to her husband's function as prefect. She had no reason to expect they would ever consist of anything else. One briefly faced with an irksome task rarely makes peace with it, the brevity itself both an excuse to hurry its end as well as an added weight to an already tiresome burden. But she knew in her heart it was more than the drudgery of duty that weighed upon her in this place. For the third time since they had moved to Judea from Rome, Pilate and his retinue had come up to Jerusalem from Caesarea for the Passover. For the third time, Procula had felt that singular, suffocating presence she couldn't quite describe. There was no escaping it here. Whatever its source, it and the other oppressions Jerusalem imposed upon her conspired with her troubled thoughts in a most discomfiting way. She sighed and lifted her chin to search for some of the late sunlight that had kissed her just a stroll ago, but in vain. Instead she felt a premature chill of the evening, and giving the walls another furtive, melancholy glance, pulled her garment about her.

"Mistress," a woman's voice spoke to her from behind.

Procula turned.

"Musa, yes," she replied.

"The evening meal is nearly upon us, Mistress. You asked me to come."

"Thank you, Musa. I did ask," Procula turned with a sigh, but felt suddenly glad for the company. Solitude had faded to mere aloneness.

Dinner would be another political affair, with Pilate entertaining dignitaries but mostly addressing security concerns relating to the Feast. It was an inherently dangerous time—hence their presence there—and there could be no leisure, whatever front they must erect to the contrary. In keeping with protocol, Procula would make an appearance befitting a Roman lady of her stature, set the guests at ease and further her husband's purposes, and, under the circumstances, demurely retire. She did not relish the charade, but at least it was a charade of her making and, she pretended, mostly on her own terms. So Procula moved with all the sense of purpose she could muster.

The two turned back towards one of the palace houses and made what haste they could, considering dignity. Procula walked ahead, with her servant slightly behind and to the side of her lady. Except to ask a few questions that would prepare her for the evening, she did not speak to Musa. But both knew that meant nothing. Procula liked and trusted her maid, whatever the circumstances, and they felt at ease with each other's silence. Perhaps it was that mutual understanding, then, that gave rise to the younger woman's concern for her mistress as they made their way along in the fading light. She saw a hesitancy in her movements, and heard a timbre in her voice that she did not recognize. By the time they reached Procula's quarters, Musa knew something was amiss. The lamplight there, now a necessity in rooms with few windows that in any case unhappily faced the east, revealed a satiny sheen to Procula's face and arms that alarmed the maid. She daren't speak, but felt compelled to. Her mistress beat her to it.

"Musa," she said, voice now clearly atremble, "I am ill."

"I feared it, Mistress," Musa answered quickly, taking her by the arm. "I will call a physician."

Accepting the help offered her, Procula sat on a couch, summoning her strength even as she conceded to infirmity.

"Call a messenger first," she said. "I must excuse myself to my husband."

Musa obeyed, hurrying from the room. Procula cursed softly. What a time for sickness.

****

Pilate was by her side before the doctor arrived. Though she would never have described her husband as doting, Procula accepted the genuineness of his concern and the softening of his usually formal demeanor for the affection she knew it to be. He was, after all, there—sitting on the edge of her couch while she reclined and tried to gather herself, Musa still fluttering about with the expected effects of comfort. Pilate allowed his wife to keep on awhile with the expressions and mutterings of resistance because he knew it futile to try and dissuade her of them. Finally, he quieted her with a soft, reassuring hiss, then turned briefly and sent Musa to find why the doctor tarried. Musa took the order—and the hint—and was away in a moment.

Procula relaxed and gazed upon Pilate with half-lidded eyes. She mustered a smile but he spoke first.

"You are pale, *Dulcis*," he said matter-of-factly.

She appreciated the term of endearment, but her smile fled.

"I am sorry," she replied. "It is so strange. I feel fine, really, but again not at all well. It is as if all the strength has gone from me."

"Fret not from a sense of your duties; I am concerned only for you," he said. "You are far too hard on yourself at such times."

"The physician is skilled and you know my constitution is hardy. It was probably the journey. I am sure to recover quickly."

Pilate acquiesced to her hopeful remarks for the time being and they sat silently for a few moments until footfalls disturbed them. Musa entered with the physician. The man greeted the prefect appropriately and did the customary honors to a reclined Procula as well, then set to work while Pilate sat and observed. The examination, as much an interview as anything else, resulted in a quick and fairly confident diagnosis. The Lady Procula, announced the physician, suffered from an excess of yellow bile. He spoke with as much cautious optimism as possible, but with the customary professional sternness recommended rest, light eating, and an herb infusion mixed with wine, regularly administered in small doses until relief was complete. As the physician sent Musa to fetch the wine he desired for his prescription, then turned to search his own supplies for the indicated leaves, Pilate arose and excused himself. He could do no more for her, and his duties called. A glance was his parting gift to his wife, and Procula pondered it mildly as his footfalls faded in the corridors. For all the trouble, a moment of contentment visited her, and she almost wished for more times like this—wishing, as always, in vain.

Musa returned with a pair of maids, the three of them hurrying into the chamber with an air of mission. They carried plates of fruit and bread, and a flagon of wine. Under the tart orders and watchful eye of the physician, the servants quickly arranged everything on a low table by the couch. The man began to doctor the wine. Presently the first odd-tasting draught was administered and the physician stood back, satisfied for the time being.

"I will take my leave until morning, Lady," he said.

Procula nodded mutely as she lay back, exhausted. Her head swam as the wine on her empty stomach went to work. After a couple more sharp directives to Musa about Procula-heard-not-what, the man left.

Meanwhile, the maids managed to find matters to attend to in the chamber, the noise of their labors and their soft but serious conversation creating a dim backdrop to Procula's thoughts. Gradually the sounds ceased and she perceived that they stood in a small circle a few paces from her feet, whispering to Musa as they asked her for more instructions. Musa hesitated a moment, and began to reply when Procula interrupted her.

"Musa," she said with resigned exasperation. The whispers stopped.

"Mistress?"

"Send them away," she said, running her hand over her closed eyes. "My being the prefect's wife doesn't mean that you can cure me any quicker with all this running about. Your continual fussing is only making things worse."

Silence.

Procula dropped her hand and opened her eyes, then closed them again. The maids were retreating noiselessly through the nearest archway. She heard Musa move her wine closer on the table, and as she straightened Procula reached out and gently took her by the arm.

"Musa, were I your very sister and you sat holding my hand all the evening, we both know it would profit my kidneys not a bit."

"I will stay and do just that, Mistress, if you desire it."

"You are a comfort to me," Procula sighed, "But no. Let us let the herbs do their work and hope that the physician's infusions do what my flesh and mind are calling for. I feel that I simply need to rest."

Musa stood for a moment, then leaned over to adjust the robe that covered her mistress.

"It is probably just weariness anyway," muttered Procula, pulling at the cloth and turning slightly—then with some impatience at Musa's idle hovering: "Go, go. I want to be alone."

Musa did as she was told without another word. The sound of the young woman's departure was momentary, and her mistress, left to herself, forced herself to relax as she invited the night to take her into sleep.

Prayer: Lord Jesus, I am often awash with the thoughts, fears, and ambitions of a restless mind. The world glitters around me, while You have presented Yourself a common man, with nothing particular that I might be attracted to You, except You Yourself. Grant me a seeing eye to pick You out of the crowd, an ear to hear You when You speak, and a discerning heart to sift through the fool's gold and find the Pearl of Great Price. Amen.

Day Ten

Whatever rest Procula hoped for, though, never came. Solitude brought no solace, and with Musa's departure the musings of the garden returned in force. She fumed at herself and turned on the couch, breathing more shallowly than her ailment warranted as she fought to drift off. Yet like a small bird vainly seeking to alight upon a thorn bush, her mind flitted comfortless from one nebulous worry to another, searching episode after episode, endlessly.

The wings of her thought grew weary. She lay with eyes closed, exhausted, and yet her mind would not be still nor were the images it conjured muddied by the failure of her will. Instead, she felt herself lifted as if by an astral wind, her thoughts taking on form and clarity and a tense alertness filling her innermost self. Her body might have been no more.

Suddenly Procula saw herself a carefree child again, an innocent girl in her mid-teens just approaching womanhood. Even in this dreamlike undream, the fragrance of her promise and the hope her parents had for her—that she had for herself— perfumed her world like a rose in full bloom. She was comely and from a good family, well-(enough)-to-do and with good connections. There was no fear for the future, and she laughed with her friends and enjoyed her youth in Rome. The restlessness of her thoughts had carried her to a place of pleasant memories, and she abided them with a detached sense of blessedness, even gratitude.

Time passed on in her thought. Presently Pilate entered her life. He was older than she, of course, also good-looking and of good fortune. Best of all, he was well-favored. Pilate was a personal friend and political ally of a young man named Lucius Aelius Sejanus. The importance of this connection for Pilate, and by him, for Procula, could not be overstated. Like Pilate, Sejanus came from the equestrian class; not as exalted as a patrician, of course, but certainly noble. Yet under Augustus, Sejanus' father had demonstrated how high an equestrian could rise, having attained the prefecture of the Praetorians, the emperor's most elite and trusted bodyguard. Thus through his family Pilate's friend Sejanus was deeply connected with the imperial court in the most promising of ways. Both his own family and Procula's warmly encouraged Pilate's overtures toward the young nobleman.

Then turmoil came. Even as Pilate courted Procula (or rather, her family), the mighty Augustus died and was deified, and his adopted son Tiberius ascended the imperial throne. Political changes were inevitable, and the ambition flowed through the courts of power as the very Tiber in December. Those were anxious days for Procula, for she was mature enough to know that anything could happen under such circumstances and often did. She overheard her parents' uneasy whisperings one night and her heart skipped when her father mentioned Pilate's name. In a very real way, her family's honor would be directly affected by how the many power struggles played out. Yet it resulted fear for naught. In that chaos, and against what any mortal could reasonably expect from Fortune, Procula watched as the emperor exalted her suitor's close friend to the Prefecture of the Guard, even as his father before him. Things augured well for Sejanus and those upon whom he smiled.

Pilate and Procula wed. Now in her memory she saw his austere face graced with a slight but genuine smile of contentment, framed by the flowering trees in the garden of his father's house after the ceremony. The laughter rang in her ears and the wine danced on her tongue. Happy faces encircled her, blessing her with joy and divine favor. And there among them stood Sejanus and his beautiful wife, Apicata. Though Procula knew what later befell that union, somehow in that remembrance the image remained sacred and unscarred. The prominent couple embodied Procula's hope for her family name, her new husband, and her unborn children. The crowd of well-wishers parted respectfully as they drew near to offer the newlyweds their own words and gifts. As Sejanus grasped Pilate's arm in fraternal affection, Apicata kissed Procula and the warmth of her embrace comforted like a promise—a promise that could not fail. Happiness was hers.

In the months and brief years that followed, that friendship continued to bear fruit. Pilate prospered in his career, and enjoyed reasonably steady if not meteoric advancement. There was little doubt that his connection with one so powerful as Sejanus helped him greatly. Procula did all she could to encourage that friendship by cultivating her own with Apicata. Sejanus' wife was her elder as well, but not so much as to be a matron. She played rather an elder sister. Oh, those were good days. Apicata was expecting her third child at the time of the wedding, and from that time she began to invite Procula to be with her whenever possible. She seemed to view her young companion as a bringer of good fortune for the pregnancy, youthful and strong and fertile. But Procula fashioned herself Apicata's protégé, and knew her friend had little to fear. She had always borne well, and things boded well for this child, too. When she rejoiced over the birth of a lovely girl child (certainly no shame after two strong sons), Procula rejoiced with her, and all the more because now she herself was with child. Yet all the while, behind the mask of smiles and happy tears, brooded the ever-present cloud of *intention*. Procula knew very well that the more Sejanus' wife favored her, the more Sejanus was likely to favor her husband. And considering how things seemed to unfold in the court, more favor with Sejanus meant favor with the emperor himself. Even as she held Apicata's infant daughter (Junilla, she named her), helpless and innocent and staring up at her with unblinking dark eyes, she realized that her doting meant profit and position for herself and the child in her *own* womb. Procula cooed and rocked Junilla as Apicata looked on, beaming.

The starry wind that propelled her through her memories turned cold. If she could have beheld her own face just then, she would have seen the furrow in the brow and the tightening of the mouth. What she saw instead was a litany of images from her life with Pilate over the following years. Their child was born—a son—and he was perfect. Why didn't her memory of that moment seem as warm as Junilla's birth? Why were her joys dampened as she remembered what should have been recalled as blessed times? Ah yes, intrigue in the political realm. It never ended. Greater success and power always met with the need for more. Procula found she had Pilate's ear more than she ever dreamed she would when she had fallen silent before his imposing presence at their first meeting. Now she spoke freely, and aside from the occasional rebuke from him to remind them both who commanded, increasingly he listened to her. The truth was that under it all he had grown to love and trust her. But hunger for status also drove them both, and he had learned that his wife was as shrewd as she was ambitious. More than once she had saved him from snares that may have hindered or even crippled him politically. She encouraged him, urged him, even drove him to act when the right opportunity presented itself, cautioned and pleaded when her sixth sense warned her of danger. She and Pilate made a good team as they ascended through the ranks.

And always there, in and out of her memories whether she willed or no, was Sejanus. It seemed that, having welcomed him as their benefactor, there was no escaping him. His finger stirred every cup they drank from in their rise. Whatever Pilate's skill, whatever Procula's subtle but vital contribution to his victories, Sejanus loitered there like a creditor, his dominant presence silently laying claim to their success and to their lives. The golden images that paraded through her mind like a triumphal procession had always been her trophies and Sejanus' vital role a source of pride for her. Even now she saw herself, time after time, smiling and nodding as Pilate confided how his once-in-a-lifetime alliance repeatedly brought them good fortune beyond hope. But a cloud covered the sun that shone on her memory of those days, and her thoughts took on a vague nightmarish quality though she knew she neither slept nor dreamt. If only she could.

Why was she uneasy with the conquests that had lifted her to the heights upon which she now stood secure? Asking the question only deepened her angst, but the answer came soon enough as her thoughts rolled, seemingly of their own will. To the fore of her forced ruminations came those things that she had conveniently suppressed, but knew very well. Yes, she had known. Sejanus was indeed their benefactor, but to call him benevolent would be a farce by any measure. Yes, he helped Pilate, even as he helped others. But above all, Sejanus helped Sejanus. He did nothing without a reason, and those reasons always had to do with increasing his own stature and power. Whether he exalted or debased, empowered or destroyed, it was always about making himself greater—an irresistible arc that continued to that day. The disquiet Procula had suppressed in those days seemed to fill her recollections—a disquiet rooted in the inescapable reality that everything Sejanus did for her husband was really something he did for *himself*. How did that make her feel? She squirmed within herself as she tried in vain to shake the oppressive cloud of conviction. *Harlot*. Procula froze, for a moment very aware indeed of her flesh and its fever. She almost opened her eyes for light but, before she could, a tide of images rose before her and she was pulled into it. Now she saw person after person, remembering names and faces and families. Victims one and all, they had fallen before Sejanus. With grim clarity the casualties of his irresistible ascendance were brought up before her. She saw them in her thought, a rotting mountain of political and sometimes literal corpses upon which he stood. And there beside him stood Pilate. As always, she was at his side.

Prayer: Lord Jesus, Your word urges me to love not the world or the things in the world. Reveal to me those affections, those ambitions, and those alliances that shame me and deaden my conscience. Remove the callouses from my too-easily entranced heart so that I might not use other people for my ends, but rather that I might be submitted to You and that You might use me for Yours. And when That Day comes, may my legacy not be one of regret, but of redemption. Amen.

Day Eleven

Procula jerked suddenly, a spasm running through her frame. She coughed weakly and tried to sit up, but hadn't the strength. A weight had come down upon her.

"Wine," she thought. She reached feebly for the goblet beside the couch, but her curled knuckles sent it clattering to the floor with what remained of its contents.

"Musa," she gasped softly.

But Musa didn't hear, didn't come.

"Please, no more," Procula choked, pleading with the storm of her own memories that had begun as a kind breeze but now rose like a gale to testify against her.

Her thoughts heeded her no more than her maid. Instead, she now saw Apicata sitting at a fountain in her courtyard garden, weeping uncontrollably. Junilla, now a fair young child, sat beside her mother comforting as a child does with sweet but powerless words. Her mother patted her, glad for her touch but no less devastated.

Sejanus was putting her away, divorcing her. As hard as this was for Procula to behold, it did not surprise her. Procula had heard the rumor from Pilate—the deepest secret he had ever shared with her. Sejanus had designs beyond where he stood, beyond what his current social station could allow him. As high as he had risen (the emperor had named him *praetor*, a rank typically reserved for men beyond his social station), he wanted more. For those in his circumstances, that meant marriage. His forefathers had married up successfully, and the connection to Apicata's wealthy father had served him well. But he had mined the union for all it could afford him and had exhausted the usefulness of its social wealth. He needed something higher for where he planned to go next.

Procula's memory waxed excruciatingly keen at that moment. She recalled staring at Apicata, her sister, her friend, all the while hearing her husband's fierce warnings ring in her ears. Terribly powerful people were involved—Livilla, wife of Drusus, the emperor's son. *The Emperor's own family*, she thought. And then she understood why Pilate had told her. It was more than idle chatter or gossip. It was a command. And so, in that moment and in the very presence of her friend, Procula made her choice. Trembling inside for Apicata and her children (especially this little lamb now by her side), trembling for Sejanus' perilous and insatiable ambition, but mostly shaking in fear for herself and her own, Procula nevertheless bared the steel in her soul and struck the fatal blow. Her sisterhood, her loving bond with Apicata, died then and there in that idyllic garden. The design she had subtly worked into their friendship now exacted its brutal price with no subtlety at all. Oh, there was still the voiced concern, the cordiality, the reassurances to visit and keep up. But even in those empty promises all was made clear. A wall had come up between them in a matter of moments. By the gods, it was painful. To see her friend already in such anguish, only to add to it herself and see her own betrayal reflected in Apicata's disbelieving eyes cut Procula to the heart. But it didn't stop her. She finished the deed and thought of as polished an excuse to go as might salvage a bit of Apicata's dignity, and hers. By the time she took her leave they were nothing more than courteous strangers. They did not embrace. Little Junilla, innocent and unaware as always, salted the wound with a tug at Procula's hand and a parting kiss on her cheek.

Procula lay numb now, the memories washing over her consciousness in rapid succession. Oddly, the only image her mind's eye could conjure was her husband's face as he whispered to her event after fearful event. Within a few months of Sejanus' divorce of Apicata, Drusus, the emperor's son, died after a period of illness. Tiberius mourned his passing, but Sejanus had hated Drusus, and no one was ignorant of their rivalry. Since Tiberius' other son, Germanicus, had already died several years earlier, all that remained to the imperial line in the way of legitimate heirs were mere children. It was all very convenient for Pilate's friend, Sejanus—*too* convenient. The rumors of Sejanus' relationship with Livilla now provided fodder for the gossip mongers (the daring ones, anyway). It wasn't long before Procula's calculating mind went to work. Late one evening a series of questions she put to Pilate earned her a severe and fearful glance, tempered with what she recognized as knowing assent. The look in his eyes told her that Drusus' death probably hadn't been from natural sickness as all had been led to believe. But for them to speak such a thing, even in secret, was beyond the courage of either one of them. Instead, they continued on the same course, Pilate ingratiating himself to Sejanus as much as ever and hoping for scraps from the imperial table to come his way. When it seemed, in the course of time, that their suspicions about Drusus' early demise were thoughts they alone entertained, their fears evaporated. Pilate assured his wife that promising possibilities shone on the horizon, so she took a breath and allowed herself some hard-bought contentment.

Then the day finally came—the time for collecting on all their political investments. Flushed with excitement, Pilate told her the news: the Prefecture of Judea had been granted him. It was an important post in the East, with implications for Rome's political situation in Egypt, Syria, and beyond. If the appointment had happened at the time of their wedding, Procula could not have accompanied Pilate. But the Senate had changed their stance in the meantime, and she and their son would soon sail with him to Caesarea. It was a great honor and all that Procula had hoped and dreamed of. For her—and Pilate himself—it came at a perfect time. Though he felt gladder for his alliance with Sejanus than ever, things were getting complicated. In the few years since Drusus' death, Pilate's powerful friend had consolidated his position even more. Tiberius had departed Rome for the countryside, and now Sejanus had taken firm control of the day to day affairs of government. (As things would go, the emperor departed Italy entirely to rule from the island of Capri just before Pilate and his family departed for Judea.) Even as Pilate explained these things to her, for once unbridled in his euphoria, Procula shared his joy, agreeing that it would be difficult to imagine a more ideal situation. No longer would they need to worry about Tiberius' imperiousness and capricious temperament; Sejanus, their friend, would hear and process all their reports himself. Certainly, Fortune had smiled upon them. Yet as she lay there remembering these things, she recalled wondering, deep within, whether the Fates had granted them only one coffer in which to put their pennies. She wondered also when the tax would have to be paid and the creditor satisfied.

Even so, with these last recollections the intensity of her thoughts began to lessen, and Procula became a bit more rational. She still felt weak, and rather odd, but she managed to straighten herself on the couch. She took a deep breath and blinked in the dying light of the lamp.

"Silly girl," she scolded herself.

It wasn't as if she hadn't mulled over Apicata's divorce, or Drusus' suspicious death, or Sejanus' other machinations before. She had—many times. This was the way of things, she told herself. It was how Rome worked and how those destined to rule actually did. She knew this, had lived this way for years, and had played a central role in her own husband's rise to power. She *had* to sever ties with Apicata and do all those other, well, *difficult* things. What other choices could she have made, really? Why shouldn't she be proud of what she had done? Would she be here now if she had decided differently? Soberly she considered the news, only months old, of the terrible purge trials Sejanus had carried out in Rome to stamp out the last of his rivals; his throne of corpses rose higher than ever. Pilate had told her sharply, in a moment when she pined for the beauty of her native land, that it was far better that he, she, and their son lived where they did, friendships notwithstanding. Besides, Sejanus grew powerful beyond measure. Even if Pilate had not been his ally, surely now she would have encouraged such a friendship after the political situation had unfolded. There was nothing to feel badly about. Thus did Procula try to calm herself, with many like reasonings and soft sighs, after such an assault by a depth of conscience she hadn't even known lurked within her. Gradually, the night terrors seemed to retreat.

A deep weariness came over her, and her eyes couldn't stay open. Her fever and her inner wrestling had left her entirely without strength, and the bitter nag of thirst plagued her throat. Not wanting to call for Musa again, she swallowed dryly and pulled her clothing more tightly about her. The lamp went out, but she took no notice. Her mind, agreeing with the exhaustion of her flesh, finally gave way and Procula drifted into the dark.

Prayer: *Lord Jesus, Good Shepherd of my soul, guide me in paths of righteousness for Your name's sake. Lead me away from fear, which tempts me into the thievery of stealing myself away from the lives of those who need me. May I always be willing to sacrifice myself before I yield to the cowardice of sacrificing another on the altar of my own insecure ambitions. Help me not to use other people, made in Your image, for my own ends. Amen.*

Day Twelve

She came to herself. No longer lying on her couch, she sat alone on broad marble stairs. Though Procula had never been there before, she had seen the place from a distance and recognized her location as the south entrance to the Temple Mount as she looked across the Kidron Valley towards that stony ridge the Jews called the Mount of Olives. It was light now, but strangely so, as if a veil diffused everything and it were morning and evening both, at the same time. All was quiet; she heard nothing but the sound of her own breathing. Procula felt no surprise at her complete solitude in this place so sacred to the Jews during such a holy season when thousands thronged Jerusalem. On the contrary, everything seemed perfectly natural to her. Within her arose, however, a deep sense of expectancy, as if the very air around her held its breath, waiting for something significant but unknown. Feeling the cold of the white stone through her garment, she stood and took a few steps to the east.

She gazed at the sky, and its muted grays were laced with pale greens and milky purples. Not a leaf stirred on the olive trees and scrub in the valley below her. The stillness in the land seemed absolute. But just as she turned her eyes to follow the trough as it continued its way towards the south, movement caught her eye.

There below her she saw a man, clad in the simple homespun cloth of a Jewish peasant, riding a young donkey. He had his sandaled feet hiked up to keep them from dragging the ground as he rode along because the animal was too small for him. In another time and place Procula would have thought the sight rather foolish, even comical, but not now. Instead, she saw a certain regal bearing in the man as he made his way calmly among the rocks. Procula stared at him, transfixed, for at once she knew him to be none other than the Prophet whose procession she had witnessed a few days earlier. The holy man did not look up at her, but somehow she knew he was aware of her. The two of them shared a connection, being the only ones in this surreally desolate holy land. The Prophet did not pause, nor did he hurry, yet he purposefully continued on his way—not towards her or the city, but across her line of sight, following the Kidron Valley south. Suddenly she wanted to go to him, to ask him…something. But just as immediately she understood from a calm, authoritative inner Voice that such was not given to her. Hers was to watch. By this point the man's back was to her, but he seemed to be going more quickly now, which was odd since nothing about his actions betrayed haste.

Now Procula recognized the beating of hoofs upon the earth—the first and only sound she had heard in that place. They were too heavy, too rapid to be those of the Prophet's donkey; she knew it could only be a horse fitted for war. Turning towards the rumor of its coming, she saw, somehow, across the rooftops and the ridges, a huge beast galloping at great speed, charging from the west down the Valley of Ben Hinnom that hemmed in the city to the south. It was a pale gray, and tall like the great horses used for a triumphal procession; upon its back sat a Rider. The equestrian was clad majestically in gold and crimson, and rode fully armored with breastplate, shield, and helm. A short sword was girt on his thigh, and in his gauntleted hand he gripped a long lance with a keen, double-edged tip of great size. Onward he goaded his mighty stallion, and lustily it obeyed. Its hoofs tore up the earth with its coming, and as it did Procula saw that many fearful and unclean things were turned up as it passed, the skulls and burned bones of small children. And it seemed they were set aflame again with hellish sparks and choking smoke in the wake of the horse and the Rider. Procula beheld the spectacle with growing horror.

"Who is the Rider?" the silent Voice within her asked.

Procula wanted to speak, to answer this Voice which was neither hers nor that of any man, woman, or child she knew. But her tongue cleaved to her jaw. She hadn't seen the face, and now her vision only granted her to see the Rider, as it were, from behind his muscular shoulder, where the plume of his helm flowed in the wind of his onslaught. She realized that she was seeing things as the Rider himself saw them.

"Sejanus," she answered, and as she heard her thought speak, the truth of it struck her like a blow to the belly.

Sejanus he was. Face unseen, by his appearance he might have been any Roman knight. But something in his bearing fairly bled the ambition, the pride, and ravenous hunger for conquest at any cost that marked him for who he was. If he knew of her presence he did not show it. He bent wholly upon his grim purpose. The Rider gained speed as Procula pondered her desperate realizations.

Suddenly she found her breath and gasped. She now saw that, before the Rider and his charger, the Hinnom Valley drew to an end, emptying into that depression where it joined the Kidron. And there, directly ahead and turning towards them, rode the Prophet on his ambling, silly little donkey. The Rider put his spurs to the stallion and lowered his lance for the attack.

Procula's heart beat in her ears and her mind raced. But now there was no seeing, no knowing what took place between the Prophet and the Rider. She stood once again on the steps of the Temple, and the dark purple clouds swirling low in the sky away to the south and east granted her the only omen of what mysteriously unfolded there. Her hands wrung each other and her fingernails bit into her flesh as she waited on the windless, noiseless perch.

Paralyzed with dread, she looked down and saw there, not a few paces away, a girl of 14 or 15 years, sitting on the steps where Procula had earlier. As she had known the others she saw, so Procula knew this one. Here was Junilla, Apicata's little girl. But now she wasn't the child she had been when she last saw her. No, this Junilla was the lovely young virgin she must surely be by now. Upon beholding her, Procula's heart wept for joy and grief; she realized how dearly she had loved and missed the child, and how much she reminded her of herself at that age. Yes, she might well have been Procula herself. Junilla sat with her knees together and pulled to one side, leaning on one hand. With the other she played at something that Procula couldn't quite make out, though it looked like she was arranging small, pretty rocks (of the sort a child might treasure) on the stair next to her.

Procula stared at her for a moment in wonder before her eyes were lifted again towards the south. The sky churned dark now and a sickening awe filled her to behold it. Junilla looked up at her and smiled mildly, then, cocking her head to one side went back to her game. Procula stood as a statue. She was overwhelmingly aware that, at that very moment, a great battle— nay, *the* Great Battle between Darkness and Light was being fought but a few stadia away.

"Yes. Just play," Procula stammered chidingly, poorly masking the terror in her voice. "Play nicely there."

But Procula had only failed to calm herself with her impotent words, because the girl took no notice of her. Junilla began to hum winsomely as she rearranged her pebbles.

It dawned upon Procula that she and she alone, in all the world it seemed, suffered awareness of the cosmic conflict that raged in that very hour. For some unknown reason it had been shown to her, but the child at her feet carried on, oblivious to it all. Though her stones glittered softly as she naively toyed with them on the marble stair, Junilla was blissfully ignorant that Life, that Luminance itself hung as by a thread in a swordsmith's forge. Procula's maternal instincts arose in her and she took a step closer to the girl. She must warn her. She would scream the alarm to Junilla, urge her child to run and hide, and if she wouldn't listen then drag her perforce to a safe place where she would be out of harm's way. But Procula's grasping panic was itself gripped by a deeper, more suffocating cloud of fear that choked her very soul. Where could they run too? What refuge would keep out Blackness if it won?

"Just play, then," whispered Procula powerlessly, again more to herself than to Junilla. "Play nicely."

It seemed forever and yet also just a moment's time that Procula stood there, frozen, watching the girl at her pointless game. She had stopped breathing and her chest pounded as she waited for Doom to declare itself.

And then it did.

A searing line parted the sky and tore all she saw asunder. Beyond it was Nothing. Darkness had vanquished Light.

Hope died within her, its death rattle echoed in her uneven breathing, but still she was not released from the horrific vision. She was condemned to see what had transpired. Transported, she now stood shaking on the lip of Hinnom, watching as the Rider bore down upon the gentle Prophet. Turning with sorrowful resolution towards his attacker, the unarmed man opened his arms and stretched them high and wide, palms outward in— *surrender!* For a fraction of a blink Procula perceived a flame in the Prophet's eyes, burning soft but bright. Then the Rider, in one merciless moment, was upon him. Procula saw the head of the lance pierce the helpless figure, lift him into the air, then cast him to the ground. He did not cry out, but Procula heard her own voice do so. She stood above the fallen one and found that she was weeping, weeping dry sobs until she felt her very lungs would come out of her. Why hadn't he cried out? Why hadn't she been allowed to hear his kind voice just once? Nay, she knew with the knowing that had guided her through this entire odyssey that he was already dead when the spear passed through him; the lance had been nothing but an impotent insult. Now his broken body lay with many wounds upon the rocky ground, and Procula his only mourner.

She heard a moan, and turned. There, a few paces beyond the dead Prophet, lay the great horse, its foreleg broken and its body writhing in its final throes. Beside it, motionless, the mighty Rider splayed facedown, armor in disarray, helmet shattered and lying at a distance, lance splintered beside him. A chill wind blew and whined among the rocks, stirring the warrior's tattered cape.

"Who is the Rider?" the Voice asked again.

Procula no longer knew. A will mightier than her own compelled her to take step after hopeless step, until she stood over the man. There she waited. The question was a living word inside of her, driving her to seek an answer. She stooped fearfully, reaching out a trembling hand and wondering how she might lift his bulk and look upon his face. Before she could touch him, though, she recoiled in horror at a dark, spreading stain that wet the earth underneath the torso and spread its sinister fingers towards her feet. Another groan, and slowly the dying Rider stirred, turned over of his own waning strength, and breathed his last.

Procula's hands went to her mouth to stifle her own screams. There before her, fallen on his sword, was her husband, Pontius Pilate, prefect of Judea. Blackest shadow felled her.

Prayer: Lord Jesus, sharpen the senses of my heart that I might truly grasp the choices that are before me. Help me not judge by the outward, but to weigh my path according to Your truth. In Your mercy give me a glimpse, if not of future consequences, at least of the gravity of my steps. By Your sacrifice, You have set before me life and death; help me choose life, no matter how unglamorous it might look, for Your glory and my good. Amen.

Day Thirteen

Procula slowly came to herself. A warm, familiar breeze now touched, almost caressed her, and the smells that filled her nose reminded her of…Taking her hands from her face (she hadn't realized she had been driving her own fingers into her eyes), she looked about her. It was late evening, almost night. Still, there was enough light for her to look about and take in her surroundings. And there was no mistaking what she saw. Rome! How had she come hither? She quickly dismissed this question for one that rang strangely more important to her right then— *where* in Rome was she?

Procula took a few steps and stared about her. The Forum. Yes, the Forum. Simple human delight at recognition of a familiar, friendly place touched her for a moment, lightly assuaging the trauma of her vision. She could not be far from the Capitol, she told herself. Yes, for there above her ascended the Gemonian Stairs. That meant that she stood near the…

Here she turned again and her nascent happiness abandoned her. The open maw of a dark doorway stood before her, and a dank, noisome odor issued from it.

The Carcer.

Animal-like, Procula backed away. This was Rome's darkest corner, a place of despair and evil endings. She nearly fled, but just then heard voices. Turning, she saw men with torches striding towards her. Between them, held in the cruel grip of their powerful hands, struggled a girl. Procula's blood ran cold. Even in the shadowy light she knew the child. It was Junilla, even as she had just seen her—a young maiden and no longer a babe.

"But what have I done? Please just tell me," Procula heard her plead. "I haven't done anything."

"Shut up, you little—," snarled one of the men, at least twice her age and thrice her weight.

"I won't do it again, whatever it was. I promise. I'll play nicely from now on if I've hurt anyone's feelings. Just give me a punishment and I'll be good."

The men shared a nasty laugh.

"Oh, you'll get yours, all right," the other man snorted. "Papa's no help now, is he?"

"Where are you taking me?" she whimpered. Then seeing the door, "No, I don't want to go in there. Where…"

One of the men went ahead with his torch, lighting the naked interior of the small prison. The other followed, now dragging Junilla. Procula's leaden feet followed, and her eyes watched, incredulous.

The men took Junilla to the edge of a hole in the middle of the cold stone floor. Below them, through the hole, sank Rome's most terrible pit, the Tullianum. It was not a place for little ones, it was not a place for women. It was not a place for…

"Ready down there, Julius?"

"Yeah, I'm ready. Only the best accommodations for our pretty guest! But send our little lady with the necklace, 'cause I forgot to bring one for her."

"Sure, just finish the job good, here and now. There are rules, you know. And big men are waiting for the word."

"I always finish, especially when there's something in it for me," Julius snickered up at them.

From that point everything happened in a blur. One of the guards grabbed a filthy rope while the other held the squirming child in a viselike grip.

"What are you doing now?" trembled Junilla, her voice now shrill. "What..."

The garrote went over her head and she was manhandled into the hole while she clutched hopelessly at their merciless arms. Junilla's disbelieving eyes, wide with terror, looked upward in vain for salvation as her monstrous wardens delivered her into the darkness below. Evil hands like claws grasped her, tearing at her fine clothes, pulling her down.

Procula shut her already bruised eyes tight, tight against the sight of the guards' leers, stopped her ears against their taunts and cheers at what they watched below. But she couldn't block out the harrowing screams, couldn't silence their hellish echoing against the damp, bare walls around her.

Icy madness took her mind as her heart fell into an abyss of infinite horror.

****

Musa came running when she heard her mistress' shrieks. By the time she got to Procula's chamber the woman had torn her bedding and upset a small table and the medicines on it, calling out between violent sobs. Musa ran to the bed and tried to hold her flailing arms.

"Mistress, Lady Procula! I am here! Lady!"

But Procula was beside herself with a panic that Musa couldn't fathom, babbling frantically and calling for her son.

"Lady Procula, it is I, Musa. Your son is safe. Your son is safe in Caesarea. I am here. All is well," soothed the maid.

Procula hesitated in Musa's arms and stared at her, wide-eyed.

"Musa?"

"I am here, Mistress. I am here and all is well. You must have had a nightmare. Everything is fine."

"But little Junilla. She's gone, she's..." she wept, disconsolate, then, frantic again, "My son! Where is my son?"

"Your son is in Caesarea, Lady. He didn't make the trip this time. He is safe and guarded in Caesarea, in the palace there. You had some night terrors, that is all."

Procula's grip on Musa's arms relaxed ever so slightly.

"Oh, Musa," she sobbed, head bowed and shoulders shaking, "Oh, my son, my son, my...my *husband.* "

"Your husband, Mistress?" queried Musa, puzzled. "Why, he is here, of course. He is well."

"Musa, where is he at this moment, where is Pilate *right now?*"

"I surely don't know, Lady. I believe he is discussing some matter with his officers. I can send to find out."

"Do, Musa. Do find out."

Musa tried to smile and get Procula to recline.

"I will, dear Mistress. Of course I will. First take a bit of wine and..." Musa looked about at the scattered utensils, then gave a glance to a couple of other attendants who had also come at the commotion. But her mistress stopped her.

"No, Musa, *now.* I must see him *now.*" It was the coolest, firmest thing she had spoken yet, so Musa stopped and looked her in the face again.

"Right now, Musa," she pled, her face wet with tears. Procula never pleaded.

"Yes, Mistress. Now. Of course now."

With another glance, Musa sent the other girls running from the room for help, then sat on the edge of the bed. She gently overruled Procula's objections with a soft hand to her damp brow. The noblewoman finally yielded and lay back, her body tense as ever. Musa felt her frame jerk with spasms of fear every moment or so.

"Dear, dear Lady, how awful a sleep you must have had! Your eyes, they're...so dark—almost bruised! I never would have thought so. You were sleeping so soundly when the doctor had us bring you here to your chamber."

"You moved me in the night, Musa?" started Procula, only then realizing she was not in the antechamber she had last remembered the evening before.

"Yes, Mistress. The doctor and I returned and you were deeply asleep. It was just after dark. He felt it best you sleep in your own bed, so the servant girls and I carried you here. You slept as a child."

Procula shuddered at the word, but Musa went on.

"They say it helps to speak of the dream, Mistress," she said hopefully. "Won't you tell me what you dreamt?"

"No, Musa, no. I couldn't, I..." Procula began to weep and shake anew.

Another girl brought a fresh decanter of wine with a goblet. Musa readied it as she spoke, but Procula shook her head and Musa put it aside.

"Comfort yourself, Mistress. You are a fair lady and strong. All is quite well. And I understand why you cannot tell of the dream. They flee the mind so quickly, do they not?"

Eyes tightly shut, Procula shook her head again and again.

"Musa, this dream, this vision..."

"So it was a dream, then?"

"Yes, a dream. But a dream unlike any other I have ever known. It isn't for the forgetting that I cannot speak of it. It is the remembering all too well that hinders me. Oh, God!"

Procula hid her face in her hands. Only then did Musa see that she had ripped the skin on her fingers with her nails during the night; fresh red marks marred their graceful appearance. Dumbstruck, she began to viscerally grasp the terror her mistress had seen with the eyes of her soul. She instinctively reached out her hand to touch Procula, though she knew that at the moment all was cold comfort to her. Procula weakly fumbled for her hand in return.

Just then the younger maids returned, announcing that they brought news. A young officer waited without, begging leave to enter the chamber. Procula gathered herself as well as she could and quickly gave her consent. In a moment the man courteously but confidently strode into the room, and bowed low.

"Lady Procula," he said.

"Yes," she replied, voice still quavering, "Where is my husband? Why cannot he come to me?"

"His deepest regrets he sends, Lady. He is gravely detained by weighty affairs at this hour. He sends his greetings, inquires after your well-being, and promises he will be by your side as soon as his circumstances permit."

"What? What detains him? I sent word that I needed most desperately to see him."

The young man, not expecting this, stood abashed, and started to bring a reply. Herself again for a moment, Procula waved his words aside in exasperation. Then she caught herself, paused and looked hard at the man.

"*What* is my husband doing?" she queried, fearfully but pointedly.

Something in her voice, some strength born of trial, made the man a boy.

"He's—he's trying a prisoner, Lady. A Jew. A teacher from the north—from Galilee," he stammered. "The priests brought him before dawn. It approaches mid-morning and…"

Now Procula's body shook like a sapling olive in the wind.

"And what, *what* do the priests want with the Teacher? What is the charge against him? What do they want my husband to do with him?"

A moment of heavy silence passed.

"I believe they say he is an insurrectionist of some sort, Lady Procula," the officer finally answered, slowly. "I believe they want him—destroyed. That is why they came to his Honor the Governor. It is a matter of the Jews, Lady, and nothing for you to worry yourself about."

"*Are they in this palace?*" Procula began to rise from her couch.

"They were, Lady," confirmed the man with trepidation, now truly afraid to say another word, "but…they just departed. They have taken the prisoner to the Seat and the Stone Pavement—for final judgment."

Procula blanched, and again her hand covered her mouth. For an instant, Pilate's dying, blood-spattered face flashed before her.

"Get me a secretary, Musa, quickly, and a runner. I have a message of the greatest urgency for my husband."

Prayer: *Lord Jesus, You have granted me the freedom to follow You, but not the freedom to know beforehand the evil that might unfold for me and others if I choose not to. Left to myself, I am a heedless fool. Redeem my life from the vicious cycle of "too little, too late." Help me, by Your kind Spirit, to learn my lessons, and to turn back to You. And direct me in my efforts to make amends for the harm I may have done to others. Amen.*

THE LIGHT

Petronius, Centurion of the Tower Guard

Mark 15:39

Day Fourteen

The light of the candle flickered softly against the walls and across the rough surface of the mess table. Petronius hadn't bothered to find a plate or shard of broken pottery on which to place it. A few drips of hot wax from the freshly lit wick and the taper found its place in front of him, anchored to the unfinished wood, granting light and a little warmth to his bleak surroundings. He had grown to prefer the candle to the ubiquitous oil lamp of the Mediterranean world because of its portability in the field, and now that he had a choice, he used them out of habit and nostalgia. The one he had just lit made little shadows as it cast its brilliance against his hand, his writing kit, and the upturned corners of the small parchment on which he wrote. Larger shadows loomed behind him in the low arches of the vault he had sought out that night. He glanced around for a moment to collect his thoughts and noticed how the shades ran from that irresistible little flame. It always amazed him how such a tiny light could conquer so much darkness. He had brought other candles because he wasn't sure if just one would be enough. But after lighting the first, he saw that it gave light and to spare, and left it alone. The others he laid aside in case his task went long.

But Petronius hadn't the inclination to meditate long on the humble splendor of the tallow in front of him. He had more important things on his mind. He was busy writing. Writing and thinking. Struggling for words and thinking exactly what he should put to the skin in front of him. It didn't come easy. As a boy he had been taught his letters by a slave his father had purchased for that purpose. He had learned the necessary skills to rise in the ranks and more greatly benefit the Caesars. In order to read his orders he had to know these things. But that didn't mean that he was a man of words. He was as he trained to be, a man of the sword, and a man of men of the sword. A weapon of one kind or another always accompanied him, and he liked it that way. He was too important a man to sit and do the work of a secretary; if he had to communicate he used an amanuensis. Pen and ink made him nervous.

Yet on this night, as the darkness of late evening wore on into the deeper darkness before the dawn, he sat writing, impelled by his own irritability. Sleep fled from him more and more lately, and although he tried to resign himself to it, he had increasingly come to see his present situation as intolerable. He should not be here, he constantly told himself. He was meant for greater things than this. Earlier in the evening, after he had retired with his men, he found himself brooding fitfully over what could have been, over what should have been. To add to his discomfiture the Festival was upon them and his garrison had been bolstered with fresh troops from Caesarea as it always was on such occasions. Normally he would have welcomed the change in routine, but this time it made him jumpy. And so, serenaded by the snores of a dozen men and the new, unfamiliar sound of innumerable bleating lambs in the dusty street below, Petronius had risen, gathered his things, and sought the solitude of the mess quarters in the lower recesses the fortress. He had finally worked up the nerve to write a letter and plead his case. Bound by the need for confidentiality he would have to write it himself.

Petronius was a young Roman officer. Born in Cisalpine Gaul in northern Italy, he considered himself thoroughly Roman even though he hadn't spent much time in Rome itself. With the aid of his father, who instilled in his son an insatiable thirst for personal glory, Petronius had launched what would become a successful military career. Attached to a legion in Upper Germany, he ascended quickly and soon enough held a rank of high centurion. But for his father's untimely death, he felt sure his sire would have been proud. Petronius consistently earned the admiration of his superiors, and his men honored his instincts and his insistence on military discipline. He was a pragmatist, not a legalist. A firm hand meant a strong century, and a strong century meant victories—for himself and for Rome. He distinguished himself by bravery in a number of frontier skirmishes, and his ability to maintain calm in battle had saved the lives of more than a few of his men. Little affection warmed his relationship with his troops; he was too focused on matters beyond them for that. He gave praise when a man deserved it, and did not hesitate to punish the negligent and careless. On balance his men spoke respectfully of him, and that was enough. A good reputation in the military went a long way and could last a lifetime, and favors gained now could be collected on later. The future looked bright for him.

But young Petronius had not been satisfied. Things had not advanced according to the ambitious schedule that he had set for himself. And so, after a number of prosperous years in Germany and a series of heartening personal victories under his belt, he began a sequence of maneuvers that he felt necessary to secure the future that he had envisioned. Since his father's death, Petronius had corresponded with the son of his father's eldest brother, a tribune in Rome and his closest family tie. As a young man he had always had a warm relationship with his cousin (a man who was nearly old enough to be his father) and had come to consider him a close ally. His position of influence had helped to make life more convenient when Petronius was a boy, adding to the network of connections that the family already enjoyed. Yet since his father's passing, what the young officer had once considered a convenient family bond now became indispensable, his only remaining chance for political alliance in Rome. Petronius felt vulnerable in a world where the leverage gained through personal associations was essential for a young man's rise to power. These sentiments led to the rather predictable strategy of striving to strengthen his ties with the man through whatever means possible. So he cultivated this relationship as carefully as he knew how, sending frugal gifts and brief letters, and trying to sound interested in his cousin's doings in Rome. When it appeared that a glut of officers in his command would limit his possibilities in Germany for some time to come, Petronius' inner clock told him that the hour had come to reap his carefully cultivated harvest. He wrote his cousin confidentially and suggested that it was time for a change, that he, perhaps, should be moved into a better position in another legion elsewhere in the Empire. It was a delicately worded note by anyone's standard, and a masterpiece by Petronius.' He was confident as he sent it off that it would not be without effect. He was right. Two short months later came the notice that he should travel to Rome for new orders. He remembered the look on the faces of several rivals as he rode off to the great city with a small body of troops, flush with the promise of something they could only vainly hope for. Even now in his dungeon he smiled briefly as he recalled the envy in their eyes. Petronius lived for such moments.

The smile faded. His trip to Rome was not what he had hoped for. Instead of the warm reception that he felt sure he would receive, he was simply granted some leave with the rest of the soldiers and told to await further notice. His relative showed him cordiality, but nothing more. Busy with his own affairs, his tone told the young officer his elder cousin was quite accustomed to being courted for political favors. Rome was a dark and perilous place. His assurances to Petronius were just short of patronizing. Yes, he had some promising connections that he had made the best of. Yes, of course there would be a good post. Yes, yes, yes. He had only to wait. And so Petronius waited, impatient as ever. Whatever his new position was, he felt sure that it would honor him greatly. He just wanted to get on with it. But reality soon dashed his high expectations; when the news finally came, he was stunned.

Judea.

Petronius gritted his teeth as he remembered the moment when the name of this cursed land first sounded in his ears. How could he have been so demoted? He had hoped for Rome itself, or even Nearer Spain. There were significant chances for advancement in such places. A man had room to move about. Even a spot like Achaia had its charm, albeit of a different nature. But Judea? From his perspective it was hard to see it as anything but the backwater of the Empire. He had tried to appeal the decision, but it was useless. His last meeting with his cousin proved most frustrating. His elder assured Petronius of the strategic importance of Judea and the real possibilities for glory there. He esteemed that if anyone could make a name there, it was his younger cousin. Certainly, if it were Rome's will to send him there, it must be for the best. Much could be learned through acceptance of the Empire's will. And so forth. His cousin's lecture had filled him with bitterness. He knew plenty about following orders; he knew more about giving them. Why was he being chastised like an errant child? What more could there be for him to master?

The shadows that hung about the ceiling threatened to close in on him, but their attempts proved futile. The circle of light kept them at bay and his hopes alive. He took a deep breath and tried to sort out his emotions from the rationale that he tried to articulate in his letter. No passionate ravings would be heard; he had to appear professional and, above all, in control. And control was a feeling that he hadn't had for some time now. As far as concerned him, his whole life and career had become like this nocturnal sojourn in the cellar mess—dark, cold, and claustrophobic. Everything seemed to be closing in on him and he could see no escape. Only the spark of his ambition, the desire to live up to—and perhaps surpass—his father's memory kept him going. Yes, his ambition kept him pressing forward.

The tiny flame, burning brighter as the wax melted away from the wick, flickered in voiceless protest against some unseen current, then returned undaunted to its former glory. Petronius felt no breeze. Indeed, he felt he was suffocating as he remembered the way events had transpired, one after another, to bring him to this point.

Prayer: *Lord Jesus, so much that I have dreamed about has not turned out as I had hoped. I confess that my disappointment has often led to me resenting You, or even rebelling against You. Too often I have pretended that I belonged to myself. By Your grace, I choose to surrender my self-will to You; my plans are Yours to prosper, change, or discard, as You will. Amen.*

Day Fifteen

At first, he had tried to put a good face on things. It was degrading enough to be sent into virtual exile, but it would prove unbearable if others saw his humiliation for it. Petronius set his jaw. He refused to be the butt of endless jokes at mess tables such as this throughout Upper Germany, even if he weren't present to hear them. So he learned as much as he could and as quickly as he could, on his own terms. He did his best to talk up Caesarea, and he almost convinced himself of the greatness of living in Herod's shining, newly-built harbor city. It was, he understood, not without its amenities. He would make it into a place of possibilities in his grand plan for personal glory. But Petronius was in for another disappointment, this time much worse than that which accompanied the initial word of his deployment to Judea. A week into his stay—barely enough time to find a place for his sandals, as he liked to say— his superiors summoned him. There had been a change, they told him. He would not stay in Caesarea. No, there was nothing to worry about, no offense on his part. He would still serve in Judea as he had requested (had he?). A post had opened in the garrison at Jerusalem, he was needed there, and thither he would travel on the morn. The decision, like that which had sent him to Palestine in the first place, was irrevocable.

And so he found himself in Jerusalem. He took up residence with the rest of the occupational troops in the Fortress of Antonia, a tower built by Herod the Great as part of the northern wall of the city. It overlooked the Second Quarter on one side and the Temple and its courts on the other. His job, and that of his men, was to keep order among the potentially troublesome inhabitants of the city. No one here spoke of Judea's possibilities. Jerusalem wasn't on the way to *anywhere*. This was the exile—nay, the sum of all his fears that he had entertained while in Upper Germany. His short respite in Caesarea vanished like a daydream as he settled into the routine of command. Petronius, for whatever reason, had been forgotten by the very people he had striven to impress.

Petronius cursed the very ground under his feet as he sat there, fuming about it all. To his mind, Judea was a rocky wasteland. The scraggly greenery that clung to the rocks seemed to cry out for a relief that he couldn't give. He often daydreamed of the sunny valleys of his childhood or the verdant forests and fields of Germany. That was what a land should be—fertile and pleasant to the eye. In contrast, very little about Judea recommended itself to him. His black mood kept him from anything but the most hateful and negative thoughts for this equally hateful land. The Jews that lived here called it a land of promise. Petronius snorted in sarcastic disdain. For him it promised nothing but misery.

Of course, the land itself made only a fraction of his frustration. What made him really hate Judea was the people. From the moment he arrived here he felt that of all the nations for a Roman to live, this had to be the worst. In truth, Jerusalem did boast some diversions. But not enough to suit him. And the people's religion ruined everything. A bevy of restrictions kept them from the very activities that made Rome great—and a soldier happy. He was not alone in his sentiments. He had heard that even the governor, Pilate himself, had been disciplined for nothing more than a patriotic show of Roman glory when he had first taken office a couple of years back. They had brought a few imperial emblems into the city, nothing more. Show me the harm in that, he thought. Yet Tiberius had corrected *Pilate* and mollified the *Jews!* Well, *they* might feel pacified, but the whole thing made Petronius furious just to think of it. The Romans were the victors; the Jews were the vanquished. He understood the principles that held the Empire together, but surely the heads in Rome could think of a better way to do things than to constantly placate a nation of religious fanatics.

The finer points of Jewish faith were lost on Petronius. Indeed, he had no desire whatsoever to educate himself in their eccentric system of beliefs. One god, one temple, one holy city— it all struck him as very, very strange. Duty dictated that he know who was who, because it could affect security. Sadducees, they were friends, or at least political allies for their own convenience. The Romans turned their greed for power to useful ends. Pharisees, they weren't so friendly. But they weren't about to take up arms. Some people were stirring those coals, and Petronius conceded that some of these peculiar people might give them a fight after all. A growing contingent of zealots had been especially irksome lately, and a few that had caused some trouble were about to be dealt with—in the final sense. After these groups came a mixture of strange elements that lived in the desert in groups or even wandered around talking about this god of theirs. This last trend had been more and more prominent recently and he always seemed to be hearing about it. Most of all, they were just people, poor people who lived like poor people lived everywhere, but for their strange faith. They didn't occupy themselves at all with what seemed important to Petronius, and at the same time seemed passionately interested in things that he couldn't make heads or tails of. He found their dietary customs and their dress incomprehensible, and they seemed fascinated to an extreme with the days of the week (oddly refusing to work or even play on every seventh day) and with certain festivals. Local peculiarities were nothing new, of course. All the Empire did these things, each nation after its own fashion. There was just something about this people that made them different (he might even have used the term "special," but not in a positive way), and Petronius couldn't figure out exactly what. As he walked through the dirty market places on patrol, he stared at their dark, bearded faces as they jabbered on in Aramaic, feverishly arguing prices, or recent events, or perhaps religion. He never knew. He did know that when he approached with his men they lowered their voices and looked askance at them. Soon he learned the meaning of one word many Jews muttered bitterly as he and his men passed—"dog." It incensed him at first, sending him into the crowds, grabbing at terrified merchants or even women in his rage. But he could never know for sure who had hurled the insults, and he finally chose to ignore them. He grew to view such petty affronts as unworthy of his time. Yet it left no doubt that he had found the common ground shared by these different groups: They all hated the Romans.

Well, I hate them back, he thought. But he didn't really hate them, of course. He stood too far from them for real hate. What he really felt was scornful apathy. If they had never existed, or ceased to exist on the morrow, he wouldn't care a mite. He had his own worries and dreams. Recently, however, he had begun to completely identify them and their dry land with the deep frustration that grew in the darkness of his heart. There was no end in sight for his service here. There was no room for advancement, no hope for transfer. The few times he had visited Caesarea had only exacerbated his inner wound. While his peers—men of equal and even lesser rank—swam in the waters of the Mediterranean or soaked in lustrous baths, he sat dying of thirst in Jerusalem. They enjoyed many of the benefits of Rome and the freedom of the Roman culture. The abundance of Rome flowed into Herod's port. They could indulge in good wine and fair women. They visited the temples at will. Most of all, they could play the game that he had become so skilled at. They were rising, falling, being promoted, being transferred, and retiring in honor. He knew that he couldn't be stuck in Jerusalem forever—at least he hoped not. But he was losing time and losing his touch. He had to get out. For all the talk of service to Caesar, he had very little patience for it. He, and everyone else, recognized such speeches as mere palaver. He didn't take them any more seriously than he took the sacrifices that his position obligated him to make. Petronius fawned after one thing and one thing alone, and that was Petronius. That was how things worked because it was the only way they *could* work. Anyone who took all this "service" nonsense seriously was an imbecile. Petronius did not consciously grapple with such an idea; it was so alien to him that it never really entered his mind. His father had taught him to consume, to absorb. His father had taught him to conquer. To do anything else was entirely out of the question.

Prayer: Lord Jesus, what wonderful plans You have for me! You know me better than I know myself, and love me more deeply than I can comprehend. You have good planned for me that my natural eyes cannot see. But I am blinder still when I push back against You. Help me now to trust You, to allow You to guide me, even if I find my present situation irksome. Help my unbelief, and direct my feet on the sometimes rocky path that leads to Your glory. Amen.

Day Sixteen

A drop of wax succumbed to the heat near the wick and began to course down the side of the candle. Like a persistent tear, it made its way past a small multitude of its defunct predecessors and onto the table. By a coincidence of nature, the hot wax found a tiny groove in the wood and proceeded another inch or so towards Petronius. He watched the glossy sheen go out of it as it hardened in front of him. Rigor mortis had set in. The flame burned on, impassive to the insignificant drama played out below. The tiny blaze had burned most of the candle without compassion and had no intention of changing its disposition now. Its victims lay like corpses on the battlefield below it, and the hill upon which they rested was rapidly being consumed. The taper stood less than half of its original height; it would not last much longer. Petronius leaned forward and fixed his gaze on the fire, staring until his vision blurred and the flame emblazoned itself on his retina. He stared until its orange nothingness was all he could see.

The candle is a fool.

The thought came to him suddenly. It wasn't the *victim* of the flame. The whole of it was one. The candle *chose* to burn, it *chose* to give itself to the fire. From top to bottom it was designed for self-immolation. No one had to coax it once the spark caught the wick. No one had to force it, like the priests Petronius had watched from the parapet of his tower, dragging goats to the altar for sacrifice. Those goats had some sense. They, at least, had the wisdom to struggle, futile though it was. They fought against the cords of their captivity until the knife fell. Yea, even the light-giving lamps of the Temple preserved themselves, suffering only the precious oil within them to be consumed. But the candle....the candle is a fool. It makes no sound, it gives no battle. It yields itself without the slightest whimper until nothing at all remains. And for what? To grant light—for another. To grant warmth—to another. To show a path in the dark place, to give courage to the frightened child, to dispel the gloom and lift the spirit of the melancholy man. It did all of this with unshakable determination and with no thought whatsoever for its own future.

Petronius blinked, then refocused on his opponent. It observed him in turn with its single bright eye, and continued with its labor of keeping the blackness at bay. Even now it did not answer him, its motives still a mystery. His silent deprecation did not turn it from its purpose nor diminish the majesty by which it illumined his benighted world. He reached forward with his right hand and dug the sharpened tip of his reed pen into the soft wax at the candle's base. Pierced, it gave way, but the candle did not budge, moored as it was in the refuse of its own destruction. It had no recourse now. It was nothing but a small, nearly formless plug of tallow on a greasy mess table. Soon the flame that flickered in the minuscule puddle at its center would run out of wick or fuel, and the candle would sputter its last and die. The soldiers who found its remains at daybreak wouldn't think twice about scraping them off with the edge of a knife and casting them to the floor. Petronius shook his head, and his hoarse whisper echoed off the chill stone walls.

"Why do you do it?"

"Centurion?"

Petronius started from his seat, jolted by the adrenaline of complete surprise. Instinctively he reached for the dagger at his hip as he turned. The chair tipped and fell to the floor.

"My apologies, sir," said one of his men, whose face Petronius recognized in the dwindling light as that of one of his lieutenants. He moved towards the chair to pick it up. Petronius waved him off in irritation, angry at himself for having reacted so. The young soldier quickly reassumed a posture of attention.

"What is it?" he asked, trying to remember himself and control his nerves.

"You are summoned, sir. There is…another prisoner."

"A prisoner? At this hour?"

The soldier nodded and began to speak, but Petronius cut him off. "Put him away then, and we'll deal with it in the light."

"It's…the prefect, sir. Your presence is required. Pontius Pilate summons you."

Petronius stared for half a moment, lips apart. His soldier was already in his armor, his helm gripped in the crook of his left arm. The light danced off the dull bronze color of his plain breastplate and the greaves on his shins. His *gladius*, the standard issue short sword the legions were famous for, hung at his side. Petronius saw his eyes glancing to one side, though he didn't turn his head. It was the letter. Centurions didn't write—ever. And to do so in the middle of the night was indeed most irregular. Petronius leaned that way and placed his fist on the table. The young man returned his gaze to a respectable, undefined point directly in front of him. Petronius cleared his throat.

"Very well. Follow me to the barracks and help me dress."

"Yes, Centurion," the soldier replied, turning ninety degrees to the left in order to let his commander pass. Petronius exhaled sharply and paused for another second, head down. Then he strode past the soldier and made his way up the steps to his quarters.

Prayer: *Lord Jesus, search my heart and deliver me from the paralysis and idolatry of always playing the victim. You and You alone have been truly innocent in Your suffering, and You freely submitted to that suffering to set me free. I want to be healed, I want to pick up my mat and walk. Open my eyes to see the Cross, the fearlessness in Your willingness to give it all, and what that absolute surrender means for me. Help me, somehow, to become like You. Amen.*

Day Seventeen

Before outfitting himself, he had his men awakened. Dawn approached in any case, and if Pilate wanted him for something the matter must be at least moderately important. He had to have men with him when he went, and the others had to be on alert anyway. Anything could happen these days with all the pilgrims in the city, and some things already had. He put on his armor wordlessly, assisted by the man who had fetched him. When he was ready Petronius turned to him, his mood already much more reasonable.

"That was smart work tracking me down, Lucius."

"Thank you, sir."

"How did you find me?"

"The light, sir."

"Of course," Petronius said.

He walked out of his small quarters with his inferior at his heels, and found a small troop of men dressed, armed, and standing at attention. He nodded to them and they fell in behind him as he descended some steps, through the passageways of the fortress, and finally down some stairs onto the perimeter of the Temple Mount. Petronius planned to walk his men about 300 meters along the massive retaining wall that held up the western side of the Mount (which was really an enormous, manmade platform), then turn onto the wall that divided the Second Quarter from the rest of the city. This wall functioned as a causeway, more or less directly connecting the Temple Mount with Herod's Palace. There resided Pilate, prefect and governor of Judea. In all it was a short journey of perhaps five or six stadia from the Fortress of Antonia by the route they took. While they marched along behind the Temple, Petronius questioned his lieutenant more closely about the summons.

"I know almost nothing about the matter, sir. A messenger of the guard at the governor's residence came and informed me that there's a prisoner to deal with, and that he could not be treated lightly. Apparently it involves the priests and some others. They are with the prefect now and have the man securely in custody. I guess they can't do what they want with him."

Petronius cursed.

"Death to the Romans until you need your dirty work done," he fumed, shaking his head.

"Yes, sir," the young soldier replied.

Soon they exited the Temple Mount, making their way along the wall towards their destination. The great towers of Phasael, Hippicus, and Mariamne loomed before them, the three of them forming the mighty Citadel that stood guard over the Gennath Gate and the palace that stretched away to the south. Herod's Palace stood between the fashionable homes of the wealthy and the far western wall of the Upper City. Pilate didn't make it his permanent home, of course. The prefect of Judea ruled from his seat in Caesarea, as befitted his stature. He only came to Jerusalem for the festivals of the Jews. A significant body of troops accompanied him as a personal guard and to allow for increased patrols of the city. If troublemakers intended to rebel, the uprising would probably begin at a time like this. Increased military presence had a marvelously discouraging effect on such ideas. Pilate had come up to Jerusalem with his wife a week or so ago, and the Passover this year basically appeared to be like so many others. After an initial inspection of the Fortress Antonia, Petronius had seen nothing of him until two days ago. Then the governor came to Petronius' barracks, accompanied by his personal guard and by a delegation of Temple soldiers and a few lesser priests. There he had supervised the turning over of the high priest's sacred vestments so that the Jews might celebrate their Passover. He remembered Pilate's businesslike attitude, and the nervous humiliation of the Jewish holy men at that sanctuary of Roman power. It might be their city, but the

Romans held the keys, and this ritual enforced that point over and over. They took their holy things, made necessary obeisance to the governor, and then took their leave. After this, Pilate had nodded briefly to Petronius and returned to his residence to wait and hope for a relatively event-free Passover. To this point, more or less, it had appeared he would get his wish. The governor would return to Caesarea the following week after the bulk of the visitors had left.

But now it didn't look like such an uncomplicated time after all, not with a detachment of soldiers marching towards his home in the dim morning light. This time Petronius did the visiting, and he was curious to see what all this was about. Perhaps it was another insurrectionist like the ones captured a short time earlier, now chained in Antonia awaiting their doom. That hadn't amounted to much—Pilate had sentenced them in minutes—but one never could tell with these people. Or maybe some sort of political intrigue plagued the governor. Petronius mulled these matters intently as he strode quickly along the wall, his men double-stepping to keep up. The city had already begun to stir. He saw women stepping out of their doors in the city below, heard their voices as they greeted one another. A few roosters crowed repeatedly in the distance. Day was breaking.

In spite of the smart marching, by the time they had descended into the palace compound and hurried his platoon the length of the expansive plaza to the southernmost end, Petronius realized his tardiness. As he approached the gate he saw a body of men, older Jewish men in robes at the front and a group of soldiers at the rear. The soldiers' formation indicated the presence of a prisoner in their midst, but Petronius couldn't see him. They were already walking away from the palace, heading back into the narrow streets of the Upper City. Petronius looked up just in time to see the figure he knew to be Pontius Pilate turn and go into his residence. An officer of the Praetorian Guard stepped forward as Petronius and his men closed on the portal.

"Greetings, Centurion."

"Greetings," said he pensively, saluting after their fashion. "What news?"

The soldier read his concern and spoke to it.

"You are prompt in your coming, Petronius. But the governor may not need so much support as we first thought. The prisoner is a Jew from another jurisdiction and has been sent to its corresponding tribunal. The decision to do so was made rather quickly."

Petronius looked visibly relieved that he had not failed in his duty. His men remained at attention, but he stood momentarily at a loss as to a course of action. Should he not speak with the prefect?

"It would be prudent for you to remain until word comes of the outcome. The high priest himself is involved," said the officer, answering his thoughts again. "Please bring your men under the portico."

Petronius accepted this word as an invitation (he was every bit this man's equal), and readily complied. He allowed his men to break file, but they remained alert and spoke little among themselves. They stood, after all, on the governor's doorstep. It would not be necessary for him to see Pilate personally unless some irregularity came up, and the matter may take care of itself. In such case new orders would come and Petronius would return to the Tower with his men. In the meantime they must wait, but that suited Petronius well for it gave him time to talk with the guards there and find out exactly what had happened.

It turned out that the prisoner was nothing at all what he had expected. Instead of some violent criminal or subversive, he was nothing more than a young rabbi, a Galilean who had come to the city for the holy days. The high priest, with many of his attendants and family members, had come with the man already in custody, vehemently accusing him. The more the situation was explained to him, the more he realized who it must be. He had heard of this man. A simple teacher from the north and supposed wonder worker, he had wandered the countryside and spoken of the "kingdom" of their god. Under other circumstances this might cause worry—revolutions had started here with such words—except for the fact that he spoke nothing of such action, at least not as far as Petronius had heard. He seemed fascinated with the heavens, and he passed this fascination on to his followers.

"Is he the one whose disciples welcomed him with cheers a few days back?" asked Petronius.

"I can't keep track of all these fanatics," answered his counterpart haughtily. "I'd only just arrived myself and I've been close to the governor the whole time. He is my concern, not this rabble."

"I think he is," said Petronius, pretending to ignore the other's puffy tone. "He's popular with the people, but he's harmless from what I understand—at least compared to some others I've had to deal with. What do they want of him?"

"Maybe you just put your finger on it. He's popular. Pilate thinks he's innocent and told them so, but these priests keep accusing him of everything you can imagine. Probably all lies, of course, but the charges are serious enough because they involve taxation and insurrection," the officer said, then paused and looked at the palace entrance. "No, I don't think I'd like to sit in the governor's chair today. Punish a prophet and cause another riot, or infuriate the priests, groundless as their case may be. Not a pleasant choice."

Petronius said nothing, but raised an eyebrow and nodded knowingly. The other shrugged. No one needed to talk about Pilate's precarious position in Judea. Another bad report to the emperor and he could lose everything he had gained by his appointment—or more. Of late, such removals from office had proved fatal to others of higher position than Pilate. Petronius had heard Pilate had friends in high places, but things were extremely volatile in Rome, regardless of one's connections.

"So, where're they taking him now?"

"Well, he is a Galilean."

"Yes."

"When the governor heard that, he did what any wise man in his position would do. He sent him—"

"—To Herod Antipas."

Another nod, with a wry smile.

"Not without reason did he get himself appointed prefect of Judea."

"Certainly not," answered Petronius, looking around at his men in the growing light. He filed Pilate's tactic away in his memory bank for future reference. A man of authority needed to learn such things to survive.

So Petronius and his men waited with the others for word from Herod. His house was reasonably close; a messenger should come soon if Herod chose to decide the case. But time wore on and no messenger came. After about an hour a guard called out, and some of Pilate's personal soldiers turned and entered the palace. Petronius and his men formed files and took up position adjacent to these men from Caesarea. The unlikely entourage approached on the street by which they had departed a short time ago. Again the priests led the way, this time accompanied by an officer and a couple emissaries from Herod. The Temple Guard and its prisoner followed behind.

"Looks like Herod knows the same trick," Petronius whispered to his new friend as he completed his formation. The man gave him a curt half-nod and a glance that said it all: This wasn't over, and it wasn't going to be clean. Pilate's tactics had failed.

Prayer: Lord Jesus, my world is full of self-important bullies. Politics, power plays, and pride all jostle to take the most prominent place on the stage of my thoughts. But You are made of a different stuff, and You make no apologies for refusing to play king of the hill with the would-be lords of this world. While the proud seek to rid themselves of Your scandalous innocence, come, Lord, and find Your home with me. I open my heart. Amen.

Day Eighteen

Pilate issued from the palace entrance and came hastily between the ranks of men that had just formed there. Herod's captain, with a messenger, stepped forward to salute him. The priests listened with interest just outside the gate, but would not enter. After a brief exchange of formalities, the messenger unrolled a small scroll and read a short message. Herod Antipas was deeply honored by the deferential gesture, but, lamentably, could not decide the prisoner's fate. At this point Petronius lost track of the rest of the message because it had to do with supposed technicalities of law, jurisdiction, and criminal offense.

But just because he couldn't follow the flowery speech and the minute details of messages that pass between kings didn't mean that Petronius missed the gist of it all. *I thank you for the offer, Prefect, but I haven't the stomach for this prickly issue any more than you do.*

Pilate received the message stoically, then took the scroll from the messenger. He said something perfunctorily courteous to the man, who bowed and backed away. Herod's captain then called forth the Temple Guard, who in turn came to deliver the prisoner.

For the first time Petronius saw him. He was a Jew, like many other Jews—nondescript, medium height and weight, bearded. He stood there amongst his captors, head down, hands tied behind him. He had been beaten, for his face was bruised and Petronius saw dried blood in the hair under his nose and on his lip. A fine scarlet-purple robe hung loosely about him. As Petronius stepped forward to take him into Roman custody (the other officer would be accompanying Pilate throughout the proceedings), he wondered. Arrayed around this man stood chief priests and their assistants, soldiers of the Temple, Herod's men, Roman regulars, and members of the Praetorian Guard. It seemed a lot of fuss for one simple teacher. Petronius met the eyes of the captain as he pushed the young man forward. The other soldier misread his glance.

"A gift for the 'king,'" he said with sarcastic reverence, and fingered the edge of the purple as his ward departed.

Petronius did not know how to respond, so he said nothing. Pilate glanced again at the scroll as Herod's men marched back down the street. The priests stood waiting, looks of impatience and angry expectation on their faces. Pilate looked up at them as if to reply, then turned to Petronius.

"Take him inside, Centurion," he said wearily. "I will be along shortly."

Petronius turned in obedience and grasped the prisoner firmly by the arm, hauling him with unnecessary roughness up the steps. He did not look the man in the face. Pilate began to speak to the priests while Petronius paused to cut four men from the ranks. He ordered them to follow, then continued on. He knew the way. Within the palace opened a court where the governor heard important cases, and Petronius had stood there before. His prisoner made no resistance whatsoever, either actively or passively. He did not stumble, and he did not try to pull away, even though Petronius felt a respectable bulge of muscle as he gripped his left elbow. The rabbi almost walked with purpose, as if he were one of Petronius' men who had been ordered to march with him. For a moment, Petronius even thought he might be leading the way. Deliberate. That was the word. There was a deliberateness to his step. It puzzled Petronius a bit but he didn't want a Jew to get the best of him. When they arrived before Pilate's chair he gave the man a parting shove.

The prisoner stumbled, head down, but caught himself and slowly straightened. He did not turn. Petronius' men stood back at attention, while their commander assumed a position a bit closer to his charge. They waited for about five minutes. During this time Petronius examined his man from behind. He found himself wishing that he had taken a closer look at him before. He wanted to see his face, but protocol did not demand a change in his position, and his men would assume that he was merely curious (and they would be right). So Petronius had to content himself with an evaluation of his form and his posture from the vantage point that he had.

In spite of the abuse he had suffered, the man stood with relative steadiness. He did not look about. His bearing seemed neither headstrong nor downcast, but simply upright in a certain anticipation. The purple robe that Herod had draped around him was slipping off to one side, and with his hands tied he could not do anything about it. Petronius doubted he would even if he could. It was a cynical insult, its elegance underscoring the scorn of its bestower. The rich carelessly spend money even on their own bad jokes. Below the robe his bare feet stood on the cold marble floor. It occurred to Petronius that he had probably not slept much that night either; the priests had obviously dealt with him before bringing him here.

Pilate walked in briskly with his guards behind him. They took their places while he settled into his seat and arranged his toga, and Petronius met the eye of the officer he had spoken with outside. He put a query in his glance, and the man looked to the side for a moment, looked back, and mouthed the word *"morte"* without making a sound. Then he gave his attention to the governor.

With one word the soldier confirmed Petronius' suspicions. Under Roman law the Jews could put nobody to death without the permission of their governor. They didn't want Pilate to judge this man; they wanted his seal of approval on a decision they had already made. But it still didn't answer the fundamental question as to why. He already knew that Pilate didn't think the man was worthy of punishment. What could this Jew have done to make the priests want him dead?

The governor leaned forward and observed the accused closely for a moment, and then he spoke. There began the strangest conversation that Petronius had ever witnessed. Clearly, the two antagonists had already met. Their words comprised a continuation of some brief interchange that had occurred before the visit to Herod. Pilate asked him some questions about kingship—if he thought and proclaimed himself the king of the Jews. The man paused thoughtfully for a moment, then chose not to answer at all. Instead, he asked Pilate a question—a silly one.

In that instant Petronius realized that the man was a fool. He obviously knew nothing of Roman laws or protocols. Pilate *could not* convict him unless he found solid evidence against him, and with his life in the balance (surely he knew that) it was insanity to play with the issue. Pilate was granting him the right to speak, to defend himself. This was the time; later might be too late. He should deny the charges directly (even if there was some truth in them), and then, if possible, lodge some sort of counteraccusation against his detractors. The law applied to all, and Petronius had seen enough trials to know how people worked the system. This man's attack on the priests may not accomplish anything other than his own acquittal, but wasn't that enough?

Pilate answered with all the dark sarcasm that Petronius himself would have used. Don't toy with me, Jew. I am here, and you are there, bruised and dressed like a clown in front of me. I will ask the questions.

The rabbi finally answered, but his tone told Petronius that he did so not out of fear for the questioner but for reasons of his own. He admitted that he was a king—of sorts: a king of another place, another world.

"So, you *are* a king?" queried Pilate in a disbelieving tone.

The young man calmly affirmed his confession once again. Yes, he said, a king of truth. Pilate made another sarcastic comment, to which the rabbi said nothing. The prefect shook his head, arose, and stalked out, muttering softly to himself.

The prisoner stood still, surrounded, it seemed, by a cloud of self-created serenity. He still did not look about at the guards, and even after Pilate's needling he showed no fear of any kind. Either that or he certainly covered it well, thought Petronius. For a moment the soldier almost wanted to approach the man and explain to him the gravity of his situation. He wanted to tell this crazy teacher about Roman law and shake him from the religious eccentricity that darkened his mind. Fool, he thought, you might very well die here if you don't start playing by the rules. Can't you tell that the governor wants to get you (and himself) out of this mess? Give him a reason, any reason, and you'll go free. Just speak up like everybody else does, and you can go back to wandering about among your people or whatever else it is you wish to do. As it is, all this talk of truth and heaven isn't helping you at all. It's your life, Petronius thought. If you don't do something quick you're sure to lose it.

Prayer: Lord Jesus, I live in this dark world. All about me walk those who still dress You as if You were a joke, sneer at You, and with their glances, words, and attitudes try to discourage my faith in You. Give me Your calm courage, Your heavenly steadiness, and above all Your merciful heart. Help me not fall for the charade of this world's wisdom; help me not be pulled in by this world's lies about strength. Amen.

Day Nineteen

After a brief interlude Pilate returned. His guards took their places again, but the governor spun around before reaching his seat of judgment and stood a few feet in front of the young teacher. Pilate fixed his eyes upon him and Petronius saw his jaw moving slightly, as if grinding his teeth in thought. The Jew made no movement, but the fine robe slipped a bit more onto the floor, revealing a simple garment of rough cloth underneath.

"They mean to rid themselves of you, Jesus of Nazareth. Will you say nothing in your own defense?"

The man did not reply. Pilate stared at him. Tension filled the air.

"Very well," said Pilate, breaking the silence so abruptly that Petronius started imperceptibly where he stood. The governor called sharply to the soldier without taking his eyes from the accused. "Centurion!"

"Prefect!" Petronius stepped forward smartly, regaining his composure.

Pilate paused, eyes still attached to the semi-comical figure in front of him. The Nazarene did not flinch.

"Scourge him."

Petronius paused for a fraction of a second, looking sidelong at the rabbi. Nothing. Pilate finally broke his stare to meet the soldier's eyes. Petronius answered and corrected his line of sight before he could read the intent of the governor's glance.

"Yes, Prefect!"

Petronius motioned quickly and his men stepped forward to seize the prisoner. They were upon him in an instant, and fairly lifted him from the floor in their zeal to obey. Judgment had been passed, the order had been given, and punishment would be meted out. They were not gentle. Why should they be? At this point a few shoves and cuffs were the least of this silly Jew's problems. Petronius waited a moment until they were a few steps ahead of him then saluted and turned to follow. After he had gone a few paces Pilate called to him.

"Petronius Severus."

It was the first time Pilate had honored him by using anything other than his title of rank to give him an order. Petronius was so surprised by it that he only half turned to the governor as he stopped in mid-stride, as he would if a friend had called out his name. Pilate had not moved from his place, his toga-draped frame still facing the spot where the teacher had just stood. Only his head turned toward the centurion, an expression of controlled anxiety on his face. Petronius thought that he wore it well—a mien that befitted his position of authority. He felt sure that he had plenty of practice with it. Pilate did not wait for Petronius to reply before completing his thought.

"I mean to spare this man's life, Centurion," he said shortly, "but these priests want blood. I have no choice but to give it to them. Perhaps a prophet bruised and bleeding will be enough to satisfy them so that we don't have to give them a dead one. But he must suffer. Do you understand?"

Petronius nodded.

"Yes, Sire."

Pilate turned back and looked at the floor where the rabbi had stood without acknowledging the answer. Petronius watched him for a moment then turned and followed the steps that his men had taken, escorting the Jew to the most painful beating that a man could ever experience.

With the prisoner firmly in the grip of his men, Petronius guided his detachment to the citadel where the ugly deed would be done. There Petronius gave the order and the victim was stripped. He remained rigid as they ripped off his clothing, common and royal, and cast them aside in an ignominious heap. Soon the man stood naked and shivering slightly in the chilly air, soldiers all around. Word had traveled quickly and almost all of the men in the *praetorium*—those that had nothing better to do— gathered for the show. It wasn't often that the Romans had permission to beat a popular Jewish holy man. The Jews had their own rules for such punishments: few blows and little blood, all in the name of brotherhood. Well, this man was no brother to them. They would suffer no limits and wouldn't use sticks or leather straps to do the job. Besides, the governor had ordered. Now the prisoner stood there in his shame in front of a post reserved for this purpose, one of Petronius' men binding his hands with a long leather strap. It was strange how angry the soldier was with the young rabbi. He treated him as roughly as possible, pulling at him and tying his wrists together so tightly that Petronius could see his fingers turn purple. Two other men held him in an iron grip so that he could not escape or struggle. But it was all for naught. The man looked down at his own hands and the progress of his captors as if he himself had a personal stake in their success. All that Petronius could see that betrayed his anticipation of the ordeal to come was some labor in his breathing.

The soldiers finished their task. They shoved the naked man into the post with a thud, and the one who had bound him deftly flipped the end of the cord over a spike that protruded from the pole some eight feet above the ground. Yanking hard they soon had him standing on tiptoe, head forced back, palms facing each other but splayed outward by the bondage that stretched him beyond his full height. Petronius had seen it all before. A fundamental of the penal system wherever one went in the empire, commanders typically administered beatings as a matter of course. He himself had ordered the scourging of German slaves for stealing, even for defiance. That, Petronius thought, is what was lacking here. The man did not seem to hate them for what their abuses. He betrayed no anger or fear, nor did he whimper or beg for mercy, behavior Petronius had always considered one of the highest forms of contempt. Even now, hanging there with buttocks bared—something Petronius knew to be of supreme humiliation for a Jew—he was still.

"Centurion, we are ready," said Lucius, his lieutenant.

Prayer*: Lord Jesus, they did terrible things to You, but they only carried out what You had purposed in Your heart to allow, that You might redeem us all. Such purity of resolve is beyond me, and yet You call me to be like You and promise the grace to sustain me. Forgive me for ever glossing over what You suffered to make it more bearable for me. Help me understand Your sacrifice, so that I might truly follow Your footsteps. Amen.*

Day Twenty

Lucius held a scourge, and its sharpened fragments, bits of bone and metal woven into its leather strands, rattled against each other as it swung in his hand. Petronius looked at him and his weapon.

"Shall I begin?"

"No," said Petronius, almost thoughtfully. "No."

"Sir?"

"This one is for another, Lucius," he said. "Call out Velius."

The message was in the choosing; this would be no symbolic beating. Velius was a big soldier, and one of the strongest men in Petronius' command. He had punished prisoners before to terrible effect.

"Sir," said Lucius obediently, and turned to call the man out of the group that stood there waiting.

The other man stepped forward and took the scourge. By now a large crowd of rowdy, joking soldiers had gathered. They had been having a good time at the prisoner's expense, taunting him for his naked helplessness and jeering him in anticipation of his suffering. Now that things were getting started they raised their voices.

"Give it to him, Velius!"

"Make the filth cry like a girl!"

The rest joined in with similar cheers.

The soldier may as well have stood alone in that courtyard, alone with his victim. He was a man who took his assignments seriously. With a grim look on his face he took a few steps toward the bound and waiting prisoner. For all his seriousness the others just got louder. Maybe this was why Petronius didn't hear the Jew cry out when the first stroke ripped across his back. As if on cue, the crowd fell silent for a second. The rabbi's frame jerked from the impact of the blow, then held steady. Velius held back for a moment, and the soldiers spontaneously broke into a whoop. Then the beating began in earnest. Up and down he went, the scourge methodically shredding the surface of the man's body. The studded thongs whipped around his sides, his chest, his limbs. In a few minutes he was nothing but a bleeding mass. Petronius lost count of the strokes, but it really didn't matter. Each blow from that whip was many, and with the strength in the flayer's arm and the nature of the instrument, the punishment had soon cut the victim to his very bones. Yet who could have known it? No screams, no cries, no whimpers, but only the occasional soft groan as the torture knocked the wind out of him. Petronius wasn't the only one who noticed. Gradually the men quieted down until all that could be heard in that yard was the rhythmic whisking stroke of the whips against flesh, then the rasping sound they made against the flagstones as the wind up came for another. Soon the man hung from his wrists, his legs no longer able to hold him. His body reacted to the blows as would the carcass of a slaughtered animal; the force of the whip, not the pain, shook his body. It was time.

"Enough," said Petronius, stepping forward.

Velius stopped in mid-stroke, lowered the whip and moved aside. He removed his helmet and wiped his brow, inadvertently staining it with a sanguine smear.

Petronius walked over to the post, drew his dagger, and cut the cord that held the man to it. He collapsed, and the soldiers broke into another cheer.

"Not so bold now, are we?" Petronius said under his breath as he looked down at his prisoner. Before he could bend down to see if the punishment had gone too far, the man rolled to one side and looked at Petronius' sandals. Then he pulled his arms underneath him and started to push his elbow against the bloody pavement to prop himself up. The centurion was amazed, and not much could amaze him anymore. He called to his men, and they moved with their customary alacrity. Soon they had the Jew on his feet.

Some men came forward with what remained of his clothes (now torn from the stripping) and the royal robe.

"May we robe the 'king,' Centurion?" they asked with sarcastic sneers.

Petronius looked and saw that they had not only readied the purple for the "King of the Jews," but they had also formed a tightly woven circlet of thorns and a reed baton. They had their permission to have some fun and they wanted to make the most of it. He saw that he wasn't the only one frustrated with Judea. He shook his head with a grin—his first all day—and with a wave of the hand gave his blessing to their impromptu coronation ceremony. He wouldn't begrudge his men a little diversion in this dismal land. Besides, if he could make this Jew look worse off it might help achieve what the governor had intimated.

Before long the rabbi stood, adorned in Herod's gift (now ruined with blood) and holding a staff in his hand. They saved the crown for last. A soldier placed it on his head with pretended pomp, then stepped back to admire him, sucking his finger where a thorn had pricked him. Everyone began to chuckle. Suddenly the soldier fell to his knees.

"Hail!" he cried.

The rest of the soldiers burst into uproarious laughter. One after another they, too, fell on their knees or bowed down, mimicking the cry of the leader.

"Hail! Hail! Hail, O King of the Jews!"

The Jew just stood there and took it. His expression spoke deep weariness, and he was weak from the blood loss and the pounding he had endured. His body shook. But his calmness remained intact while he looked down upon those who mocked him so cruelly. Petronius saw a look of sadness in his eyes, and against all reason he perceived that it was not self-pity, but rather a sort of benevolent condescension for the violent men clamoring stupidly at his feet. It occurred to him that nothing obligated that Jew to hold their ridiculous scepter and play along with the joke. For a trice Petronius saw something that he only then realized he had never seen in another, but what every man recognizes when he first encounters it. Petronius saw nobility. It stunned him. In that piercing instant all the pomp and glory of Rome seemed a vanity, and all the power of its vast armies a boy's game. The man lifted his head and began to turn it toward Petronius. The solder's heart skipped a beat.

Just then the man in front of the teacher cried out, "Your crown is slipping!" Jumping to his feet he snatched the baton from his hand and in one swift, horrible blow brought it crashing down on his brow. The weakened man crumpled to the pavement, blood pouring from his forehead. The crown had done its work. Others laughed hilariously and began to fight over the honor of adjusting the crown of the "king." Again and again the baton fell, pounding the thorns into the rabbi's head. He hadn't the strength to resist, and the men resorted to holding him up. Some kicked him when he fell; others struck him in the face or pulled at his beard. Most just stood around and had a good laugh. Only when Petronius glanced at Lucius did he realize that he himself wasn't doing a very good job of playing along. An expression of slight bewilderment replaced the mirth that had covered his lieutenant's face. Petronius coughed and forced a laugh from his inexplicably tight throat.

"All right! All right!" he said. "That's enough! We have to get him back—our king has a pressing audience to keep. We've done our job and you've had your fun."

Comically disappointed but obedient to the command, they stepped away, laughing and joking, and some began to filter back to their respective posts. Those who had come with Petronius remained. At his order two of them jerked the prisoner to his feet again. He obviously couldn't walk on his own, not at this point anyway. With one last look at the broken man—he hardly resembled one anymore—Petronius turned and headed back into the palace. The men fell in behind him, dragging the stumbling prisoner between them.

Prayer: Lord Jesus, I cringe at these unspeakable stripes, which were only the prelude to Your greatest sufferings. It is too painful to know what You endured, and I would rather look away, rather not consider the specifics. I ask Your grace that I might understand what Your earliest disciples understood, that I might also behold Your majesty. Help me to look on Your wounds such as they were, and so be healed. Amen.

Day Twenty-One

By the time they reached Pilate's chair, Petronius was thoroughly furious with himself. He, a centurion and a seasoned warrior, had gone soft. He was acting like a little child. What were these absurd feelings within him? Had he been away from battle so long that a little blood and some diversion at the expense of a crazy Jew made him go weak at the knees? What was wrong with him? As he presented himself and the prisoner before the governor he resolved to hate this stranger with all of his might. No one, least of all a condemned prisoner, would turn him from the pitiless discipline that governed his life and drove him forward to glory. He had an image to preserve and this puny preacher of proverbs had caused him to tarnish it. Just when his own reason was about to speak to him of the irrationality of his thoughts, the presence of the governor demanded that he speak. His own voice cleared the slate of his mind.

"The prisoner is ready, Prefect."

Pilate looked up at the Galilean, then at Petronius, then at the accused again, examining. He said nothing, but nodded slightly with his lips pursed. He rose and they stepped aside as he came down and walked through them toward the entrance where the priests must still be waiting. His toga dragged the floor and Petronius noticed that the edge of it stained where it ran across the spot where the rabbi had been standing. The scourged man had left a trail of bloody smears on the marble floor to show where he had been. Pilate turned before going too far.

"Bring him," he said tersely.

Petronius and his men followed, and soon they stood on the polished stones that paved the entrance to Pilate's residence. The priests waited there, their ceremonial purity still intact outside the gate, and a crowd had gathered behind them. The soldiers stayed behind at Pilate's bidding while the governor walked toward the holy men, then paused. Too far back to hear all of what he said to them, Petronius could only make out some reference to the man's innocence. Pilate then turned and motioned for them to bring him forward.

Petronius took him hard by his lacerated arm and he heard the man's breath pull sharply between his teeth, but he offered no resistance. They both went forward about half the distance toward the gate, then Petronius saw that the governor wanted the Jew to come alone. He let him go, and the man shuffled forward, then stood still before his accusers. Petronius saw only him.

"Behold, the Man!" cried Pilate.

Without a moment's hesitation they answered, "Crucify! Crucify him!"

Crucify? Why on earth would they want the man crucified? True, Petronius lost no love on Jews. And at the moment he was trying to stir up a particular dislike for this one. But nothing this man had done could justify such a death. It was reserved for only the vilest of criminals and could last for days. Rome exempted her citizens from it, and in most cases of non-citizens (like this man) there was no need for it. He had done nothing but offend their political prejudices or violate one of their religious codes. With Pilate's approval they could stone him, and that would be painful enough. Besides, it was their way of doing things. In Petronius' judgment it fit the case, if indeed this man was some sort of religious offender. Pilate might have to yield to this for the sake of political expediency, and Petronius thought that this was what they were after all along—Roman approval and permission. Now he realized that they also wanted Roman *methods*; only Petronius and his men could carry out such a sentence.

The chorus gained strength while Pilate shook his head. He had failed again. Finally he turned and motioned to Petronius, who quickly stepped forward and grabbed the prisoner again, then ushered him, stumbling hard now, back inside. Pilate did not follow. They waited at his court within while he parleyed with the priests without.

When after a few minutes Pilate returned, Petronius and his men reassumed the places they had taken at the beginning, with the centurion a few feet directly behind the rabbi. The governor seemed nervous, as if the priests had gained some sort of ground on him. He didn't take his seat, but paced a bit in front of the prisoner, looking him in the face. Finally he stopped in front of him.

"Where are you from?" he queried. His voice had an odd quality that sent a chill down Petronius' back.

The man remained silent, but swayed slightly in spite of his best efforts to remain still. A shudder ran through his frame. Petronius knew that an unshakeable cold had begun to grip him. That always followed a scourging, that and other things. He saw that the man literally stood in his own blood, which had dripped down his legs onto the beautiful floor. The governor waited in vain for a response. All was terribly still.

Pilate finally broke the silence in anger. Who did he think he was? He stood before the Roman governor of Judea, a man who had the authority to kill him—crucify him—or set him free. Would he not have the sense to fear even that? Had the scourging taught him nothing at all of the Roman ability to make a man suffer?

"You would have no authority against me," answered the Jew with astonishing clarity and strength, "unless it had been given to you from Above; therefore he who delivered me up to you has the greater sin."

Pilate, speechless, stared at the man. The Jew said nothing more, and for the moment his body ceased its minute convulsions. Petronius could see the face of neither. After a moment Pilate grasped his robe and strode past the Jew, past the centurion, and out to the gate. There was no describing his visage. It was a curious mix of fury, confusion, and something else. Petronius had no difficulty whatsoever identifying that other element. Every fighting man knows it, has grappled with it, has instilled it in other men. After several battles Petronius got to the point where he could practically smell it, and as the governor passed Petronius thought he smelled it in him. Pilate was afraid. Fear followed him like a wretched vapor, poisoning the air around him and seeking to sicken others with its contagious effects. It hit Petronius like a quiet wave, and the centurion, whose gaze had followed the prefect as he passed, kept his head cocked to one side while he mastered himself. There was something about this simple rabbi...something very, very different. What was it? By what power did he unnerve the rulers of men?

When after a minute he righted himself and looked forward again, he found himself eye to eye with Jesus of Nazareth. The teacher had turned just enough to look his captor full in the face. The centurion froze. Petronius could not have broken that gaze if his life had required it, and he knew in that breathless moment that the man had chosen to look upon him and had had no interest in the governor's exit. Petronius stared unblinking, a prisoner to something that was beyond him. A single, pregnant drop of crimson fell from a thorn imbedded in the man's brow. The fringe of Petronius' vision followed it as it coursed slowly down his forehead, across the eyebrow, and around to the edge of the temple. The wounds it found on the way enabled it to retain its volume. Gaining speed it made its way down his cheek and finally disappeared into the matted chaos that had been his beard. Through it all the eyes never changed. Petronius could see that the white of one of them had gone red with a hemorrhage that was spreading across its surface. In a fleeting, futile thought he hoped against his own will that the Temple Guard had caused it and not his own men. After this, his half-conscious introspections fled under the piercing power of the rabbi's countenance. What he saw there shook him, not for the ugliness or desperation of the victim, but for the inexplicable stirrings that suddenly rose within him. From far back in his memory he felt something coming to the surface. He was a small boy again. There was his mother, playing with him as a child, running and laughing with him on the hills behind their home in Italy. He fell and hurt himself, drawing blood from his hand. She kissed him and rocked him, holding him against her breasts and humming until he drowsed in the afternoon sun. Then she carried him home. He remembered how she had looked at him then, drying his tears and comforting him. It was so long, so very long ago. Wide-eyed, Petronius blinked once. How could it be? How could this Jew feel pity, feel compassion, for him? How *dare* he? The rage of old hate fought for air, but died, suffocated by a force greater than the soldier's ability to explain. He could endure no more. Petronius looked away.

Prayer: *Lord Jesus, even weak, You are infinity stronger than I; appearing as common, rare beyond price; ugly with Your blood and bruises, still more beautiful than anything I have ever beheld. And because such might, wealth, and glory were too much for me, You humbled Yourself so that I might be able to receive Your mercy. Deep calls to deep, oh Lord, and so by Your grace birth humility in me that I might answer Your gentle call. Amen.*

Day Twenty-Two

A company of the Praetorian Guard returned to the court, this time without the governor. They, along with Petronius' men, were to accompany the prisoner to the place of judgment, the *Lithostrotos*. There the fate of the prisoner would be finally decided. Petronius knew what this meant. Unless Pilate had some other trick to play, there would be no trial to speak of before the people. The fact that they must take him there told Petronius that Pilate had tried one last time with the priests, but had lost. His position was too shaky to take risks, and he would not sacrifice his office for the sake of a stubborn Jew who hadn't the sense to defend himself. Before long an entourage of soldiers and priests, together with the governor and the doomed rabbi, found its way out to the Pavement. People were out and about now, and the sun had just broken over the hills to the east of the city. Bystanders, encouraged by the priests' attendants, gathered to watch. By the time they had ordered their ranks a large crowd had gathered.

Finally, Pilate took his place and the people took theirs in front and below him. The priests stood there to one side, and Petronius could see they sensed the moment of triumph they had been politicking for was at hand. Pilate conferred with a couple of his assistants, briefly consulting and giving orders, though Petronius knew not what. As they nodded obediently and turned to go, a messenger—Petronius recognized him as an officer from the Lady Procula's attendants—strode up quickly and spoke to one of them. His urgency caught Petronius' attention, snapping him from the daze he had walked in since the episode in the palace. After a brief exchange, they immediately passed the courier on to the governor. Petronius saw that as he bent and whispered to Pilate the man presented him with a small scroll. Pilate immediately took and opened it, reading intently and ignoring for the moment all else about him. The whole matter was most unexpected, and for a long breath all the actors in the drama—priests, soldiers, and crowd—seemed to pause in their respective roles while this improvisation played itself out. Only the prisoner at his arm, he observed, mysteriously seemed to continue in his own pacific realm. Pilate thoughtfully closed the letter, his noble face lined and his expression dark. Glancing again at the rabbi, Pilate's eyes betrayed that haunted, hunted look Petronius had seen in the palace. All waited. Pilate mastered himself, lifted his chin and surveyed the scene in front of him. With lips pursed, he gestured for Petronius to bring Jesus before them.

Pilate stood and raised his voice.

"Here is your king!" he shouted, waving with his hand.

The priests and scribes responded with jeers and more calls for death, at which Pilate nodded knowingly, then glanced to one side. Here the prefect made a final throw of the dice, his acquiescence to their demands ironically having given him one last chance. A delegation had already approached him with their annual request—the request for pardon. During the Festival the governor could grant clemency to one doomed man of the people's choosing. In truth, it was a thoroughly Roman idea to serve Roman purposes, a way of currying favor with the masses and discouraging uprisings through a show of goodwill. Now that Jesus of Nazareth stood all but condemned, he might be spared by the voice of the people themselves, if they chose him. But the tradition implied that a choice must be presented them; who else might Pilate offer them? Then Petronius himself stood amazed at Pilate's machinations when he saw some of the Tower jailors—his own men, accompanied by the assistants he had seen earlier—stand forth with the insurrectionist ringleader who had been just been thrown in the dungeon, awaiting crucifixion along with a couple of his men.

"Whom do you want me to release to you? Which will you have? Jesus Barabbas or Jesus of Nazareth?"

Here Pilate took a terrible risk. What irony, thought Petronius. To offer the release of an insurrectionist to placate the people under the pretense of avoiding another insurrection! But he knew from this ploy that Pilate feared the fallout of the rabbi's death—and something more, it seemed—far more than he feared Barabbas, and he wanted to make the choice as obvious as possible. Surely they would choose...

"Give us Bar-Abbas!" they shouted in reply.

Petronius couldn't believe his ears. Barabbas was nothing more than a common killer, disguising his brigandage with religious doublespeak. Anyone with sense knew that he and his type would be the death of this city and this people. Petronius, looking across his prisoner's bowed head, saw the undisguised frustration on Pilate's face. His political cunning had availed him not a bit.

"But what shall I do with this one called the King of the Jews?"—yet Pilate already knew the answer.

Deafening cries of "Crucify! Crucify!" came from the crowd, filling the court and echoing from the sides of the surrounding buildings. The Jew stood still through it all, though now he finally appeared affected, his figure bent and overcome by the moment. Petronius watched him with amazement as he endured the abuse they heaped upon him. He had led these people, he had taught in their markets and in their temple. Everyone had heard of it. His wisdom had silenced all who listened to him. Surely he could say a few words with what remained of his strength, turning the crowd to see things his way. Surely there was some will left in him to speak up for himself and save his own life. What did he have to gain from his silence? No, thought Petronius, I am not meant for Judea. I will never, never understand these people. A people who kills their own heroes was bad enough. That could and did happen in Rome. But a hero who lets them do it when he has the power to escape with his life—*that* Petronius could not fathom in the least. He felt such a storm inside of him that he could only be relieved that another occupied the center of attention. He saw Pilate trying to dissuade them from their bloodlust, but it was useless. With a word Pilate summoned a slave, who stood by while Pilate washed his hands in ceremonial repudiation. At this the crowd grew quiet. Pilate finished with a verbal self-exoneration: No word of innocent Jewish blood would reach the emperor. It was the crowd before him that had done the deed. Incredibly, they agreed.

Prayer: Lord Jesus, what awful choices this life forces upon us. But none is so terrible as the very real, very present option of choosing something other than You. For all the times I reached over You to hungrily take hold of rubbish, Jesus forgive me. Cleanse me from bloodguilt, oh God, God of my salvation. You have yielded all for my sake. Now let me yield all for You. Amen.

Day Twenty-Three

After this, things proceeded mechanically. Petronius put Lucius in charge and saw to it that the condemned was taken to the Tower in preparation for execution, as others had been taken before him. The people followed his movements and crowded in so as not to miss a moment of the spectacle. The soldiers who did not have immediate charge of the prisoner kept the multitudes at bay. Petronius watched the drama briefly, then, accompanied by a single common soldier, went in to the governor. He had gathered the priests and was writing out the sentence on a parchment, as was customary, so that it might hang with the condemned man as a warning to others. For whatever reason, the holy men had a great deal of interest in what Pilate put down there. Petronius stood at a respectful distance and watched as the governor put the final broad strokes on the paper. The priests read it and immediately began to protest. He was no king, they said irately. Put down that he merely claimed to be a king.

Pilate had yielded enough to them for one day.

"What I have written, I have written," he said curtly.

The old men stepped back, grumbling but powerless.

"Centurion!"

"Prefect."

Pilate rolled up the scroll and handed it to him.

"You will see to it that the sentence is carried out forthwith."

"Immediately, Sire."

He turned and walked down the steps to the pavement below. The crowd had already thinned considerably, and Petronius and his guard found it easy to make their way back to the barracks. When they got there they could see the people milling around, trying to get a glimpse of what was going on inside the half opened gates. Roman soldiers shoved angrily at them and shouted orders. When Petronius' men saw him, they did their best to open a passage. He fought his way into the courtyard, holding the scroll aloft.

Once inside, he could see that a lesser centurion, a young man named Marcus, had already assembled the rest of the guard that had not been directly involved with events to that point. They were readying themselves with spears and forming files to make the short trip outside the city wall to the execution site as uncomplicated as possible. The rabbi was already stripped of his purple robe—Petronius could only guess what had happened to it—and knelt on the ground. He faced away from Petronius, who could see his whitish garment now saturated by his own blood. A few men tied the crossbeam to his shoulders and arms and forced him to his feet. The condemned man tottered precariously, but managed to stand. In his mind's eye Petronius saw him as he would appear but a few minutes hence: hands and feet nailed to the rough wood, head down, belly distended. Petronius had witnessed that horror more times than he could remember, watched as gravity tore the limbs from their sockets, the chest heaving with indescribable pain as suffocation and heart failure set in. By cruel cunning it was a torture perfectly conceived to slowly kill while stripping the victim of all self-worth and decency.

"Everything in order, Petronius?" It was Marcus.

"Yes. Everything is in order." He couldn't take his eyes off the doomed man in front of him. Calm determination still radiated from his rapidly weakening form.

"Good. Well, we still have the two others, you know. I have prepared for them anyway."

As a matter of fact, Petronius had forgotten about them altogether.

"Of course."

"This third one is a real surprise. He's drawn quite a crowd, but I imagine we can handle it," Marcus said, looking about with youthful confidence.

"Yes, I'm sure," Petronius replied, detachedly.

They were silent for a moment, surveying the final ordering of the troops before they gave the final word for them to issue from the gate. Now Petronius could see the other two men, naked to the waist and bleeding from their scourgings, their crosses already tied across their shoulders. One of them was weeping uncontrollably. Soldiers pushed them along, barking at them and poking at them with the butt of their spears. With a bit more prodding and bullying, the procession was finally ready to depart.

"Is that the sentence?" Marcus asked suddenly.

"Wha–?"

Marcus pointed to the scroll in Petronius' hand.

"For the prisoner. His verdict."

Petronius looked down at the roll of parchment in his right hand as if it were the hand of another man. A flash of realization hit him.

"The letter!" he blurted out. He had left it, unfinished, on the mess table for anyone to come along and read. Gods pity him if someone had already found it. His mind raced as he tried to remember how far he had gotten and what would be the consequences if what he had penned there got out among the men.

"What?"

He turned to Marcus suddenly.

"You've got this in hand."

Marcus looked at him blankly.

"The executions," Petronius said impatiently. "You can handle them. The men are under your command."

He was not asking, but neither was he commanding. His words affirmed, but it was the closest to begging that he would ever come with an inferior. Marcus stammered a bit. This was very unexpected. Petronius had walked through the whole process, and to him Pilate had personally handed the written sentence. Shouldn't he be present for the completion of the affair? In the end the lesser man's vanity won him over. The honor of command would be his.

"Yes, Petronius. Everything is under control. Do what you must."

"I am grateful."

He shoved the scroll into the astonished Marcus' hands. It was the first time Petronius had ever expressed gratitude for anything, but he didn't realize it. He turned and began to stride as quickly as his pride allowed him toward the entrance of the tower. As he neared the door he heard Marcus shout an order and, in response, the immediate jostling rattle of several dozen armored men coming to attention. Another shout and the gates sounded as they began to swing on their hinges. The sounds of the crowd poured in. Petronius turned and looked back. Between the hulking frames of two of his men he saw the bent form of the young teacher. He fought to move forward under the weight of the cross. Petronius saw the top of his head, a matted mess of blood and thorns, rising and falling as he put one foot in front of the other. A soldier pushed him. The men closed ranks, and Jesus disappeared from his view. Petronius stood transfixed, then swallowed a dry swallow and went into the fortress.

He made his way quickly through the passages and toward the stairs that would lead down to the mess. A force had stayed behind to guard the Tower, but Petronius encountered no one. An acrid haze filled the halls and burned the back of his throat. It mattered little because he was too distracted by his thoughts to notice anything around him. In spite of his overwhelming fear of humiliation over the letter, the events of the morning began to whirl inside his head. So much had happened so quickly. He saw the rabbi's bruised face again, the blood, his eyes. He heard his silence before Pilate, the priests, and the people. The memory of that still acquiescence shook him again. It surged within him like a deafening roar. He saw, he heard, and the mystery of it all began to overtake him. He furrowed his brow as he began his descent, and a whisper—the voice of his own conscience— escaped from the knot in his stomach and hurled itself into the tangled center of his brain.

"Why?" it demanded in hushed anguish. *"Why? Why? Why?"*

His sandaled feet pounded the stones to the beat of the interrogation within his heart. At last, head down and teeth clenched he reached the bottom. As he turned toward the corner of the cellar he had used he ran into a soldier hurrying out. The man fell back against the wall and grasped at a column. A wooden pail clattered on the floor.

"Centurion! I…your pardon, sir. I didn't see you."

"No matter, soldier. It was an accident."

The man reached out and picked up the bucket. A waft of smoke drifted between them.

"What is going on down here?" Petronius asked sharply, looking around for the source of the fumes.

"A bit of a fire, sir. That's what the water is for," he said, lifting his vessel. "Don't worry, though. We have it under control."

Through the smoke Petronius could see two other men emerging from the corner room, also carrying buckets.

"A fire? Who started a fire? What for?"

The man coughed at the smoke and shook his head in irritation, finally relaxing a bit. Petronius recognized the look of a man who had just cleaned up after an unnamed neighbor, but wasn't about to take any blame for him.

"I don't know who it was, sir. But it appears that some fool left a candle burning on the back mess table along with some fuel for it to work with. It set the whole cursed thing ablaze!"

Petronius took a faltering step toward the source of the smoke, then stopped short. The answer he was seeking hit him, and with a last glance at the soldier and his approaching companions, the centurion turned on his heel and raced back up the steps on his way to Golgotha.

Prayer: *Lord Jesus, help me see You crucified. By Your mercy, don't allow my slippery heart to evade what You did for me by painting it with misty religious colors two thousand years old. Give me a glimpse of the fullness of Your sacrifice, and so implant Your sincere fire in me. As You astonished those who saw You face to face, may I be astonished now, and somehow through me, may You astonish still more around me. Amen.*

THE PROMISE

Demas, the Zealot

Luke 23:39-43

Day Twenty-Four

Judgment had already been passed. There was no hope. He knew this well, understood that his time was very short now. He had not slept, of course, but he was no nearer to inner resolve for his wakefulness. Since sundown the day before the desperate energy of his mind had generated nothing but aimless, circular thoughts, phantasms that wore themselves out with rousing battle cries that would never be heard and hard questions that would never be answered. Bound hand and foot, thirsty and short of breath in the fetid air of Antonia's deepest prison, Demas languished. The darkness in his cell echoed the suffocating despair in his soul.

Yet a drowning man will grasp at anything, and for the last hour his tortured introspections had something fresh to lay hold of. Three of them had been caught and condemned—he, his companion, Matthias, and their leader, Jesus called Bar-Abbas. Together they had been thrown here, knowing that daybreak would bring their grisly deaths. They had spoken little because Bar-Abbas had chosen not to speak, brooding instead and pretending to sleep. Then, without any warning, the soldiers had come. They had taken Bar-Abbas alone, and there was something about the way they escorted him from the cell that made Demas wonder. Hadn't the sentence been handed down, the three to be hung together as a portent to any who might choose their rebellious ways? But Bar-Abbas had not returned, and like the pathetic light that filtered its way from a small grating somewhere down the corridor into the dungeon where he was chained, these happenings pierced the monotony of his suspense and made Demas think that something might be afoot. It couldn't be called hope, but it was a new development he hadn't expected, a broken stick with which he could parry the thrusts of madness that had stabbed at him all night.

Demas turned his head and looked across the cell at Matthias. Though they were only few feet apart, for the darkness he hadn't been able to see him for hours; now he could make out his dim form. Both of them sat on the floor, feet shackled, wrists manacled to the wall by a short chain run through a low-set iron ring. The cruel arrangement forced them to half-sit, half-lie on their sides. Matthias' had his head thrown back and Demas thought his eyes were shut, but he ventured a low whisper anyway.

"Matthias!"

His counterpart stirred and lifted his face.

"What."

"What do you think they're doing with Bar-Abbas?"

Silence.

"What difference would it make for us?" he finally said, a dull anger in his voice.

Demas said nothing in reply. Disillusionment washed over him as he realized that it had come down to merely that—their fate. They were finally and fully trapped now, caged animals awaiting their slaughter. But a dark end hadn't always seemed so inevitable, at least not as he recalled things. At the outset they had been, in their own thinking, the very beloved of God and the instruments of his will in the land.

Bar-Abbas was a powerful leader. He had a purpose—a vision—and he had a powerful presence that enabled him to pass that vision on to his followers. Like so many others, he seethed over the Romans in the land, weary of their pagan ways defiling the holy inheritance of his fathers. Was God with his people, or not? Weren't his promises true? If God reigned (and he surely did), then the burden lay upon the men of Israel to *act*. They should arise and march, and God would be with them as he had been with the heroes of old. But here was where Bar-Abbas' purpose burned the hottest, where his charismatic rage became most articulate. The men of Israel *didn't* act. They *colluded!* Priests, tax collectors, merchants, and common folk alike actually cooperated with these vile dogs. But what they did couldn't stay the hand of God, preached Bar-Abbas. The signs revealed that God's time drew near. There would be no more waiting in the name of piety and submission, no more excuses in the name of faith. God would come to Israel when Israel came back to him, and that meant purging the evil from the land. His favor was upon them and they could not fail.

Staring into the darkness, Demas remembered how Bar-Abbas first had spoken to him. There had been a meeting arranged at a house in Jericho. It was night, and Bar-Abbas had stirred those present and encouraged them to believe and prepare for action. Demas had heard about Bar-Abbas, and now that he listened to his words he felt a zealous faith stir in him that he hadn't known before. The God of their fathers was with him as ever! He needn't live as he had, oppressed and ashamed. Though he had said nothing, there was no mistaking Demas' enthusiasm, and he realized it as Bar-Abbas increasingly caught his eye. When the meeting concluded the leader took him aside and inquired more of him and his thoughts. Demas felt flattered, if also a bit nervous. There was no use hiding the fact that his father's business relationships had made his upbringing more Gentile-friendly than many devout Jews would feel comfortable with. His very name oozed the Greco-Roman culture his father had embraced. Some less fierce in their hatred of foreigners than Bar-Abbas had spoken ill of his family in the past for their associations. Yet Demas was also a true Hebrew, his father having gone to extra lengths to see him schooled in the truths of the faith under the Pharisees. What he had learned in their care now stirred and came to life as he listened to this preacher of revolution—alive in a way his father never would have foreseen. For his part, Bar-Abbas the pragmatist saw in this young recruit a rare combination that he knew would be invaluable to him: a solid Jewish pedigree with some training in the Holy Writings, respectable facility in Greek and experience in Gentile affairs, and, most of all, fiery religious zeal.

At first, Bar-Abbas seemed only to do what he condemned so many others for: he talked. But Bar-Abbas hardly settled. Far from it. This formative period proved crucial for Demas, and through speech after angry speech, the vision became complete, the fever to do something great in God's name irresistible. Now the stories of Israel's ancient heroes took on fresh new meaning for him. What had been inspiring tales from his childhood became present realities of immediate significance. The armies of Joshua—Bar-Abbas' namesake—marched through his soul, expelling the Amorites from the Promised Land. David slew the champion of the uncircumcised Philistines and gained the kingdom that would never pass away. In a way, Judas "The Hammer" Maccabeus loomed larger still, a more recent hero who had resisted pagan occupation, purified the Temple, and reestablished Jewish independence. But the greatest of all for Demas, the symbol whose spirit he most admired and the hero he sought most to emulate, was Phineas, son of Eleazar and grandson of Aaron, Israel's first high priest. Phineas' glorious hour had been granted in the time of Moses, when Israel sinned at Peor by mixing with the hated Moabites. While others wept and pined, he took up arms. With a single thrust of his spear he had slain the corrupt Israelite and the wicked idolatress who had seduced him, halting the plague that had befallen the holy people. *God himself* had exalted Phineas for his zeal and granted him perpetual priesthood as a reward. Demas began to dream of such a thing, of being the one that made the fateful thrust, struck the blow that turned the tide and saved the nation. He longed for God's praise, wished for just one chance to show his devotion. So zealous did he become, so dedicated to the imitation of that former hero, that Bar-Abbas took to affectionately calling him "my Phineas," and praising him to others in their small but growing band of revolutionaries. Demas could not have felt more proud if his own father had robed him in a coat of many colors.

Prayer: *Lord Jesus, protect me from my own cravings for praise. My insecurities are not the stuff of harmless childhood immaturities, but rather a deeper refusal to trust in Your love for me, leading to catastrophic consequences for me and others. Too often have I been charmed by the flattery of fools. Search me and know my heart...see if there is any offensive way in me, and lead me in the way everlasting. Amen.*

Day Twenty-Five

Guerrilla actions began bit by bit. King David himself didn't move until he heard marching in the treetops, explained Bar-Abbas. Time and place meant everything in a holy war. Listening for those angelic footfalls was the key to their victory. Of course, Bar-Abbas never really explained how this worked or how he heard from God, and nobody ever asked. It remained a mystery. What was not mysterious, however, was how this theology translated itself into action. Consistently they found themselves targeting the Jewish civilians Bar-Abbas saw as accommodators rather than Roman troops themselves. Remember, Bar-Abbas once chided, Phineas' spear smote the wicked Israelite *first*— then slew the pagan whore in her turn. There was more than purely spiritual principle in play, though. Many of these corrupt Jews also happened to possess significant wealth—their riches were a sign that they were "fornicating with the Moabitess"— and that money would fund their efforts. As Bar-Abbas pointed out, it was the precious metal of Korah's censers that Moses used to cover the altar of the Lord. Bar-Abbas had wisdom to explain everything.

Demas pulled at his chains, but the pain of the iron digging into his wrists was still the lesser. For at that point in his memory he was forced to recall his first doubts. He had joined Bar-Abbas to serve the God of his fathers and to liberate Israel. He had dreamed of a restored kingdom, a place where Heaven met earth as God blessed the noble deeds of his chosen warriors. He had thrown in his lot with these zealots because in an evil age he wanted to be *good*. But the more he did in Bar-Abbas' service, the less good and the less noble he felt. It was a violent affair. Oh yes, the Scriptures spoke of war in God's name, but something nevertheless gnawed at his conscience, telling him that *this* wasn't *that*, and he knew it. Lines that Demas had in his soul, stone boundary markers that had to do with respect, caring for his fellow Jew and the sojourner, and keeping faith, well, these were moved over and over until he didn't even know where they were anymore. The mission, the vision of an Israel pure and free from the infidel Roman justified all, or should have. But a heaviness grew in his heart over the trail of grief and fear that their actions left—sorrow never caused to their occupiers, but always and exclusively to his own people. These thoughts turned deep inside him, and he never spoke them. Outwardly, he was the same young Phineas he had ever been—or thought he was.

Then, a few weeks back and as Demas' inner crisis became acute, Bar-Abbas proclaimed that the hour had come. They would follow their God to Jerusalem at Passover. In that holy time and place God would surely be with them, the crowds of pilgrims would arise and join their cause, and Heaven would vanquish the Romans and cast them out. Bar-Abbas' plan was simple. They would enter the Court of the Gentiles on the Temple Mount, target the infidels who dared to defile God's Holy City with their unclean presence, and cut them down. In order to avoid confusion, only a handful of them would strike the first blows, together, and the place where the blood was spilled would become the rallying point for the multitudes. The rest would stand ready with more weapons hidden in their garments, to help their compatriots or arm the others, as God might be pleased to bless their obedience. Those who would lead the attack would be Bar-Abbas himself and three others, including Jonathan, Matthias…and Demas. Something in the way Bar-Abbas spoke his name made Demas' heart skip a beat—and not from the gravity of the announcement alone. Demas had caught on the edge of his leader's lingering glance a sort of rebuke, or a hint of conquest. Had he known of Demas' wrestlings? Was this his way of bringing a wavering warrior back into line? He didn't know. But if such was his intention, it was masterfully done. Finally, thought Demas, we retake holy ground wielding the sword against those who truly deserve to fall by it. Finally we attack the Romans and drive them from the City of God. His doubts were swept away and he felt more loyal to Bar-Abbas and more committed to his revolution than ever.

Demas closed his eyes as what had happened played for the hundredth time in his sleepless brain. They had arrived, had drawn near the southern gate to the Court of Women. Bar-Abbas looked about, then pointed to a pair of men in the crowd there, men clearly not Jews but nevertheless dressed as pilgrims. More civilians! Demas' eyes cast a questioning glance back at Bar-Abbas, but his chief would have none of it now. They were Gentile dogs, he had savagely spat, and their defilement of the Temple must be atoned for by their own blood. God would be with his people and the final battle would begin here. Demas obediently cast the last of his hesitations aside and followed. The first man, who appeared larger and stronger, fell to Bar-Abbas' and Matthias' small swords, the second from Demas' thrust. The blade pierced the man's belly, and he crumpled at Demas' feet with a gasp and a cry. Demas stared at his victim and did his best to feel like a Phineas, but it just didn't come. As the crowd scattered in fear, Bar-Abbas began to cry out and call the people to himself, proclaiming that God's kingdom was indeed upon them. Arise, men of Israel who are zealous for the land, arise!

But the men of Israel there weren't as ready as Bar-Abbas had convinced his fellow revolutionaries they would be. Incredibly, it seemed the crowd had just come to the Temple to worship and pray—not to riot. Not a one answered Bar-Abbas, not a one drew near to join his uprising. The only response they heard was the piercing cry of a woman who ignored the threat and ran to throw herself, wailing, on the dying man thrust through by Demas's blade. Trumpets sounded. Would God come to their aid and send the fire on the altar as in the days of Elijah? But it was not Joshua who sounded the blasts, not God who answered. The Romans were upon them in a moment, far more prepared, it seemed, than anyone else for Bar-Abbas' long-anticipated hour of revolution. In the end the four of them managed only to wound a couple of guards before the Romans slew Jonathan and took the rest of them captive.

That had been yesterday morning. The authorities held court within a few short hours and their doom quickly published. They would be crucified on the morn. The speed and efficiency of the whole affair led Demas to believe that not only had the Romans been more than ready for them, but they intended to make them an example during the Passover itself. It was no accident that the Romans ruled the world, and they would brook no insurrection. This was brutal anticlimax, not only to months of preparation and careful planning, but to a lifetime of hope. Worst of all, standing there before Pontius Pilate, Demas learned that his victim had indeed been a simple pilgrim, come to worship the One True God. The man's Jewish brother-in-law—the widow's brother—testified that the man was a Greek who had been circumcised and lived in full compliance with the law of Moses. His crime, the man choked out, was the color of his skin and hair. Up to that point, Demas had acted as defiantly as Bar-Abbas, confident in the rightness of their cause and in God's deliverance. But upon hearing the name and the story of the man he had murdered, shame filled his heart.

Now Demas sat, awaiting his death by public torture, his mind a tangled knot of half-resolved convictions. He had concluded that, however their revolt had turned out, the Promised Land must be cleansed of its impurity, and to his dying breath he would believe that God's people must rise up and take the kingdom by force. While his confidence in Jesus Bar-Abbas was wounded, to be sure, at his core his loyalty and admiration remained unshaken. They had lived together, they had fought together and, if God willed it so, they would die together. Yet Demas' view of himself, paradoxically, had not survived the night. Never before had he felt his life such a loss, such a waste, such a futility. The man he had killed was no defiler of the Temple courts; on the contrary, he had come near as a devout believer to be sanctified by them. Demas' doubts, long suppressed, now consumed his mind. Even so, who could know? Perhaps God would yet bare his mighty arm and save, just as he had overwhelmed the frailties of their fathers.

The outer door clanged and he heard the shod feet of soldiers coming through it and down the passageway. Night had gone and his nightmare began.

Prayer: Lord Jesus, You are real. Forgive me for reducing what it means to be Your disciple to a series of tired clichés, autopilot jargon that misses You and ends up leaving a trail of casualties behind me— people I should have helped but didn't, and people I shouldn't have hurt, but did. Retracing my steps is impossible for me, so work in me that kind of godly repentance that leads to You and leaves no regret. Amen.

Day Twenty-Six

Within a few minutes the guards marched Demas and Matthias—with many cuffs and curses—into an outer courtyard. No sun fell there, for above it loomed the mighty Tower of Antonia, the very symbol of everything they hated. It was a bitter cup indeed that in its shadow they should meet their final defeat.

There were four soldiers to each of them, plus some sort of officer giving orders and a handful of others standing by. Demas could see plainly from their features that a couple of them weren't ethnic Romans, which probably explained why the commander gave his orders in Greek. This meant that Demas could understand, more or less, what was happening.

Near a far wall were planted several whipping posts. The men guarding Demas hauled him to one of them, while Matthias' guards did the same at the next pole over. Forcing his manacled wrists above his head, they lifted Demas and unceremoniously hung him by his bonds from a hook near the top. His feet barely reached the ground. The pain in his hands and arms was unbelievable, but more significantly it was at that point Demas' lungs first felt the bitter constriction that would mark the final hours of his life.

A cry and a shout rang out. Matthias had resisted, clasping his bound hands together as a single fist and trying to strike one of his guards. Demas' head instinctively craned sideways to see what was happening just as a club came down on Matthias' shoulders. He fell to the pavement and before he could move the largest of them savagely but skillfully kicked him in the belly. The other raised his club again but the officer shouted at him.

"None of that! Don't do him any favors, boys. We know his kind. He's got some holiday waiting for him and we want his bones to last him as long as they will."

Limp and gasping, Matthias soon dangled beside Demas.

Demas felt rough hands ripping his clothes from him, and soon he was naked except for that cloth wrapped around his loins as an undergarment. A guard pulled at it to strip him completely, but the commander stayed him.

"Nah, just get on with it. This will have to be quick. Running behind with all these changes," he said.

As the soldiers stepped way, Demas heard the noise of the morning bustle beginning beyond the wall. The Passover crowds had begun to move about. A voice rose for a moment above the indistinct blend of footfalls, hoofs, crying lambs, and wooden wheels rolling on the cobblestones. Strangely, it was at that banal sound and not the first flesh-rending blow of the scourge that the fear of death fully laid hold of him. The multi-lashed whip fell again and again. Demas heard Matthias' grunts become howls next to him, and his own cries sounded like drumbeats in his temples. Aside from the pain that turned his thoughts into a lightning storm of utter confusion, two things came to Demas as the metal barbs of his tormenter's stroke shredded his body. First, it occurred to him that wounds he was receiving would never heal—his soul would leave his body long before these stripes did. It was a thought unlike any he had ever known before, or had understood his mind to be capable of. The other thing strangely stood out even stronger in his tortured thoughts, like a precious coin irretrievably mislaid: Bar-Abbas was not there with them.

The interminable scourging finally ceased and their guards took them from the posts. Shaking and bleeding heavily, they were forced to kneel on the flagstones. After removing the manacles, the guards stretched out their arms to tie the *patibula*—the crossbars that they would carry to the execution site—across their shoulders. More soldiers had come into the courtyard now, and they were organizing and preparing themselves for the march to the execution site. Security was obviously high. Directly in front of Demas stood the officer who had directed things, and Demas, burning within from more than his wounds, and with nothing to lose, looked up and stared into his face when he paused for a moment in his supervisory pacing. Seemingly by chance, the man looked down and met the gaze of the doomed zealot—a gaze neither pleading nor rebellious, but something else. The man stopped and cocked his head, returning the query with merciless sarcasm. Demas immediately spoke, his own voice strange to him.

"Jesus Barabbas," he said evenly, in accent-free Greek.

An evil smile slowly dawned on the soldier's face, then he laughed.

"Alright," he crowed, "since you ask so pretty. Turns out your hero got a break and won't be joining the festivities today. It was one Jesus or another, and yours was the luckier of the two."

Dismissively, the man went on. But Demas knelt dumbfounded, momentarily oblivious to the pain of his knees grinding into the pavement, trying to make sense of what he had just been told. Then the gates opened and in came a large troop of soldiers. It was much greater than the one already gathered in the yard, and it carried in its midst a badly beaten man. As the guards finished tying the beam to Demas' shoulders, others brought the man forward and shoved him to the ground. Then Demas recognized him. This was Jesus of Nazareth, the teacher from Galilee whom the crowds had so warmly received into Jerusalem but a few days back. Given a moment's respite as the soldiers brought a *patibulum* for their new charge, Demas stared at him. He had been abused far more than Demas or Matthias had been, his face bruised and swollen and his beard a bloody, patchy mess. A wreath of thorns crowned him. The Nazarene did not struggle or look about him, but simply gazed at the ground while they lashed the wood to him as they had to the others. The enormity of what had happened finally dawned upon Demas. Bar-Abbas had abandoned them. He would not be there as he had promised, he would not die with them. Their loyalty had gone unrequited, and their God had forgotten them and left them utterly alone. There would be no parting of the heavens, no apocalyptic salvation. Uncelebrated and unmourned, they would die under the gloating eye of the uncircumcised. Demas hung his head as irrepressible sobs rose from the very center of his being.

"Get 'em on their feet!" someone yelled. "Let's get going!"

Other voices echoed the call, and the gates opened. A large crowd waited outside. The guards moved forward, pushing the people aside, making way for the escorts and their doomed wards. His guard shoved him, and the butt-end of a spear jabbed Demas in the kidneys.

"Must stop weeping," he said to himself, futilely. "Must die bravely."

Stumbling forward, he tried to think of a great hero of Israel who had bravely faced death by the hand of the heathen. All that came to mind was the mighty judge Samson, begging with his last breath that God remember him one more time as he stretched out his arms and brought down the Philistine temple. It was no use. He would be hanged on a tree and die naked under the curse of God and man. Crucifixion took every last thing from a man before it tore the life out of him. Blackness of soul like midnight overwhelmed him.

Soon they were out in the street. The Romans enjoyed driving their victims in front of them, the more prized, the more prominently displayed. Had things gone unchanged that almost certainly would have meant that Jesus Barabbas would have led this morbid parade, followed by the others. But as things turned out, the Romans forced the Galilean Jesus to take the lead. Demas saw him moving ahead under heavy guard, and when the people caught sight of him a collective cry went up, some in derision but mostly wails of mourning. People lined the way, calling out and moving with the procession as much as the guards and the space allowed. Once they had gotten a distance away from the Tower the soldiers had more success in keeping order, though many people, especially keening women, flocked to behold the spectacle and cry out after them.

The procession moved along, nearing the gate by which they would exit Jerusalem's perimeter wall. Crucifixion was too horrendous, too unclean to take place within the Holy City. Demas now trudged along closer to the Nazarene, but a few paces behind him, with Matthias to the rear. The Teacher staggered as he walked, much weaker from the severity of his ordeal than the zealots. Blood soaked his homespun garment. There now, the man had fallen hard, face down into the dusty street, pinned under the weight of the crossbar. He could not rise. After his escorts had kicked him a few times in vain, a centurion—Demas knew him from the skirmish on the Temple Mount the day before but had not seen him this morning until now—stepped forward and sharply rebuked them.

"Tell me, you idiots, what good will it do you if he dies here? Now get that thing off him and get the man on his feet!"

The men nearly cowered at his word, scrambling to obey him. The officer who had spoken to Demas earlier tried to look commanding but he clearly stood in the presence of his superior.

Demas watched as the Nazarene was pulled to his feet and relieved of his burden, his frame shuddering and his hands trembling as if it still lay upon him. The big centurion looked at the broken man hard for a moment, then cursed and looked about him. Suddenly he reached into the crowd of worshipers trying to enter the city gate and took hold of a random pilgrim. The officer demanded that he carry the cross for the Nazarene, the man's brief and pointless objections silenced by threats. Frightened and humiliated, the pilgrim passed his own belongings to his family, took up the beam and fell in line. With a shout and more barking of orders, they began to move again.

If not for his own despair, Demas should have felt terribly sorry for this fellow Jew being force-marched to his death. But Demas knew a bit of him, at least by hearsay, and sympathy did not immediately come to mind. Bar-Abbas had spoken about this Jesus, and what he had said was no compliment. Widely known in his own land, this Galilean had also made a name for himself in Judea. Reputedly, he was a skilled teacher, a man of great charisma and wisdom. He was also supposed to be a wonder worker who could heal—rumor ran that he had even opened the eyes of the blind and raised the dead. As every Jew understood, these were the miraculous signs that accompanied the coming of Messiah.

Upon hearing these things and the murmurings of his own followers, Bar-Abbas made a point to speak to the matter. So this man spoke and did well. What of it? What good was it, he said, to have such gifts from God and not use them for his cause? Here was a man whom the crowds adored and who commanded tremendous respect from people of all kinds, but did nothing with it. What did he actually teach? What was his purpose? What did it matter! His lack of action spoke volumes. Whatever else his motivations, he could not be seriously dedicated to the grim business of rescuing the nation and establishing God's kingdom on the earth. Open the eyes of blind, indeed! He was obviously blind himself, fumed Bar-Abbas. He was an aimless wanderer, too weak and too naïve to leverage the influence he had been given.

Even then, Demas perceived Bar-Abbas' jealousy toward the man. Oh, his guerrilla leader was charismatic to be sure. He had his followers. But if he could stir the pot, Jesus of Nazareth was a spellbinder. What zealots couldn't rejoice that his words had silenced Sadducee and Pharisee alike, both useless together? Yet if Bar-Abbas had possessed such abilities they would have been silenced by more than a riddle; the nation would have arisen as one, and the Romans would be no more. Yea, then they would have seen the glory of God. Only earlier this week Bar-Abbas had stood with his men, seething as this prophet entered Jerusalem on a donkey's colt to waving palms and cries of "Hosanna, O Son of David!" Son of David, indeed. He was no messiah. He *couldn't* be. Let him ride a warhorse into Jerusalem, Bar-Abbas had declared, and I should be his most faithful disciple.

Now, as Demas beheld him through the eyes of crushing disappointment in his *own* Jesus, he did not see *this* Jesus in any better light. If anything, his scorn grew all the more. Bar-Abbas had failed in the very place where Jesus of Nazareth had marveled the multitudes. This Jesus was an affront to the very spirit of Phineas that had driven him. Why didn't the man do something with his power? Why didn't he turn and raise an army, even now? What a spear he could wield! But no, his disciples were women and fools, and as he went along he still concerned himself with them. Even now, as they left the city and approached the execution site, he turned and spoke softly and comfortingly to those who followed, inconsolable.

There was a quality to his voice—it was the first time Demas heard it—weary and dry though it was with torment and thirst, that sounded in his spirit. Here the man was not concerned for himself, not lamenting his own lot. He was concerned for them and their babes. Like a shepherd he briefly tended them before he was forced on his way. Something in his compassionate condescension, something in his demeanor and look affected Demas and momentarily cleared his mind of everything else he had thought of him. Indeed, mystery shrouded this man. But after pondering for a bit Demas brushed these thoughts aside. Couldn't this "messiah" have averted their tears? If prevention is better than cure, is it not far superior to empty words, too few and too late? No, Bar-Abbas must be right about such a man.

"Alright, let's get to it," a voice called out.

They had arrived at Golgotha.

Prayer: Lord Jesus, forgive me for all the times I wanted You to ride a warhorse instead of a donkey, the times I wanted You to use Your wisdom to wound rather than comfort and heal, the times I wished You would fight back rather than carry the Cross. Lord, all too easily I have accepted another Jesus, because believing You to be as good as

You are has been too hard a task for me. Give me Your grace to know You as You really are, and believe. Amen.

Day Twenty-Seven

In front of them stood half a dozen large wooden poles driven securely into the ground. Notched at the top with a slot, these were the *stipes* that were cut to receive the very *patibula* that the condemned carried to the site. Permanently planted and impossible to avoid at these crossroads outside a major gateway to the city, even empty the *stipes* served as a constant reminder of Roman retributive power. Demas saw that the cross he would be hung upon, hideous with nail scars and stains, had been used before and, he knew, would very likely be used again after it had wrenched the life from his body. When it came to executions, the Romans were as economical as they were theatrical.

They were also terribly thorough and efficient. If fear of crucifixion was a method they employed to keep potential malefactors in line, it was also a weapon they used right up to the moment they made good on their threats. In this case, it took the form of being forced to watch as the sentence was carried out on others. There was no way for Demas to deal with the effect that watching the Romans crucify the Galilean had upon him. He didn't have time to even try and conquer his terror, because he was next.

They didn't waste time untying him. With one swift jerk the soldiers stripped him of his undergarment, the only shred of dignity that had remained to him. Now stark naked and trembling uncontrollably, he was knocked to his knees then thrown on his back, his legs twisted under him. Demas tried to play the man, but shrieks emptied his lungs as they drove the nails through the base of his hands near the wrist—first one, then the other. The soldiers then hoisted his whimpering, convulsing frame by the *patibulum* and dropped it with a thump into the top of the *stipes*. The iron-bound mallet they had used to drive the nails now secured the crossbeam in place by a wooden peg. Demas never knew his body to have the capacity for such agony, and then it got worse. Grasping then hanging from his legs, each in their turn, a Roman soldier—all the heavier for his armor—stretched his body taut as one of his cohort nailed their victim's heels into the sides of the post. The crucifixion now complete, they stepped away. Through sweat, tears, and a sort of semi-blindness brought on by unspeakable pain, Demas beheld his tormenters. To say he looked down upon them would be an exaggeration; the cross was not very tall, and his feet hung but a generous handbreadth from the ground. The younger centurion stood there with them now and had a scroll (which Demas knew to contain the charge against him) that they would post over him as a warning, just as they had posted one over the head of the Nazarene. It hung unrolled in the commander's hand, and while the soldiers hacked at a branch with which to fasten it above his head Demas saw for a moment what was written there. *LESTES*, it read in Greek—*insurrectionist, brigand*—along with its equivalents in Aramaic and Latin so all passersby could take note and be afraid, or curse and mock if they chose. The executioners briefly surveyed their handiwork.

"Long life to you, rebel scum," one of them sneered, punctuating it with a curse and spitting in Demas' face before he walked away.

Now they crucified Matthias. He cursed and shouted while the Romans stretched him out.

"*Do* something, Messiah! If you are such a miracle worker why don't you work one of your miracles now?"

His desperate goading ended in anguished screams as he was secured to his cross. The bitterness and grief boiling within Demas burst forth and he joined the tirade.

"If you are truly the Son of David, why don't you show it and rescue us all?" he gasped through his pain. "Save us by your great power."

With effort, Demas lifted his face and looked to his left. As always, Jesus said nothing. His head hung down and his countenance was solemn and sad but, he saw, he was neither provoked nor shamed by their contemptuous words. A nail of doubt stabbed at Demas' heart. Suddenly his scornful words sounded empty and foolish in the face of such noble and determined surrender.

Soon Matthias hung on the other side of the Nazarene, and the soldiers, after a customary check of their perimeter, settled down to monitor the long ordeal. Their first order of business was to divide the spoils they had gathered from the victims, as was their customary right. They squabbled and gambled at the foot of Jesus' cross, laughing loudly while they threw the dice over the garments. Their greedy, bawdy ritual only added to the humiliation of the crucified. It was meant to.

"Father," Jesus said softly but clearly as he looked down at the ridiculous spectacle, "forgive them. They do not know what they do."

The soldiers went on in their games, oblivious to his words. But hearing him, Demas hung dumbstruck. This was not merely unexpected, it was otherworldly. It became clear to him now that what he had been taught to believe and who Jesus of Nazareth really was were two very different images. This man on the cross next to him was doubtless unlike any he had ever known. He had nothing passive about him; his actions and words, his stillness and his silence were all as purposeful as any guerilla attack Bar-Abbas had ever carried out. But here lived something Bar-Abbas had never displayed in all of his violent raging. What had it taken for Jesus to say that about his torturers? To actually pray mercy upon those who had nailed his flesh to the wood and laughed about it? Yet it appeared to tax him not a bit. Nay, it flowed from him, effortlessly. Here was manifest irresistible strength of another kind altogether. Demas felt that for the first time in his life he was in the presence of real revolutionary power. By it, Jesus had guilelessly turned the tables and taken command of his enemies from the inconceivable throne of a Roman cross. His mind a maelstrom, it struck Demas that he had just witnessed subversion the subtlety of which lay beyond the furthest reach of his thought or craft.

The upheaval in Demas' spirit as he now hung silently next to this enigmatic rabbi mixed curiously with his physical agonies. His mouth was parched with a thirst beyond description, his nostrils filled with the stench of his own slow death. Though he had been stretched upon the cross, his abdomen now protruded and his knees bent as his weight slowly pulled his arms from their sockets. His body was collapsing within itself, his heart raced in his chest, and it was nearly impossible to draw a breath. To do so, he was forced to push up off the nails that secured his feet to the wood, lift the chin which seemed glued to his chest, and gulp for a breath of air. It brought a whole new world of suffering upon him.

There was no plumbing the depths of his shame, his nakedness and weakness on display for whoever cared to stare at him, Jew or Gentile, man or woman. But humiliated though he was, Demas could see he was hardly the center of attention. A modest crowd huddled at a distance, watching the affair and trying to comfort each other. Since, he desperately observed, neither mother nor brother stood there grieving him, he knew these must be those who loved and followed the Nazarene. Some wept and knelt in the dirt, their faces muddy from their dusty hands. But those who hated him were bolder, and they had gathered close to gawk and mock. Many were just people who came by the crossroads, spat their curses as if it were their civic duty, and went on. Such were public executions. But there were others that were more determined in their disdain. Prominent among them was a cadre of priests and other religious leaders, insulting him and gloating.

"King of Israel! Messiah! Come off that cursed tree if you are the Chosen One!"

"Destroy the Temple and rebuild it, will you? What work will those hands do now?"

"He saved so many, but this one who called himself the Son of God cannot save himself! Save, King of Israel, that we might believe!"

And so it went on, and on. A crucified man has no reason to hold his tongue. Demas heard Matthias cursing back at those who mocked him, shouting about the liberation of Israel, calling his detractors cowards and worse. What did he have to lose? The priests were right. No one came off a cross. No one. But Jesus said nothing to those who counted him their adversary, replied not a single word. As before, he looked no more shaken by their slander than if they hadn't spoken at all. On the contrary, in Demas' eyes he almost seemed ennobled by it.

The soldiers had withdrawn and posted themselves some paces away. Now Demas saw a few older women and a young man at the foot of Jesus' cross. These were those of his disciples who were not ashamed of their connection with the dying man and did not dread the Romans, or if they did they loved more than they feared. One was obviously his mother, quietly weeping and rocking while she knelt there, holding her breast as if her heart would break. While the catcalls continued, Demas heard him speak gently to them. Again, he showed no self-pity, no concern for himself.

The thunderstorm in Demas' heart had become a torrent. While Matthias kept on with his cursing, Demas looked at Jesus. Who was this crucified man next to him? How would events have unfolded that morning if it had been Bar-Abbas on that cross instead? It occurred to Demas that without realizing it, he had been comparing this Jesus to the one he had walked with for the past year. Bar-Abbas failed the test miserably. Now he glanced across the Nazarene's twisted frame and saw Matthias, heaving and muttering. Suddenly, the enormity of his folly was revealed to him. The real comparison was not between Jesus of Nazareth and Bar-Abbas, or even Matthias. The real comparison was with himself. Then he saw Demas for the first time, as if mirrored in the parting waters of a crystalline river. There he beheld not a godly man, sincerely zealous for the holiness of Israel, but rather a vainglorious, self-serving terrorist. He had wanted honor and power for himself, not for the God of his fathers. He hadn't been serving God at all, but his own cravings. The memory of crime after crime came up before his eyes, and now Demas knew himself as nothing but a highwayman and a thief. Yes, he had plundered and stolen things. But most of all he had stolen *hope*. He had played the savior, building up the expectations of common folk that his revolution would redeem the nation from her ills. But Roman crimes did not make him innocent, and Israel's cause did not make his actions just. He remembered his deep shame upon learning his victim on the Temple Mount had been a pious believer; now he felt criminal that such a thing would matter to him at all. Had the man been a heathen skeptic, yet Demas would have stood guilty of innocent blood. Pain filled his heart as he realized that not only was he Phineas no more, he had never even remotely resembled him. Everything he had lived for had been a lie.

He lifted his downcast, tear-filled eyes to steal another glance at his neighbor, only to find that the man already looked upon him. Their eyes locked. Demas couldn't breathe. He wanted to cover his face with his hands in shame, but could not, to turn on his heels and run, but was unable. The cross held him captive to the Nazarene. It seemed that Jesus' very nakedness stripped away the façade of who he had been, unmasked his falsehood and laid bare his innermost motives. Under that fiery, piercing gaze the only thing left was *Him*.

Matthias' voice broke the moment, again echoing some of the more recent taunts the religious leaders were hurling.

"You fool! You waste! If you are the Messiah do something to save us all! Call your God down and do something!"

It was enough. His heart afire, Demas steeled himself, paid the price for a lung full of air, and rebuked his compatriot with all the strength he could summon.

"Don't you fear God at all—you who are doomed to die by the same death sentence? It is nothing but justice that we hang here, receiving our due for the crimes we have committed. But this man has done nothing wrong."

Matthias, stunned by his comrade's contradiction, fell silent. But he was not as surprised as Demas, who heard his own broken voice continue.

"Jesus, remember me. Remember me when You come into Your kingdom."

"I tell you the truth, this day you will be with me in Paradise."

If Demas had not been prepared for the faith that gave birth to his words for Jesus, he was rendered dumb by the words he received in response. Something washed over him from the inside out, buoyed him, cleansed him. Of all the places to find comfort, of all the places to find friendship and salvation! His dying body groaned no less desperately than before, and the heat of the late morning sun beat down upon them mercilessly. But somehow he felt stronger. There is a fatalism with which doomed men look upon each other—a disease of the eyes that haunts their every mutual glance. It was a darkness that had infected Demas' vision ever since they had left the Tower courtyard. Part resignation, part despair, it is a look that speaks more than words, an impotent camaraderie of death and forever farewell. He looked at Jesus again, and again their eyes met. But the death-look had left Demas and never returned.

Prayer: Lord Jesus, thank You for the power of the Cross that sparks faith under the worst circumstances and in the most unlikely places, and snatches us from the power of death, even at the last. I am grateful for the starkness of Your sacrifice, the blinding light of Your truth that unmasks my ugliness, and gives me grace to respond with repentant supplication. And thank You that for the voice that tells me I will be with You soon, soon, in Paradise. Amen.

Day Twenty-Eight

At midday it began to grow dark. In a matter of minutes, dark clouds covered the sky. It seemed nature herself was rebelling against the violence that was being committed in her midst. As one horrific hour after another passed, it became darker and darker until mid-afternoon was a dismal twilight. A wind came up, blowing dust about and chilling the air. At this some people grew frightened as if by a portent and started to flee the scene. Others pulled their cloaks about them and remained, spellbound. Above it all, Jesus' voice suddenly rang out, clear and strong.

"Eloi, Eloi, lema sabachthani?"

His cry caused a stir among the soldiers and some of the other bystanders. Demas heard them chattering in Greek about Elijah, but he knew what Jesus had really said.

My God, my God, why have you forsaken me? What a terrible cry of anguish and abandonment to leave those holy lips. What could it mean? Had Demas' newfound King bowed to despair?

"I thirst," Jesus' parched voice rasped softly.

Someone ran and got a sponge that had been sitting in a bucket of sour wine the soldiers kept on hand, and lifted it to him on a reed.

"Leave him be," someone laughed coarsely. "Let's see if Elijah returns from heaven to save him!"

But the man came anyway. Jesus received the drink, and as he watched, something stirred within Demas' breast. From a dark recess in his spirit, his memory as a student of the Scriptures awoke, shook itself, and stirred to life inside him. Now as then, Demas responded to prompting of the rabbi. To cite the first verse of a psalm was to instruct the pupil to finish the whole.

*My God, my God, why have you forsaken me? Why are you
so far from delivering me, from the words of my groaning?*

"It is finished," Jesus said. "Father, into your hands I commit
my spirit."

Demas saw his head drop and his body go utterly limp. A
tremor seemed to shake the very earth, and a great rumbling was
heard, rising and falling in the distance. People cried out and
some ran in fear. Away to the south, across the rooftops of luxury
in the Upper City, Pilate's wife Procula trembled and wept for
fear in her chambers. But something had taken hold of Demas'
innermost being.

*O my God, by day I cry, but you do not answer, and by night,
but find no rest.*

"Truly, this man was the Son of God," said Petronius,
Centurion of the Tower Guard, and hung his head in sorrow.

*But you are Holy, enthroned on the praises of Israel. In you
our forefathers trusted; they trusted, and you delivered them. To
you they cried out and they were rescued; in you they trusted and
were not shamed.*

Now Jesus' disciples and others who watched in sorrow over
His crucifixion wept aloud and beat their breasts, comforting
each other as they limped away, crippled by grief. The Place of
the Skull became increasingly deserted.

*But I am a worm and not a man, scorned by mankind and
despised by people. All those who see me sneer at me; they curl
the lip at me; they wag the head; "He committed himself to the
LORD; let him save him; let him rescue him, for in him he
delights!"*

Demas' mind continued its quotation, but now he saw that
the soldiers gathered for a discussion with some officials that had
come, along with some well-dressed Jews. After a brief
exchange, the centurion in charge nodded. He summoned two of
his men, and they took up a spear and a heavy club. Then they
approached Demas' cross.

*Be not far from me, for trouble is near, and there is none to
help.*

The priests, ever concerned with ritual cleanness, had made
their case and Pilate given the order that the deaths might be
hastened because of the Passover. If left alone, a crucified man

might last for days, but breaking the legs meant that death by asphyxiation set in much more quickly. It was an unintended mercy for the victim who wanted nothing more than for the ordeal to end. But who could gratefully receive such a gift? One soldier slid the shaft of the spear between Demas' knees and twisted. He gasped in agony, then cried out feebly, too weak to scream when the other brought the club down with all his strength, just above the knee. His other femur was shattered in like fashion.

Many bulls encircle, strong bulls of Bashan surround me; they open wide their mouths at me, like ravening and roaring lions.

Demas slumped, broken now and completely unable to lift himself for the pathetic gulps of air that had kept him alive for the last six hours. His breathing became impossibly shallow, and the pressure that had been building in his chest became a crushing weight impossible to bear. But he could still hear, and now he heard Matthias' moans, as if at a great distance, when the soldiers broke his legs as well.

What would they do to the Teacher? Surely they would leave him in peace. With all his remaining strength Demas twisted his head to see. The soldiers grasped his knees and shook him, and one even reached up and took him by the beard, turning his head from side to side. There came no response.

"He's dead, I say. The man's dead," said the one holding the spear.

"Hard to believe it. Never seen anyone go that fast."

"Well, no use talking when there's a sure way to know."

With those words he stepped back and immediately thrust his spear deeply into Jesus's side, its tip piercing upward towards the heart. The image stuck in the mind's eye of the repentant zealot. Demas choked and coughed weakly, his airless lungs unable to produce a sob. For now he beheld, and now he found in his final moments the Hero he had sought, and sought to be, all his life. Here beside him shone the Zealous Priest, the Holy and True Phineas. Sin's guilt and shame both had been put to death by a single stroke of the spear, and atonement for it made. God's hand had been stayed, His wrath turned aside, and the plague on the nation lifted. It had been lifted from Demas.

The lance withdrew; blood and clear fluid streamed out.

I am poured out like water, and all my bones are out of joint; my heart is like wax; it is melted within me; my strength is dried up like a potsherd, and my tongue cleaves to the roof of my mouth, and you lay me in the dust of death.

Satisfied, the killers walked away. The King of the Jews was dead. Jesus' mother let out a cry as if her own heart had received the blade. As for Demas, he was fading fast. His heart pounded unevenly, and with every breath he exhaled more than he could take in. His extremities trembled involuntarily and his jaw went slack.

But Thou, O LORD, be not be far away! O Thou my help, hasten to my aid! Rescue my soul from the sword, the only life I have from the paw of the dog!

His spirit leapt within him, even as his body ceased to struggle. His eyes, half closed, dimly beheld the dust at his feet that his own body had defiled. Inaudible mumblings rose in his throat, but he was too spent to speak them. His mind rambled and then caught itself.

For He has not despised or abhorred the affliction of the afflicted, neither has He hidden His face from Him, but heard, when He cried to Him.

"He has *not* despised...He has *not* hidden His face..." Demas' consciousness whispered urgently. His shoulders and his back were a wasteland of agony, his arms were on fire, his wrecked legs throbbed and pulsed, his skin was clammy and chill, his mouth was a desert. But incredibly, unbelievably, peace descended upon him, bathing his spirit like a soft shower out of season.

The poor shall eat and be satisfied; those who seek Him will praise the LORD! May your hearts live on forever!

This day you will be with me in Paradise. This day you will be with me in Paradise. This day you will be with me...

Demas' heart could take no more. Unable to think, on the edge of consciousness, his pain began to ebb as his memory gave way and another Voice guided, finished the recitation. It was strong and tender, tranquil and mighty, sublimely divine, yet near and warm.

All the ends of the earth shall remember
and turn to the LORD,
and all the families of the nations
shall worship before Him.
For the Kingdom is the LORD'S,
and He rules the nations.
All the wealthy of the earth will eat and worship;
before Him shall fall prostrate all who go down to the dust—
even the one who could not keep himself alive.
Descendants shall serve Him;
it shall be proclaimed of the Lord to the coming generation;
they shall come and preach His justice
to a people as yet unborn,
that He has done it.

****

The darkness peeled away like a torn veil, like a weak and filthy garment that had in its spite not only refused to cover his nakedness but had rather increased his shame. He was gently but suddenly lifted, his broken and twisted self now standing free, his legs effortlessly coursing with youthful strength, his arms feather-light and raised high in childlike wonder.

"Oh Jesus, Messiah, my King, my God, my Friend," his lips began. "I love…"

But his words were overwhelmed by a symphony, the gushing well of his own joy bursting forth in musical laughter that joined the song which filled that Place. He saw it dance before his eyes like so many roses of Sharon in a summer breeze, heard the ineffable colors of the emerald rainbow stretching over this Promised Land, his outstretched, astonished fingers caressed by the intoxicating fragrances of endless Eden. But before all, Demas beheld the Face, shining like a thousand thousand suns in clemency and welcome. And then, suffused in cool, blinding flame, as for the first time he tasted the milk and the honey of true understanding. In that infinite instant he was both fully consumed and completely made whole as his heart burst with unbearable blessedness.

Prayer: *Lord Jesus, whenever I feel abandoned, whenever I feel You are waiting until the last minute to rescue me, help me remember the Cross. You reign over a Kingdom that sets this upside down world right-side up. Only beholding the Pierced One will work in me what I need to overcome the vertigo of divine reversal, the realm where loss becomes gain, where brokenness is crowned as glory, and where sinners like me are scandalously received as sons. Thank You for daring to present Yourself clearly as crucified. Amen.*

Part III

Simon Peter the Disciple, and Stephen the Archdeacon

And they conquered him by the blood of the Lamb, and by the word of their witness, and they did not love their lives, unto death.

~Revelation 12:11

THE QUESTIONS

Simon Peter, Disciple

John 21:1-22

Day Twenty-Nine

The final miles of their return pilgrimage lay before them. They made their way up the western shore of the Sea of Galilee towards Tiberias, and hours before midday the heat began to tax them. They were weary for the journey. The previous day had been a long, hard stretch because they had pushed to reach a home sure to receive them—one of the disciples' relatives. The humble ground of that safe house, just south of where the Jordan flowed from the great lake, provided a measure of natural peace for its homeliness. After an early breakfast, they had given their hosts a parting blessing and headed north under a bright and balmy dawn. Though the nearness of home made every mile seem interminable, a steady pace would have them there with time and to spare. They had until sundown to reach Capernaum; the next day was the Sabbath.

Simon Peter led the way, his headship of the Eleven assumed in the Lord's absence. He looked over his shoulder at them and the half dozen or so pious women of the inner circle who had accompanied them to Jerusalem almost three weeks ago. Andrew was closest to him, then Philip and Nathanael, with the rest in small groups strung out behind; the sons of Zebedee brought up the rear with Mary Magdalene and the Lord's mother. A few of the disciples returned his gaze, both conveying and searching for something in each other's hearts that all of them knew dwelt there, but none of them yet fully understood. Faltering still, Simon pretended his gesture was merely casual and allowed his eyes to slip to the shining waters on his right and linger there for a long moment before fixing himself once again on the road before him.

It had been nearly a month since he had trod these roads, heading south. But in his home country again and smelling the waters he had known since his childhood, his memory wandered back, not just three weeks, but three years. Simon had first encountered Jesus in Judea, of course, through his younger brother's acquaintance. He never thought anyone or anything would captivate Andrew like John the Baptizer had. But Simon had misunderstood his brother. And when he came face to face with Jesus of Nazareth he understood how wrong he had been. The Teacher had given him a welcoming look and called him *Kepha*—"Rock"—and not for the last time. That was an unforgettable moment, even if Simon hadn't begun to comprehend the meaning of it. The real turning point, however, happened not in Judea, but in Simon's own land, on the shores of this lake in Galilee.

****

It had been a long and profitless night on the lake. Tired, hungry, and stoically disappointed, Simon, Andrew, James and John, along with a few hired hands, dragged their boats ashore and pulled out the empty nets for the obligatory cleaning and repairs. Focused as usual on his work, Simon hardly noticed the gathering crowd. By the time he did, Jesus was almost upon him. To his surprise, the Teacher, showing neither haughtiness nor hesitation, climbed into the boat. While a startled Simon beheld him, Jesus, in that same spirit of unpretentious authority, asked the fisherman to put out from the shore a bit that he might speak to the people unhindered. Wearily, but without delay, Simon complied. After the brothers and their men maneuvered the boat so that they might weigh anchor parallel to the shore, Jesus sat amidships and began to teach the crowd. He preached God's kingdom, of the urgent decision that was breaking upon them all, of making choices with their lives and not just their words. If the crowds were captivated, Simon was a prisoner. True, he saw James and John leave their work and stand at the fore of the people, unmoving and entranced. But they might wander away if they pleased. Peter's obedient hospitality, on the other hand, had made escape impossible; standing in the stern, gently pushing at the tiller to keep the boat steady, he and Andrew were the only truly captive listeners Jesus had that morning. There could be no polite begging off, no anonymous slipping away among the crowd. He had to hear the Teacher out. Simon had never sat under teaching like what he heard that morning, not from the sagest rabbi he had ever had the privilege to encounter. Then came the greatest surprise. After the Master finished his lesson and dismissed the crowd, he turned and told Simon to push into deeper waters and let down the nets. Andrew looked at his brother, and Simon, humble by tone but in so many words, informed the Teacher about the realities of fishing on the Sea of Galilee. The night had been futile; in the light of morning and under the circumstances the effort would waste even more of the day, not to mention another fouling of the nets they had just cleaned and mended. But nevertheless, to humor him, Simon would once again comply with the Teacher's wish. Jesus looked on with a gaze of placid lordship, and said nothing.

Within minutes, Simon was falling at the Master's knees. His nets had been filled to breaking, his boat to sinking, and the sons of Zebedee had had to answer his call for aid, though to no avail. Astonishment overwhelmed them all. Simon's simple but tenacious mind grasped in that moment that he was dealing with someone entirely beyond his small world on those waters, entirely too lofty for him to aspire to attain. "Depart from me, Lord," he begged, head bowed, "for I am a sinful man." Truly, fear was the only sane response. Yet Jesus, speaking for the first time since he had given the command, swept aside Peter's objections with a mixture of compassion and confidence that pierced Peter like a blade: "Do not be afraid. From now on you will fish for men."

Simon Peter abandoned his nets that day, as did his brother and their partners. If he had grasped anything through that miraculous blur of events, he understood now that his was to follow, not to fish. But the wonder that he first encountered on that day proved only the beginning. How could he recall it all? Everything had become a single blur to him. The towns and the inescapable crowds, the parables and the mysteries revealed, the signs and the wonders. Jesus had drawn the multitudes, instructed the simple, and silenced the wise. The healings were beyond counting, and in truth they were more than healings. The unclean were cleansed. The eyes of the blind opened and saw. How could Simon shake, as long as he lived, the amazement that came upon him when the multitude ate their fill from a lad's meal that the Lord had easily held in his hands? What would happen next? Where would these things lead them? Surely God's kingdom had come in power, and they would see its glory wax full with their own eyes.

Here Simon's memories grew quieter and more intense. He stared at the dust his sandals kicked up before him as they entered the streets of Tiberias, and blocked out the murmuring of the disciples around him. The Lord had chosen him. He could neither deny nor boast of it. The electrifying feeling that accompanied those early days of realization reached to the very bottom of his soul. All the disciples experienced the miraculous, yea, the Lord commanded that they walk in it themselves by his name. And so they had gone out by twos, healing and driving out the demons. But Simon knew he had special favor with the Master. On this lake the Lord had called to him in the storm, and Simon had left the others behind in the boat and walked on the waters. Only Simon and the sons of Zebedee had been allowed to see him raise the girl to life again, and again only those three had seen Jesus transformed by the glorious vision on the holy mountain, seen the vision of Moses and Elijah. Such things were so far beyond him that he hadn't had words then, and didn't have words now. But the moment that defined him and glorified him before his brothers was when words were granted him: *You are the Messiah, the Son of the Living God.* Even now the Lord's response, and his glowing affirmation in the new name he gave Simon, rolled like thunder within him. Peter, the Rock, the solid one, the disciple who had heard directly from the Father. The Master's words burned his heart: *I will give you the keys of the kingdom of heaven...* What doubt remained? If the demons yammered for mercy, and famine, blindness, even death itself all yielded before the Teacher's softly spoken word, who were they to doubt or resist? What else could the Lord have meant when he promised they, the Twelve, would sit enthroned, judging the tribes of Israel? What were they to do but breathlessly anticipate the shining vision of heavenly power he prophesied?

Prayer: Lord Jesus, so often it seems to me that of all the prayers I could pray, saying, "Depart from me, Lord, I am a sinner" is the only one that makes any sense. But You remind me that not even the truth of my sinful shortcomings in greater than Your love. Open my ears to hear Your words, "Do not be afraid," and to surrender my faithless self-pity in exchange for the courage to know that I have not chosen You, but You have chosen me. Amen.

Day Thirty

Then the strange and fateful talk began. Talk not of glory and honor and the Messiah's miracle working power restoring the splendor of David and Solomon, but of suffering, ignominy, death. Simon could make no sense of such talk. Who was more well-received than the Master? Not only did these words clash with Simon's own hope and vision, they flatly contradicted the glorious future Jesus himself had promised them. How could both predictions comes true? Surely the pressure had become too much for him. Surely he merely needed some encouragement...

Nay, Lord. These things will never happen to you.

Who has understood the Lord or instructed him as his counselor? Who might sit and explain to him the way? What folly—even then—to think that he could fathom the mind of Jesus of Nazareth. How quickly and firmly the Lord had rebuked him when he acted as if he were in a position to dissuade him of his painful and mysterious plans. Peter flushed at the memory, for those harsh words, too, had been spoken in the presence of his brothers. The rebuke felt like so many others delivered by Master, chiding him and the others for lack of faith. And like those others, a lesson followed hard on its heels:

If anyone would come after me, he must deny himself, take up his cross, and follow. For the one who tries to save his life will lose it, but the one who loses it for my sake will find it.

The oft-repeated promise of impending kingdom glory that punctuated these words just confused Peter all the more. As anyone living under the Romans well knew, the man took up his cross did so only because he was soon to be stretched out upon it. How could they follow the Master to glorious reign as dead men? And Simon wasn't the only one suffering from messianic vertigo. In the course of time, and increasingly, many who had followed so closely, who had become friends and advocates, fell away. All the undercutting of victories with perplexing predictions of death, all this talk of eating his flesh and imbibing his blood, proved too much for many. Once, when the Lord confronted the Twelve over their intentions after a large crowd had departed, murmuring and casting confused glances over their shoulders, Simon had again been the spokesman. *Lord to whom shall we go? You alone have the words of eternal life; you are the Holy One of God!* Who wouldn't consider his words the model of fidelity? And yet Jesus, if not cold, seemed unmoved. With his enigmatic reply he once again asserted his absolute prerogative over them as well as his knowledge of their hearts. He was the same Jesus who had opened the very heavens to Simon, whose warm affection for him came through each time he called him *Kepha*. But increasingly the young rabbi revealed a hidden but fiery purpose, an unblinking focus that proved all the more troubling in that it betrayed no sign of being at odds with the selfsame personality that had won the favor of the masses. But the Twelve (or so it seemed) really believed what Simon had said, and made no move to leave the Master, and for his part he seemed neither surprised nor flattered by their loyalty. He merely set his face towards Jerusalem, the place he spoke of so fatefully, and pressed on with his greatly diminished entourage behind him.

The weighty events unfolded so rapidly from that point that it would take almost as much time to tell them as it had taken for them to happen. Not that they seemed at all clouded in Peter's mind. On the contrary, their succession marched in orderly, crystal clear vision before his mind's eye. The dramatic events of Lazarus' sickness, death, and coming forth from the grave led to what the Twelve thought for certain would be a return to the popularity they had once enjoyed. People thronged to Bethany, fighting for a glimpse of Lazarus. The chatter was everywhere, and it seemed like old times, managing the crowds and helping make way for the Master. But when they sat to celebrate in the risen man's home, Jesus responded to Iscariot's attack on Mary with the same foreboding language. *She has anointed me for my burial.* A darkness fell upon Simon when he heard those words, but their cryptic nature ultimately could not compete with the buoyancy within them over the surging of the happy, welcoming crowds. It was as if Judea had never been a place of danger to the Master, and the Holy City was ready to receive her rightful Lord.

In that charged atmosphere Jesus called Simon and John aside and gave them orders about his upcoming entry into Jerusalem. Peter could feel through his exacting, nay, *predictive* instructions that some great happening bore down upon them. He was not disappointed. Soon the Master fulfilled Peter's expectations, riding through the midst of the Passover crowd, with disciples old and new waving the palms of victory and peace, and throwing their garments down before the humble King and his lowly steed. When his enemies objected to the crowd's deafening cheers, Jesus, laughing and smiling, rebuffed them with the Scriptures. No one had ever seen a day like it. The Jesus of old had returned, the one they had known from the beginning—before the ominous words and dwindling numbers had confused them all. The Son of David had come to claim his inheritance.

It lasted a day. When Jesus began the next morning in the Temple courts by overturning the money changers' tables and scattering their wares, the favorable winds quickly changed. True, the crowds pressed in as delighted as ever. But a new element had emerged in the opposition that deeply troubled Simon. Sadducees, Pharisees, and Herodians alike—sworn enemies of each other—seemed to join forces to try and take the Teacher down. They plied their most calculated, their cleverest, their most persistent attacks—and they were no match for Jesus. But while Simon and the others alternated between joy at his mastery of the situation and their nagging concern over what revenge these power brokers might seek for the public humiliation he inflicted upon them, the Lord showed no sign of either bending to the plaudits of the masses or quailing at the hostility of his foes. He neither deliberately provoked nor pacified. Jesus spoke the blunt truth with color and passion, and, it seemed to Peter, kept his eyes on an unseen mark ahead of him. Privately, the Teacher delivered words of doom and hope like none they had ever heard. How would this all end?

Prayer: *Lord Jesus, Your paths are indeed wonderful beyond my power to trace them out. Grant me the grace to enjoy them as amazing rather than resent them as merely unexpected. What should I expect from You except that You would exceed my ability to grasp You? Help me to rejoice when it is time for it, without fearing a trap; help me accept the difficulty of twists in the road You have for me as opportunities for You to do even more than I thought You would. Amen.*

Day Thirty-One

They bought fresh bread and a little fish in Tiberias, and drew cool water for their midday meal. They must eat hurriedly; they had to reach their homes on the north shore before the sun went down. Sitting in the shade of some trees north of the town, the others talking softly around him, Simon lost himself in thought again over what had happened at that portentous meal two weeks back, and its aftermath. Waves of emotion washed over him, emotions that mingled with each other and confused themselves even as they pressed upon his heart.

Fateful words, fateful actions, fateful prayers. As Jesus spoke of wonderful and doomful things beyond their bearing, even so Simon could not restrain his impetuousness. He objected, he resisted, he loudly made his promises and swore his oaths. He was determined to be the strong one, the leader of his brethren in their Lord's darkest hour. Sadly, lovingly, the Lord answered him.

Unless I wash you, you have no portion with me.

Simon, Simon, lo, Satan has demanded to sift you all as wheat. But I have prayed for you that your faith fail not. And when you yourself have turned back, strengthen your brothers.

And, excruciatingly,

Will you really die with me, Simon? Before the rooster crows you will thrice deny you know me at all.

Oh, Gethsemane. If only Simon had taken warning from the painful failures that overtook him in that idyllic, haunted grove. If only he could have prevented that chilling prophecy from fulfilling itself through him, like an ill-fated figure in a Greek tragedy. The shame was still heavy, the ache not yet fully assuaged by the overwhelming events that had unfolded since that terrible night. In spite of himself, Peter still wrestled, still hid within his heart the full revelation of weakness that came to light in those dark hours before a hopeless dawn. His strength unmasked itself as clumsy violence the Lord had to rebuke and reverse; his loyalty a distant skulking under cover of night; his bold and noble oaths turned into cowering curses at the surly voices of slave girls and strangers. Had he ever been that disciple who had seen the glory and confessed the Messiah before them all? Even now the grieved, knowing look in Jesus' eyes scalded Simon's memory. Never again would the crowing of the rooster ring the same in his ears.

The 14th of Nisan dawned. Simon Peter saw Pilate surrender the Lord and the soldiers lead him away, but he did not follow. He and the others, overcome by terror and shame, hid their faces and slipped away in the crowd, then made their way to their rooms to tremble and wait. They heard the inevitable horror late that day from John, for only John had braved the ordeal, he and their women. Simon stood there numb as he waited for their youngest member to tell the story, his voice breaking. But when he finished, Peter just turned away. Andrew's sorrowed touch and the questioning eyes of the others only made it worse. He could not look the Lord's mother in the face, could bear her silent gray grief even less than the sobs of Magdalene and the others. They had stayed with the Lord; he had not. His disgrace was complete.

In the endless hours that followed, paralyzing fear and suffocating despair fought within him for chief amongst his feelings, but that battle never did resolve itself. All their hopes, all their illusions of kingdom glory, of Israel restored, of God breaking in and delivering his people, lay mangled and lifeless in a borrowed tomb. Simon could not bear the nagging, clawing thought that whispered in the center of his mind, the thought that Jesus had just been another fraudulent messiah, leaving Simon and the other disciples as another band of duped fools who had been naïve enough to believe the lofty talk and the magic tricks. And like those messianic fools before them, the authorities would catch them, sentence them without recourse, and crucify them along with the fool they had followed. Fits of weeping took him, shaking his body and breaking his health as his soul rose within him in a pathetic attempt to fight off these nightmarish doubts. But as miserably defenseless as he felt, as inverted as his world had become, a tenacious anchor remained firm within him. Though his mind skidded futilely from one miraculous proof to another, one held true, wouldn't budge, remained firm against the inner assaults that battered and threw him. With the very fingernails of his memory he held onto what had happened on that lake some three years back when the Master had rent his nets asunder, and with otherworldly love in his eyes had called Simon to follow. He had failed utterly in his Lord's hour of need, and now his Lord was gone. But this scrap—he swore to himself with tears—this miracle worked expressly for him, he would guard.

Those three days passed tortuously, like a continuous night. The women carried out a few secretive comings and goings to get supplies (though most ate very little, their thirst was great), but also to complete the preparations for the Lord's burial after the Sabbath. Women were women; they posed no threat to the powers that be, and their veils more easily disguised them anyway. But the men dared not venture forth. In the course of things they received word of Judas' self-destruction, news that tore at the wound of his betrayal; one more ugly detail drove home to them that things had not been what they seemed. The Master was no more, and now his Twelve were undone as well. They also heard about the soldiers the Romans had sent to keep the tomb. It took Simon a moment to realize that the guard had been posted with them in mind. Someone less ashamed of himself might have laughed at this revelation. Their enemies had seen them with the Teacher for days, and even common folk had recognized them by face and accent the night the priests' men had taken Jesus. They remained in the city because their fear had convinced them that the gates of Jerusalem were guarded against them, and the Romans searched for them amidst the Passover crowds. Surely spies lay in wait for them even now, seeking a reward for their betrayal just as Judas had. The disciples' had no recourse but to lie low and let the multitude abate, and hopefully trick their pursuers into thinking they had already gone. When the excitement had ebbed, they would make good their escape.

Prayer: Lord Jesus, forgive me for presuming upon Your lordship. In my weakness, I have pretended that Your Cross was a talisman against struggle, disappointment, and defeat. But You are the Lord of Resurrection Life, not of untroubled life. I surrender, then, all the grand promises I've made to You. It is the faith that You've graciously planted in me that is my victory—You Yourself are all I need. I cling to You. Amen.

Day Thirty-Two

Simon was only dimly aware of the women's departure in the darkness before the dawn on the 17th of Nisan, the morning after the long Sabbath. Exhaustion had taken him to a place of drifting in and out of sleep, interrupted by sudden night terrors and long periods of wakefulness. Even now, looking back, he could not remember when or how much he had slept and how much he had watched in those cramped, sweaty, suffocating rooms. His nightmares and his waking thoughts seemed one and the same. In any case, he had not been there for the last hours of the Master's life; he could not bear to see him in the first hours of his death, even if fear didn't crouch like a beast outside the door. It was dull dawn when they pounded on the door, whispering and crying out with an urgency that could only mean more trouble. Peter arose quickly and opened the door to them, and so saw their faces as they burst into the room.

Five women, breathless from running. Five women talking all at once, contradicting and confirming and repeating each other—frightened, bewildered, but also speaking with a kind of hopeful wonder. Long moments passed with the disciples gathered around them before any sense could be made of their words. No one rushed them or lost patience with them; the new life in their eyes told the men that something momentous had happened.

In the end they told their tale, but when they finished the disciples had nothing but gibberish about an open tomb, and guards laid low, and beautiful men in shining garments bearing incomprehensible tidings. *You seek Jesus of Nazareth, who was crucified, but he is risen,* they had said, *he is not here.* This made no sense. The disciples asked for the story again. *Why do you*

seek the living among the dead? He is risen—just like he said.
More foolishness. By the time the same disbelieving questions
were asked a third time, Peter pulled the door open. A quick look
over his shoulder on his way out, and John's eager eyes met his.
Then the race began.

The eastern sky shone a pale golden-gray above the Mount
of Olives, the sun's early light gilding the trees that crowned that
ridge. But the disciples only caught a glimpse of this glory as
they ran through the streets of Jerusalem. The light that dawn
afforded them came at a price, as the multitudes had begun to
stir. They ignored the offended glances of the pilgrims they
passed, oblivious to their own dignity; more than once they
barely avoided collision. As they turned a sharp corner Peter
glanced up the narrow street they had just run down and saw a
woman hurrying after them as best she could; it was Magdalene.
They did not slow for her. The Gennath Gate was wide open, and
the early traffic that milled about there mostly crowded inwards;
the disciples went against the flow. In spite of himself, Peter
navigated the bottleneck with his face down, still concerned as
much for his anonymity as for their haste. But the guards looked
bored and paid more attention to their gossip than to the lowly
worshippers passing them by. Once free of the gate, Simon lifted
his head and ran with all his strength. His eyes smarted from the
wind of his speed, the tears running back across his temples, and
his lungs burning in the crisp morning air. He and John strove as
two starving friends might run for fresh bread on yonder hearth:
neither would begrudge the other's success, but at the last each
ran for his own belly and as his own man. As they neared the
garden where they knew the Lord had been laid, youth and a
lighter frame finally bested Peter, and John left him behind. Only
for a moment was he hidden from view, then Simon caught up
and found his friend.

Excepting the presence of guards in a faint or shining
messengers, all appeared as the women had described. The tomb
lay open, its great stone completely removed to one side. The
garden was empty but for a few birds, who sang exuberantly,
oblivious and carefree. John, stooping, peered inside. As Peter
pushed past him, he absently noticed the remains of the ropes
and shattered clay seal that had warned all comers of Rome's

might and wrath lest its ward be violated. It might as well have been a discarded child's toy for all he cared; for the moment, heavenly fears gripped the disciples, pushing them beyond the reach of earthly ones.

Peter looked around the low cell, a shaft of sunlight lancing past him and setting the opposite wall aglow. Now John entered. White linen strips, some bearing the expected ugly stains, lay on the floor, and the cloth customary for the head and face neatly folded to one side. Peter turned around three times, looking up and down and staring first at the walls and then at the cloths as if the very intensity of his desire for an answer might summon one. Resignation set in. The mystery would not be answered here. As they stepped from the tomb Magdalene drew near, her face expectant. Tears of grief, hope, and bewilderment filled her eyes. Peter shook his head slightly and slowly walked past her. John followed. They would leave her to seek her own answers, and to mourn.

****

Now, in their journey back home, Simon and the others approached the little town of Magdala, a little more than an hour's walk north of Tiberias. The town gave Mary her surname to distinguish her from the other Marys in their midst, and had been her home, though she made clear she would go on to Capernaum with the others. As they drew near, Simon recalled what happened next that resurrection morn. They had not been back an hour when Magdalene was at the door again. If she had been confused and hopeful before, she was transformed now. Joy had eclipsed grief, and meaningful purpose her former confusion.

I have seen the Lord! He is risen and he lives! He goes before us into Galilee!

Once again they heard her, but once again they did not believe her. They had heard Peter and John's report—what they had seen and what they had not seen. The women suffered hysteria. For his part, Simon did not blame them, even as Magdalene's unwavering countenance sent tremors through his doubts. His hopes, indeed, his entire life had been turned upside down when they had murdered his Master. The trauma of it all had shaken him, spirit, soul, and body. His life, as he had known it, was over. But the whole of it rang true. As terrible, as horrifically agonizing as it had been, the loss had made rational, human sense. But angels and apparitions? This made no sense. Risen? Alive? Impossible. The wonder worker may raise the dead, but who would raise the dead wonder worker? Simon's exhausted mind, no less spent for the astonishing events of the morning, now puzzled hopelessly over this fresh enigma.

Crouched on the floor with his face in his hands, Simon glanced over at Mary, sitting with the other women around her, comforting her in the isolation her faith had brought upon her. She did not weep, but only shook her head and urgently whispered to them. Presently, she looked up and into Peter's eyes. It was too much for him. He arose and walked into a small side room of their borrowed home, shutting the door behind him. He needed to be alone.

Peter tried to gather his thoughts, but as he sat down on a low pallet against a wall, he stepped, as it were, into a stream of consciousness barely his own.

You have in mind human things, not the things of God...unless you bear your own cross, if you do not give up everything you have, you cannot be my disciple...if anyone strikes you on one cheek, offer to them...not seven times, but seventy times seven...if any of you would rule over the others, he must become like this child, and the least among... what does it profit a man to gain the entire world and yet lose his soul? And what can a man give in exchange...for the Son of Man did not come to be served, but to serve, and to give his life a ransom...I am the Good Shepherd, I lay down my life for my sheep; no one takes it from me...do you understand what I have done for you? Now that I, your Teacher and Lord...the Son of Man will be betrayed into the hands of sinners and will be beaten, spat upon, and crucified...but on the third day...

Nay, Lord. These things....shall never happen to you. Nay, Lord. Nay, nay, nay...

Kepha.

All the teachings, all the prophecies, all the events of the last nine hours, the last three days, the last three years hadn't been enough to prepare him for this. He looked up at the speaking of his name, and though it was now the heat of the day, a cool, electric tingle coursed through his skin from his brow to his heels. What is it to recognize, unlooked for, a long lost friend in a strange place? First one sees a stranger, then the heart perceives while the mind still doubts, then they agree to familiarity if not identity, then finally comes the light of knowledge, and with it, the heart grants itself permission to rejoice and, sometimes, to fear. All of this happened inside Simon Peter within the blink of an eye.

There stood Jesus, not two paces from him. Like a lighting flash in the mind, in that moment Peter perceived him as he had when he came across the waves that stormy night. Was this a phantom? Then the phantom spoke.

Peace. Do not be afraid. It is I.

It was really Jesus, fresh and clean, warm and alive. The Lord was risen indeed. Impetuousness conquered fearful paralysis, and Peter fell, clasping desperately at his Master's wound-marked feet, his spirit flooded with love and holy awe. He choked and haltingly whispered some nonsense; Jesus, gentle as only one immeasurably strong can be, was spare and direct in his reply. Then he disappeared. He had granted a mere visitation, not an audience. After staring at the place where the Lord had stood, momentarily overcome by the encounter, Simon arose and rushed into the other room.

The following hours brought such a full mixture of wonder, inexpressible joy, doubt, questioning, and constant, excited talk that Simon still could not recall who reacted how to his testimony and his confirmation of what the women had been saying all along. Just as they began to wonder how exactly they might live with all of this and tell the others, Cleopas and his wife, Mary—the Lord Jesus' aunt and uncle—burst in upon them. They had seen Jesus on the way to Emmaus, and had come back to share the news. What would happen next? Heaven itself answered that question when, into this marveling din with nary a door opened or a shutter rattled, stepped the living Lord.

Now all the disciples shared what Mary Magdalene and Simon had seen, save some not of the Eleven and Thomas, who was away. He remained the same Lord they had known, yet completely different than they had known. Their Master seemed at once more solid, more palpable, while also more heavenly, more...*other*. And yet, as always, he assured, confirmed, revealed, and rebuked. He instructed them from the Scriptures and spoke sweepingly of the things to come. But he spoke by his mercurial departure every bit as much as by his word; if they had thought for even a moment that things would return to how they had been, his going taught them otherwise. He would not remain amongst them in the same way he had.

The earth had shifted under their feet. But they were not the ones traversing walls. Fear of the priests and their Roman allies still weighed heavily upon them. After much discussion, they chose to remain in the city another week—until after the Feast of Unleavened Bread had run its course and its crowds had dissipated—before heading north to Galilee as the Lord had commanded. He had, after all, not spoken of times. He only impressed upon them the need for that journey home, then the urgency to return to Jerusalem where the Father's plan would be completed. Perhaps the Lord would come the next day and sup with them and reveal even more of his thought.

But the Lord did not come the next day, nor the one after that. What could it mean? The long, hot days stretched into a week, the rumor of the Passover multitudes gradually lessened, and doubts began to get the best of them. Had they imagined something? And even if they had not, how could they follow a risen but nevertheless absent Master? Thomas, who had seen nothing, only worsened the trouble. Their imagination had summoned an apparition, or an impostor had made fools of them, but their Lord was no more. Firmly, immovably as befit his character, the Twin refused to yield without the grittiest of firsthand evidence: he must place his fingers into the very nail marks, and his hand into the gaping hole left by the Roman lance, else he wouldn't believe. Overwhelmed by his own bewilderment, Simon did not argue with him.

On the eighth day—one week to the day since the Lord first appeared—Thomas had his answer and in the presence of their divine Master, the rest forgot their own questions. As Jesus, majestic and ever-living, towered in benevolent rebuke above a repentant and confessing Thomas, something broke in the disciples' midst. A decided end had come to this chapter, this first schooling in the new Kingdom Age that had descended upon them. Here stood no Lazarus, raised to someday die again. Here stood Life Himself in the flesh. And the Messiah's wounds, once ugly evidence of powerlessness before worldly government, served now as witnesses—yea, the very weapons—of the unvanquishable authority and strength that had always been his. The Lord had commanded, and they would obey. They finally mustered the courage to cast off the fears that had kept them in their self-made prison, and Peter voiced the decision for them all.

The next morning they left the city unmolested, their faces set upon the road to Galilee.

Prayer: Lord Jesus, I submit to the great truth that though You come to me on Your own terms, You do come as promised, You come in time, and You come in power. As You make these things clear to me, move me past a doctrinal Resurrection and into the pristine inner air of Resurrection as encounter with You. Let the arguments and the debates fall away in Your presence, and all those voices be silenced as You speak. Amen.

Day Thirty-Three

As they had come from their homes, so they returned. Traveling down the precipitous road to the Jordan Valley, they passed among the other pilgrims that streamed from Jerusalem now that the sacred week had run its course. They reached Jericho by nightfall.

Early the next morning, while they made their way out of the city towards the north, Simon first heard the talk. As they passed a slower group of pilgrims, the name "Jesus of Nazareth" sounded upon the edge of his hearing. Reflexively, he turned and looked, but the people had not addressed him or any of the other disciples; they merely spoke among themselves about what had happened. It was the first of several such instances, the kind of overheard, idle public conversations that the ears might perceive but, usually, the mind disregards for their insignificance. Such-and-such happened to so-and-so, and it means (or doesn't mean) thus-and-so for me. The death of Jesus of Nazareth had become fodder for gossips. Some of them fretted, others scorned, most apathetically filled the time. But for Peter, heading back home, such talk struck his newborn and fragile faith with unexpected force. Verbal assault, even violence itself he had come to expect. Yet for mundane chatter that neither attacked nor sympathized, but simply reduced the high and holy to the vulgar… for that his soul had no parry.

The talk of others was probably the worst thing that immediately troubled Simon's mind, but other things buffeted him as well. Everything from the hard memories of his denials and the Lord's sufferings, to the unchanged landscape around him, to the dust on his feet and in his throat played upon Peter's doubts and muddled the ecstasy of the Lord's visitations. And Jesus did not walk in their midst as they headed north. The temptation to deny the Lord altogether had given way to the subtle idea of making him a natural thing of the past. How did the loss of him differ at all from the loss any man feels for a dead friend? It would feel so much easier, so much more normal. A battle raged in Peter's heart—the battle between the rarified air surrounding the risen Lord that any other sane person on that road would call a dream, and the sensible world everyone knew and lived in. Jesus' death had indeed unmade Peter's world beyond recovery; now that his heart trembled with the surreal joy of seeing him again, the rest of creation had surely been set on its head. Yet the Jordan flowed as it ever had, and the warm breezes stirred the thickets on its bank, and the bleak but beautiful hills beyond it made his eyes smart in the sun as always. Who rises from the dead? What did that really mean? All of it transcended Simon's ability to grasp, and in its desire for resolution his mind sought rest in the familiar and the common, even at the cost of the rare and the precious. Thus did his thoughts double back upon themselves, and thus by the time they reached Capernaum, Peter found himself a thoroughly conflicted soul. He knew with a surety that the Lord had risen; he wasn't sure he knew anything at all.

The sun hovered low over the flat-topped mountain to the west by the time he reached his home. After agreeing to meet the next day, the others had gone to their own dwellings or had found shelter as guests. Though Andrew remained with him, Peter begged for a respite with his wife, Mara, who had remained at home during this Passover with her mother, whose advanced age had prohibited the pilgrimage. So Andrew rested in the shade outside for a time, looking out over the lake.

Never had a husband and wife experienced such a meeting as awaited Simon. His weary delight at seeing her resembled the natural kind that any young man feels after being away from his woman for several weeks, and her initial response mirrored his. But as she embraced him pain flashed upon her face, and she buried her eyes in his shoulder and began to sob. By the mouth of swifter pilgrims word had reached her days ago about all that had happened in Jerusalem. Peter perceived that she wept as much for his loss as for anything else; she wept out of compassion for her husband. Quickly he hushed her with assurances, smiling into her bewildered, tear-stained face as he sat her down and began to tell his tale. Awkwardly, excitedly, he explained that Jesus was really alive. No, the reports were true: Judas had indeed handed the Lord over, and yes, the authorities had humiliated and killed him. But he had risen on the third day, just as he said he would. Simon himself had seen him, as had others, and the Master had spoken with them several times and told them he would meet with them in Galilee. Mara's eyes might have compared to those of a child born blind staring at someone who had just described a sunrise; she did not disbelieve, she had no way to comprehend what she heard. He had seen this look on her face before, but never had the gulf been so vast between the words and deeds he had witnessed in the presence of his Master and the realities of her simple life. Yet in the end, humbly, joyfully, she accepted. Besides, her husband's contagious elation had swept over her, captured her imagination. With a believing smile she wiped her eyes and declared it too good to be true. But it was true, Peter responded, clasping her hands. Now stirred with excitement, Mara did what anyone might expect of such a young wife: hungry for details, she asked for the full story, as much as he could tell her. And—quite nearly looking over Peter's shoulder—she wondered aloud, naturally, where the Lord Jesus walked just now.

Peter the evangelist, recounting the unshakeable evidences, now showed the conflict storming inside of him. His expression betrayed him, and haltingly he told her that though the Lord was risen indeed, things were different now. Thus far he revealed himself only to a few, and only briefly and at times. In the saying, Peter himself seemed less satisfied with his answer than his patient wife. Again she looked at him, searching his face as he now looked more at the floor between his feet than at her. At length she spoke.

"The Teacher always has his own way about things," she said softly.

"Yes, he does," Simon murmured.

Mara waited. His hitherto hidden failures now weighed upon Peter as he wondered how to give his wife what she wanted to know of the events that had brought them to this place.

"I am very weary, Mara. I will tell you everything tomorrow."

Once again slightly confused, but knowing her man well enough to know that further talk would be useless at the moment, she rose to complete her preparations for the evening meal.

Prayer: Lord Jesus, You call me to know Your glory in an inglorious world. And You have commanded me to unveil You to others even as I sometimes struggle with the often drab veil of my daily life. Lord, You know what it is to walk among the children of men. Help me get past my ups and downs, and to put more stock in You than in how I might feel or whether I understand what You are doing. Thank You for being patient with me. Amen.

Day Thirty-Four

The next day brought a restless Sabbath for Simon. He could not bring himself to go to synagogue, close as it stood to his dwelling. He felt ashamed not to do what all his sense of religious obligation urged him to do, but another shame mastered him. If he could not stand up under his own wife's gentle questions, how could he bear the faces of the townsfolk? They had already suffered from the stares and whispers of some as they entered Capernaum the afternoon before, he and the other disciples. He had no stomach for them in the house of prayer where Jesus had taught and delivered the oppressed, not without the Master there with him. Instead, Peter hid in his humble house, searching his own heart for answers that did not come.

So he sat, idle for respect of the seventh day and unable to work out the energy of his inner wrestlings. He realized how much heavier his conflicted thoughts weighed upon his heart in his own home. As doubleminded as he felt on the road, the sweat of travel had been an outlet for him and had given him and the others a task to accomplish. The Lord had told them to go to Galilee; to Galilee they had come. But now that he had returned, Peter realized that no one about him would see his homecoming as anything other than what had to be done. The vaunted mission to Jerusalem had ended in disaster, and now the departed Teacher's abandoned disciples had come home in shame. Of course they came down to Galilee. Where else would they go? How else would they live, and their families eat?

In the still of midafternoon after a light noon meal Peter stirred from a brief and unsatisfying nap. A soft breeze touched his brow, and he lifted his head, hoping that with the opening of his eyes Jesus would appear—Jesus in the flesh to answer his questions, still his doubts, and prevent the need for more talk or explanations. Jesus, standing there, would be the explanation. But he did not hear the Lord calling his voice, only Mara speaking softly with Andrew in the other room. She had asked nothing more of Simon since the night before, keeping especially quiet as Peter brooded and sighed. But he knew he would have to tell her, as he had promised. He knew he would have to get it behind him. Besides, the others would arrive soon, perhaps wondering if Jesus had come to him again, and in any case asking what they should do next. He rose from his pallet and went to his wife and brother.

He told them both all he could remember, hoping to lance the festering wound inside him. Andrew already knew about the threefold denial. During the nightmare of the three days and three nights he had admitted that to the others; as painful as the confession had been, holding it within felt like a white-hot iron in his belly. But now he told details of Gethsemane that even Andrew had not known, things he couldn't bring himself to say before now. He told of his own shameful failure to keep vigil, the hideous details of Judas' betrayal, the arrest, and his absurd swordsmanship then flight. And then he told as fully as he ever had—deliberately, phrase after phrase as if pulling nails from his own flesh—how literally the Lord's prediction about him had come true.

Mara said nothing, but only looked at him with tears quietly coursing down her cheeks. Not in the slightest did her husband retract his testimony of the Lord's return to life, but she understood now why he had suddenly fallen silent the day before. He knew she wanted to know from him, and not just from the gossip of the townsfolk, what happened to Jesus after that. He began slowly, but, sympathetically and much more effectively, Andrew broke in and briefly told the rest as well as he could. When he finished, the three of them sat in silence for a moment; so much to say, so few words that might say it rightly. Finally, Peter got up, nodded—half to them and half to himself— and quietly walked out of the door towards the lake. Suddenly he didn't care what any passerby might say to him.

****

Peter looked out across the Sea of Tiberias. The sun stood about where it had when he came into town the day before, and shining through the slight haze of late afternoon it gave the distant green hills a golden cast. The afternoon light played upon the rippling water, empty of any sailing craft for the Sabbath. Absently, Peter thought how beautiful it all looked.

Failure overwhelmed him, betrayal, more failure, still more failure, then denial after denial. Tears welled up in Simon's eyes again at the thought. Stepping a bit closer to the water, he gazed in the direction of the place, now muted by the light, where Jesus had first called him to follow and he had left his nets. But no, Jesus did not linger there, walking as he had so many times, teaching them and laughing with them. Jesus had been crucified in Jerusalem, and he no longer walked with them, and no amount of staring at the old familiar places would summon him back. But, objected Peter's mind, the Lord had risen! The Lord had come to him and to the others as well! He rehearsed the events of the 17th of Nisan, one after the other, carefully and deliberately like a small boy clumsily but carefully learning the notes of a simple tune on a toy flute. He then played the refrain that came a week later when the Lord confronted Thomas. In the end the melody sounded in his mind slow but harmonious. Yet just as he tried to enjoy the tune, the agony of Jerusalem arose within him again, and his tortured mind again confronted him with his failures, the scandal and the scorn of the crowds, and, above all, the harsh reality that they were on their own.

For perhaps an hour Peter meandered along Galilee's shore, trying and failing to find resolution and peace. As the Rock, he needed to be solid, he needed to lead the others. But lead them where? He suffered the whiplash of colliding and irreconcilable realities, realities that none of his forebears had ever dreamed of facing. But Simon did not dwell on his fathers or their encounters with the Living God; he could not behold Moses' burning bush nor hear the whispering voice that prodded Elijah in the cave. He had seen the Lord and heard his voice, and had walked again on the waters of a pure and ecstatic faith. But now he could do no more than sink as he saw the wind and rising waves of an unrelenting natural world around him. Jesus did not appear to raise him, and Peter's flailing hands went unaided.

"Simon?"

Peter turned. There stood Andrew, with five others behind him: John and James, Nathaniel, Thomas, and Matthew. They all looked at each other for a moment.

"I'm going fishing," Peter said plainly.

After a pause, Thomas spoke for them all.

"We'll go with you."

******

Where were his nets? Where had he stowed them? The nets he had turned his back on, never to lift them again? No, but the Lord had called him to follow, and the tools of that trade had been left behind. With a lump in his throat Peter pulled them out with the help of the others in the last light of the setting Sabbath sun. The mood of his companions shrouded itself in a similar gloom, but noiseless gestures and light, businesslike conversation about the task at hand kept them moving. As they spread the nets on the shore, their rent seams fairly shouted in the ears of Simon's conscience the memory of what had caused them.

Depart from me, Lord, for I am a sinful man.

Do not be afraid. From now on...

His eyes swam, but he wiped them and tried to ignore the ache in the pit of his stomach.

He who puts his hand to the plow and looks back...

They performed the necessary repairs, arranged the nets for casting, then loaded the boat. Peter had done it so many times before, that after beginning he found it easier with each moment to find some refuge in the rhythm of it all. As the last of dusk faded to night they pushed off into the calm waters of the Sea of Galilee.

They fished at night, as Galilean fisherman often did, for the simple reasons of avoiding the punishing rays of the sun and for a better chance of surprising the fish. But the work was still hard, and the long hours of night did not hurry by. Not that the elements gave them cause for complaint. The air was dry, the temperatures pleasant, and the winds blew just enough to keep them moving wherever Simon turned the tiller, but not so strong as to stir the waters above a gentle roll. The sails caught the breeze and the boat glided effortlessly from one favorite spot to another, a clear sky and a canopy of stars giving them a confidence they wouldn't have had on a cloudy night. But though the familiar toil should have provided the distraction the Sabbath could not, the night on the lake provided no escape for Peter's anxious soul. The Lord had sat with them in this boat, preaching to the crowds, traveling the shoreline to get from village to village, even crossing to the land of the Gentiles to set the oppressed one free. When trouble had befallen them not even the waves could keep him away. Now they felt his absence like a gaping hole in their midst; they did not speak of him.

Lord, don't you care that we are perishing?

Why waste breath to lament the empty nets? These were his home waters, but it wasn't the first time he had labored all night with nothing to show for it. Peter tried to shrug it off as the light dawned over the lake and they headed back to shore near

Capernaum. But he couldn't help but feel the weight of failure on his shoulders more heavily than ever. He had failed as an apostle, that much he knew. But now his first stab at plying the trade he had known since his youth had also come up short, even under ideal conditions. He might as well have been riding a leaf caught in an eddy of the Jordan, spinning, spinning, but going nowhere. What would happen to him and the others? Yes, well he had known the futility of regretting time lost on the Sea. But he was about to learn as much about the barrenness of nostalgia.

"Have you any fish, lads?"

The voice rang clear across the water, the question as old as fishing itself. A friendly stranger asked after their welfare, and perhaps wished to make an early morning purchase. They looked up and caught a glimpse of him, standing there in the dim morning light at the edge of the water.

"No," several of them answered directly, and no more. Sound carries well on the water but two hundred cubits is too great a distance for extended pleasantries.

Heavy silence. The men continued at their minutia, finalizing the last of their chores before making land.

"Throw the net on the right side of the boat, and there you will find some."

It was senseless, of course. The light already danced across the rippling waves, and the tiller stirred the waters on that side of the boat as they maneuvered out of the deeper waters. Not even a single fish would be so foolish... But Peter found himself—quite nearly watched himself—lift the net and, with the help of the others who moved in a trance like unto his, poise it on the gunwale. As he cast it with the deft skill that only a lifetime of practice bestows, Peter caught John's frame out of the corner of his eye. Zebedee's younger son had begun to obey the stranger's order as the others had, but then paused and stopped, tense and motionless, staring at the water's edge. Peter turned and looked at him, then continued around, following his gaze until he, too faced the shore. The stranger stood still, a distant figure whose face returned the salute but whose features were indistinguishable. Peter squinted and shaded his eyes from the glare in a vain attempt at recognition.

Suddenly the others gave a shout, and Simon started like a man from a dream. Now he was the fisherman again, and saw what every fisherman waits for. The water boiled and the nets teemed with fighting, flapping, jumping fish. He shouted back and the others pulled, but there was no hauling it in: heave as they might, the catch was heavier than they could bring aboard, the net too small to contain it.

"It is the Lord," John declared simply, a look of sublime awe on his face.

Prayer: Lord Jesus, I confess my faith in You can be so inconsistent. Even when You have worked wonders for me, very quickly I can lose sight of the truth and grow weary in well-doing, looking for yet another sign from You. Lord, I am grateful for Your unending patience and understanding that I am dust. Forgive me for looking back over my shoulder, for yearning for my nets that I so dramatically abandoned to follow Your call. And help me trust You, the Lord who appears in His time, and on His terms, for my good. Amen.

Day Thirty-Five

In that instant Simon Peter saw it all. He would not suffer to wait that Jesus might come walking to him across the glassy sea; he would not allow himself to be outstripped as he had in that footrace a fortnight ago. Grabbing his short tunic he wrapped it around his naked chest, tied it rudely, and dove into the water.

The lake's surface rose and smote him with its usual bracing chill, but he warmed to it within a few vigorous strokes. Not that it mattered to him either way. The Simon of two and a half weeks ago would have imagined that, were it necessary, he would have swum through fire and knives to get to his Lord. But this Simon swam as through his own tears, only wanting to get past his disappointments and doubt. He wanted to swim back to how it was before. He wanted to put as much distance between himself and those now-shameful nets as he could, as quickly as he could, and be close to Jesus again. The gasps he took between strokes were truer to his mind than the impressive labors of his broad shoulders.

Within a few minutes he stood dripping on the pebbly beach, panting and wide-eyed before his Master. The others came close behind, and before either of them had spoken a word, two or three had leapt from the boat and were pulling it through the last of the shallows onto the shore. While the others finished the job, James and John came, their ankles in the water still, and stood behind and to one side of Peter: the veterans three of Gethsemane. As in that dark hour, so now in the light of daybreak they knew not what to say.

He who had been a stranger tended a fire of hot coals, already spread with fish and bread. How had they missed the fire in the pre-dawn gloom?

"Bring some of the fish you have just caught," he said, lifting his head and looking Peter in the eye.

No shaming, no rejection, not a hint of scorn. Simon nodded obediently, turned, and jumped into the boat. This he could do. Thomas and Andrew helped him gather the remarkably sound net, and he hopped out again towing his catch. There they fully beached the net and spread it out, quickly tallying the great fishes with practiced eye and hand. One, plus two, plus three, plus four, plus...153 total. So even now the sign of resurrection revealed itself: henceforth all they did at his command, everything done in his name would be marked by the day of his costly victory. How could it be any other way?

"Come and eat breakfast," Jesus said to them.

So they came. They sat in a semicircle around the cooking food, taking comfort from the hot coals. Peter sat to the Lord's right, glancing at him as he broke and blessed the bread, and the fish. When they saw the Lord begin to eat, Peter and the others began to partake as well. They ate quietly, the silence somehow both awkward and peaceful, pregnant with anticipation yet in no way tense. Between hungry bites—their appetites revived as they ate—they exchanged furtive glances one with the other. No one would have called the Lord's demeanor detached, certainly not unaware, but he sat there obviously beyond their quiet wonderings in some unfathomable way. Their last meal they had shared together they had eaten in haste; it was the Lord's Passover. Now there was no haste in him. He was the Lord; beyond question he was the Lord. But as before, as with

Magdalene, as with Cleopas and Mary on the road to Emmaus, his outward appearance alone was not that which granted them recognition. It began to dawn upon them that it wasn't even the main thing. To question him because they now knew him with a knowing they hadn't known before would be folly. Why not ask from whence came the food? Had his invitation indeed expressed the hospitality of one that purchases and prepares, or rather the word of one who creates and provides? Some things you just do not ask Jesus, not when you already know the answer lies beyond you and, at the same time, readily within your grasp. They knew; he knew that they knew.

The Master leaned forward to stir the coals, and the small rocks beneath him sounded softly as beach pebbles will when they are ground underfoot. The stick he used did its work, and the pungency of charcoal filled the air—a smell Peter couldn't help but recall from the painful night of his failures. The humble meal continued. As the contagion of Jesus' calm took hold more and more, Peter realized that the most surreal thing about this morning with his Lord was its undeniable reality. The Son of the Most High sat cooking him breakfast, and everything was as normal as it could be. Taste and smell, sound and sight and touch: Jesus Christ risen from the dead had set the natural world ablaze with the miraculous. The resurrection meant that the world had become—perhaps always had been—a much more wondrous place than Peter had ever thought. Creation had just been waiting for its Maker to come that it might reveal its true nature. A ghost leaves no footprints because it is not of this world; Jesus risen does because the world is entirely his. Verily did the stones cry out.

****

Breakfast ended. For a few moments the Lord was silent. The soft sounds of the morning and the shore continued around them, and the disciples looked at one another, and at him. Then he lifted his voice and spoke.

What is that in your hand?

Elijah, what are you doing here?

"Simon, son of John, do you love me more than these?"

It is true that some make questions to lay a trap, whilst others do so because they sincerely desire to cure their ignorance. But Simon Peter was being lessoned, as his forefathers had, in the truth that when God asks a question it doesn't mean he wants for an answer. It means he knows that you want for the light of how he knows you, and it means he wants to confront you with that knowing. As his fathers were bidden to reply, so Simon, too, stammered an answer.

"Yes, Lord. You know that I love you."

"Feed my lambs."

Peter blinked hard and said nothing, for he knew there was nothing to say. The Master paused again as Peter looked down at the dying fire, daring now and again to regard the Lord's profile. Then, again...

"Simon, son of John, do you love me?"

Another question; the same question. Whatever questions we ask of God, even the most strident complaints and accusatory queries, are but child's play compared to these questions he asks of us. They might be clumsily thrown potsherds hurled during a tantrum or a benighted melancholia rather than the surgical incisions he applies to the wounded heart. The surgeon's knife cut in the selfsame place this second time, going deeper still. Simon swallowed hard and looked at his own feet.

"Yes, Lord," he whispered again, "you know that I love you."

"Shepherd my sheep."

So, men were not to be fish, nor he a fisherman any longer, not even in holy figure-talk. If he truly loved his Lord, he would smell of the sheepfold now, not the nets. The Lord was peeling back his past and tossing it on the coals in front of them. Time itself seemed to bow before the Master. Now he lifted his chin and looked Peter full in the face.

"Simon, son of John, do you love me?"

A third question. A third chance. Oh, the searing sorrow of conscience, of seeing oneself reflected back in those inescapable eyes. As the Lord had granted Thomas his terrible wish, so now he granted Peter's once futile wish that his denials might be reclaimed. And in the reversal the Lord gently and carefully chose his words according to those used by his weak-willed but earnest disciple. The divine surgeon had reached his mark and painfully, piercingly, the cancer of self-flattery and self-loathing was being excised. Boasting, failed Simon was being vanquished and cured by crucified and all-powerful Jesus. Peter managed to answer,

"Yes, Lord. You know all things. You know that I love you."

"Feed my little sheep."

Did the Lord now redeem and save, or did he call and appoint? Did he concern himself with Peter's life or with those souls in need of a shepherd? Did Jesus address him as disciple or apostle? Such silly questions. It was all one. The Lord went harrowing the nether regions of his soul, trampling the shame and the ugly residue of his spiritual self-sabotage underfoot. Peter's inner objections were swept aside just as Jesus ignored his spoken ones three years earlier—after that first miraculous catch of fish near this very beach. How summarily, almost cavalierly did the Master pass from penance and proof to complete restoration and commission.

He does not cry out loud, or raise his voice in the streets; the bruised reed he will not break, the smoldering wick he will not snuff out...

Oh, the power of those wounds...wounds still, and never to be scars. Blood shed, and not just tears. In and by those wounds all other wounds, even self-inflicted wounds, are healed. Though he could hardly have spoken it clearly then, Peter came to realize that even as his shame died at the cross, so his dignity had risen from the dead, and, resurrected, now sat beside him on that idyllic shore. Simon Peter was restored, the Rock in the midst of his brethren.

"Truly, truly do I tell you that when you were a young man, you would gird yourself and walk where you willed. But when you are an old man you will stretch out your hands, and someone else will gird you and lead you where you do not want to go."

I am the Good Shepherd, I lay down my life for my sheep; no one takes it from me.

Who in his right mind calls weakness strength? Who gambles his life away at the peak of his power? Who holds the favor of the crowd in the palm of his hand yet exchanges it to tread the way of shame? Who is it that dares death even for the sake of one's dearest friend, much less submits to it for a hateful enemy? Who barters for heavenly dwellings with earthly coinage and closes the deal?

Jesus crucified and Jesus risen confirmed those promises of Kingdom reign like nothing any around that fire could have imagined. But Jesus crucified and Jesus risen had also turned those promises completely around, transformed them, clarified their truths. So this is what it meant to adore a crucified Messiah. Peter daren't flee the cross, he daren't scorn it for a safety that the Lord had now exposed as mere daydream. He daren't run the fool's errand of preserving that which was forfeit from the beginning, at the cost of eternity itself. Jesus had handed Peter the keys to the Kingdom with a nail-pierced hand.

The chilly air of that morning race to the tomb two weeks back seemed to burn the lungs of his spirit anew as he grappled with the Lord's portentous words. How could it be? How was it that victory did not merely *follow* defeat, victory did not come *in spite* of defeat, but rather victory broke forth by *embracing* defeat as the world called it? All the rules had been rewritten, it seemed, and Peter felt like the first pupil to learn them. The truth of the resurrection, viscerally, was being driven home to him. Death has no power, and sacrifice as true discipleship became as irresistible as gravity itself. Oh, what folly not to see it! All die; not all rise to new life. And the promise of the latter had made the former a detail—important only as it might serve the glory of God.

The Lord stood up, and turned. He fixed his eyes on Peter, then lifted his right hand in summons. For a second, the wound Thomas had insisted on probing caught the morning light.

"Follow me," Jesus told him.

He continued as Peter got to his feet and made to catch up and keep pace with him. Peter could hear the others begin to rise behind him, begin to follow after. His mind reeled. For a moment the last vestiges of the old Simon fought for familiar air, the air of the world he had known where conquest made victors and surrender meant defeat and kings surveyed their kingdoms from thrones and not from Roman crosses. That Simon—the Simon who argued about who was the greatest and heralded his devotion and swung the sword in the Garden—spoke as a man pulled under by unbreathable living water.

"What about that man?" Peter turned and looked at John, who along with the others was following several paces behind them.

Jesus looked upon him with eyes of gentle fire.

"If I will that he remain until I return, what is that to you? You follow me."

Prayer: Lord Jesus, I love You. You know that I love You. And You know in what way I love You. I am grateful that by knowing me so fully, You also make Yourself known to me. You wipe away every last thing that has ever made me ashamed of myself, and You stand me on my feet in Your presence so that I can not only hear, but also obey Your command that I follow You. Help me to stop comparing Your call on my life to either my past or somebody else's present, and may I glorify God right to the end. Amen.

THE VISION

Stephen, Deacon of the Earliest Church

Acts 7:54-60

Day Thirty-Six

After several days of rain and clouds, the morning skies over Jerusalem swept themselves clean in a flawless dawn. The harmless ghosts of his last dream dissipated from Stephen's waking mind, and he let them go without contention, rising with the light. He spent time in prayer and ate his bread, then left his house and headed for the Temple. Though the sun shone brightly, there remained a comforting chill in the air that made his cloak about him feel just right; midwinter rested upon the Judean highlands. Walking down the narrow streets amidst the early morning bustle, the cobblestones under his feet, Stephen might have looked every bit a young Jerusalemite to the casual observer. He had indeed adapted in many ways to his new home, though his choice of attire had more to do with climate than culture. The reality persisted that, at heart, he felt a foreigner in the city he had adopted and chosen to love as his own. But his life was here now, and he embraced the sojourner status as his new norm.

Weaving his way up an alley, he stopped and rapped gently—once, twice—on a homely little door. Normally he wouldn't make such a call alone. Even now he went to meet a few of the other deacons, with whom he typically carried out the duties of his ministry. But this was a special case, and on his way, and his heart was particularly involved. He heard the soft rumor of movement, slight footfalls, then the halting rub of wood on wood as the rope latch was pulled. Her face always looked at him as if she were meeting him for the first time, just discovering that someone really wanted to show her kindness after all. Then she smiled her infectious, partially-toothed grin and loved him with a reverent but affectionate kiss on the hand. Today was no different. Apollonia was a head shorter than Stephen and thrice his age, slight as a bird and looking very much like one at times—especially at moments like this with her eager features just visible in the morning light that made its way into the opening of her hovel. She was a widow, of course, without family and without resource. Stephen had taken to her and she to him, and no one in the church begrudged them the common bond of the same maternal city. She opened the door wide, beckoning, and he entered, ducking for the doorway and uttering a blessing. She made him sit in a chair he himself had bought for her and offered him bread and water to refresh himself. He demurred on the bread but politely drank her stale water, smiling at her with gentle eyes. They chatted briefly in Greek, exchanging the usual pleasantries. But before Apollonia could ply him with her usual motherly questions, Stephen blessed her and her home once again as a goodbye, squeezed her hand, and begged her leave to depart. Sad but not grieved, she consented. She watched him go, then glanced down at a small silver coin in her palm, glimmering in the wan light of the alley.

It struck Stephen as he stepped out onto the main street again that had he known Apollonia when they both lived in Alexandria five years ago he likely wouldn't have given her a second thought. She was a widow even then, living off the last of her departed husband's reserves before her (now dead) son had brought her to the Holy City. In contrast, he mused, the Stephen of that time had been very different indeed.

The son of an ambitious father and a sensitive mother, Stephen grew up in a prosperous household along with several younger brothers and sisters. They were at once faithfully Jewish and thoroughly Egyptian—the very embodiment of Greek-speaking Jewry scattered across the Mediterranean world. His family could speak Aramaic as well, naturally, because Judea and the rest of Palestine made up the market for the Egyptian goods his family traded in. His father had schooled him in that tongue from an early age, not only for business purposes but because he felt Stephen "ought" to know it. It took time for Stephen to understand that obligation. In any case, he grew up speaking Greek as his first language, and deeper than that, he was colored by the countless cultural intangibles that make a person who they are. Life as a Hellenistic Jew was as natural for Stephen as both swimming and flying were to the waterfowl of the Nile. He had never known another way, and never imagined a reason to. Stephen's biculturalism was accentuated by the fact that from his adolescence he had accompanied his father on business to Jerusalem and other population centers from the Negev to Damascus. By the time he reached his twentieth year, his father sent him almost exclusively as the family agent (and even when his brothers did go along, he as the eldest remained the leader), so that Stephen came to know the Egypt of his birth and the Promised Land of his forefathers with near-equal familiarity. His Aramaic became more and more fluent, and he grew to relish his visits to Judea. Jerusalem became especially beloved, where Stephen carried on a brisk trade in papyrus and linen with men both sacred and profane.

He couldn't remember when his thirst for the Scriptures began to truly shape his thinking. Naturally, as a boy he had been taught at their synagogue in Alexandria, reading the Torah and the Prophets as a sacred duty. The Septuagint, with its easily-read Greek phrases, made things easier still for him, but Stephen had always excelled in his letters. While his brothers completed their schooling then allowed themselves to be caught up in the endless lure of commerce, something took within Stephen's heart that the busyness of trade never could strip away from him. Being around those scrolls only deepened his interest, so that he spent nearly all his extra hours poring over the holy writings. In them Stephen discovered a unified story with endless connections amid the lines that, in some enigmatic way, played the same haunting tune that ever seemed just beyond his ability to capture or express. So he pondered and he yearned, the Scriptures cooed and they wooed, and his fascination went on. Somehow, in some tantalizing way, Jerusalem itself intensified his fever. The very stones of the city seemed to cry out to him, stir his deepest longings, fill him with anticipation for something or for someone. Being there made real to him the things he had read and wondered about, put flesh to the bone, as it were. It happened there—on the last trade journey his father had taken with him, coincidentally—that Stephen had lain awake one night while his family slept around him and truly cried out for the first time to the God that he had prayed prayers to since his childhood.

The mysterious music swelled within the ear of his heart, but still he could not discern its chords.

Yet for all this Stephen's life would appear to outsiders, and even to himself, respectably mundane. If his brothers murmured now and again about "Stephen the Scribe," his command of business affairs always mitigated their bemusement over his passion for the Scriptures. They knew full well that his growing skill in trade and the handling of the family purse secured their future and made the prospect of caring for their aging parents all the less worrisome. Life hit its stride: lucrative connections multiplied; Stephen was betrothed to the daughter of one of his father's business allies (a fine young woman named Alis); his family felt every bit as proud of him as they had expected they would. The path before him was comfortingly predictable.

Then everything changed.

Prayer*: Lord Jesus, You know me fully—my background, my personality, my flaws and my foibles. You know those parts of me that are most inclined to be wayward, and those that yearn for You. Call me to Yourself, O Lord, and fill the gulf between where I am and where You want me to be. Work the miracle in me that will make a life of surrendered service to You as natural as speaking my native language. Amen.*

Day Thirty-Seven

Stephen had heard of the Galilean prophet's execution that Passover. He and his entire family had made the pilgrimage to Jerusalem that year as usual, and the city buzzed with the retelling of those events for days afterward. But Stephen himself hadn't witnessed anything firsthand, and even if his father did not share his hunger for the holy, Stephen couldn't help but agree with him on this score: would-be messiahs came and went like so many songbirds sold at market, and this one almost certainly should be counted in that number. Stephen dismissed the matter from his mind.

Seven weeks later he returned to Jerusalem for the Feast of Weeks—Pentecost—this time alone. For a few years now, because of their health, his parents had limited their pilgrimages to the Passover and the Feast of Booths, and most of the time his brothers stayed with them. Stephen, in contrast, always tried to attend everything, even the lesser feasts; the Holy City drew him as always. Pentecost was not to be missed, but business concerns took him there anyway.

On the morning of the Feast itself, he walked among the crowd, approaching the steps at the southernmost end of the Temple Mount. He had taken the same path many times before, and as an experienced pilgrim he knew how to navigate the crowds and how to flow with them, how they behaved. But that morning, he soon realized, the crowd did not at all behave as it usually did. There on the steps of the Temple, off to one side of the great entry arches, swirled an anomaly, a knot of people circling some undefined eye. As Stephen drew closer he could see that the crowd there was growing, saw that at its center, at the top of the stairs, stood a group of young men. Now he could hear their voices raised above the general din of the multitude, their hands raised, their faces uplifted. Stephen, fascinated, decided to investigate. He stepped aside and joined the growing throng. He could see that around a core of a dozen or so men there milled scores of people, men and women, all loudly praising God. Stephen's heart turned within him; he wove his way through the undergrowth of the amused, past the copse of the mildly curious, and into the thicket of the truly captivated.

Astonishment met him. There, not two paces away, stood an older woman who was obviously one of these exuberant, mysterious worshippers. Stephen had long ago learned how to intuit a true Gentile from a Hellenist such as himself, and a Hellenist from a native Judean. His practiced glance weighed a dozen details at once and determined in moments from whence someone hailed, and therefore (usually) how to approach them. In this case, the divining was easier than usual. He observed rather than concluded from her attire and her grooming that the woman before him was a Jew of the land, probably a Galilean peasant. For a moment he thought her beaming face met his, but for all her ecstasy she might have been looking right through him. Instead of averting her gaze as such a woman usually did, she closed her eyes and, her expression suffused with inexpressible joy, raised her voice unrestrained in an utterance of passionate praise to God. Such was the beauty and liberty of her worship, such was the art of the verse that spilled from her lips, that Stephen forgot himself and stared. He felt the holy music rise within him, ringing through his soul, calling back to his heart's memory his most intoxicating times of searching the Scriptures—searching, but only *almost* finding. Then all at once it struck him: this aged country woman was not speaking Aramaic, but rather *Greek*. And not any Greek, not the pidgin trade Greek some men here clumsily used to close a business deal, no. Here spoke an orator, a poet, a songstress. This rustic woman articulated flawless Alexandrian Greek—dialect perfect down to the finest lilt of her cosmopolitan voice—stringing together in glorious catena verse after verse, now from the psalms, now a paraphrase from Isaiah, now from the Law, exalting God Almighty and thanking him for his goodness and salvation. Stephen, quite literally, could not believe his senses.

Then he perceived that others in the crowd around him experienced the same wonder, as they, too, heard local Israelites shouting God's glory—not in their own tongue—but in the languages of the lands from whence the pilgrims had traveled for the Feast. A few scoffed and turned away, but Stephen ignored them, his eyes turned towards the spectacle unfolding in front of him.

Now a broad, strong-looking young man—he might have been an older brother to Stephen had he had one—stood and raised his hands and called over the crowd in Aramaic. The man he later came to know as Simon Peter proclaimed a message that morning that even to the present day Stephen could never forget. It wasn't just what Peter said, and it wasn't just how he said it. It was the sum of those things in the moment, an event, an encounter with a Power that reached into Stephen's belly and revealed itself as far more and greater than anything that met the eye or the ear. That prophetic message about Jesus of Nazareth pulled together everything he had read, answered the unanswerable, filled in the missing pieces so that it all finally made sense. The holy music in the writings that had haunted his soul no longer tarried just beyond the reach of his yearnings, demurring like a beautiful song he had heard in his primal innocence, only to have it slip away somewhere on the road to adulthood. Now the song rushed in, lifted and carried him, one chord after another ringing inside him. It had a name—*Jesus the Christ*. Its lyrics were courage and cowardice, subtle betrayal and subtler surrender, shameful suffering and death then impossible reversal unto life and eternal kingship; its melody was bottomless sorrow and soaring joy. It was Mystery revealed, but also Mystery compounded by that revelation rather than undone by it. Here was the One Ballad, the Love Story, the Epic you grew up thinking you knew, only to realize that nothing could be more contemptible than the passive contempt with which your familiarity had treated the Most Holy. As Stephen heard Peter tell the story, his own complicity dawned upon him. The Christ, the Son of God had come and his own people had treated him like a common criminal. Conviction that transcended the details of where they were, what they said or did, or even how they felt on that day seven weeks ago settled upon the hearers. What must they do?

****

One of the Twelve baptized Stephen that morning, along with hundreds and hundreds of others who heard Peter's sermon, into the name of Jesus Christ. The walls of the ceremonial baths in the shadow of the Temple Mount heard that name over and over that day. And what Stephen felt upon confessing that Jesus of Nazareth was the long-awaited Christ ran far deeper than emotion, though his emotions certainly hummed with it all. There was no describing the energy he felt, no expressing the bond he experienced with the others around him who had also believed. The following days buzzed with excitement as one amazing thing after another unfolded before his eyes, and his spirit drank in the teaching of the apostles.

But the question soon returned to mind, albeit with another meaning altogether: what must he do? He had a family that awaited him, a betrothed, business obligations. His life lay in Alexandria, not in Jerusalem, as much as he loved it here. But just as obvious to Stephen loomed the inner sense that he could not go back to the life he lived before—which he now understood had been no life at all. From an apostle's lips he listened to a parable the Lord had spoken while he yet walked among them, a story of soils fertile and barren.

And some seed fell among the thorns...

No, Stephen told himself. Never. One could not give up breathing. One could not choose to go back into the darkness of the womb after being born and seeing the light. What he felt coursing through his soul not only fulfilled his own longings, but the hope of a nation, indeed, as he understood it, the deepest meaning of what it meant to be alive. As he prayed, a conviction rose within him that surpassed the euphoria of conversion: the cost of this new life, and the price of this peace and purpose was the realization that he no longer belonged to himself. The Spirit of the Living God burned within him, and Stephen could not betray that calling. The God of his fathers had manifested himself in fulfillment of the prophets in a way no one had anticipated, but now that he had been revealed, how could one turn away? Something great transpired in Jerusalem, day by day—even hour by hour—and he knew the Spirit within meant for him to walk in the midst of it. Stephen would remain in Jerusalem.

He wrote the letter and sent it by a courier.

As driven as Stephen's father was, he had always loved his sons, and his bearing inspired respect rather than fear. For this reason and others Stephen joyfully welcomed him and two of his brothers, Arsenios and Jason, when they arrived at his door some three weeks later. After his family refreshed themselves from the journey, the inevitable began. Naturally, the son deferred to his frail father, though in truth it fell to Stephen to do the talking. And just as predictably, his father quite nearly acted as if no letter had been written and received, and played this trip like any other trade mission to Judea. He spoke of business details, asked how things had progressed with the usual contacts, and suggested they would all be able to return to Alexandria in a week or so.

"Father," Stephen said softly, "As I wrote in my letter, I will not be returning to Egypt."

This was no disrespect. Rather, Stephen knew his father well and obliged him by doing what he had asked in everything he had and hadn't said. His father wanted to hear the story from the beginning, face to face, and Stephen gave it to him.

By the time Stephen had finished, his father looked stoic, Arsenios looked peeved, and the younger brother, Jason, looked like he wanted to hear more. There was silence for a few awkward moments, then his father spoke.

"Well, it's not as if we couldn't certainly use a permanent tradesman here in Judea. I had rather planned on Arsenios for that role..."

Arsenios said nothing.

"Father," began Stephen, "I have no desire to take anything away from my brothers...."

"...but there's no doubt you will do very well at the task."

"Father, business is not why I am staying in Jerusalem."

His father looked at him.

"Does this mean your family no longer matters to you?"

"Father, of course that's not it, it's just that..."

"And what of Demetrius' daughter? What of Alis and your contract with her?"

His father's tone had taken on an edge. Stephen knew that relationship meant a great deal to him, and tossing it aside— divorce, essentially—was no light matter. It could damage his father greatly, and indeed, his entire family, if he offended the parents of his intended. But this was one matter of which Stephen felt unsure. He had not only entered into a formal betrothal with Alis, he still felt drawn to her. He hoped that she might join him in Jerusalem and come to know what he had experienced. Now he told his father of this hope

The sun might have come out in the room.

"Well, it's settled then! You will stay in Jerusalem, I will speak to Alis' father. We will make the arrangements. Now, about the linen shipments..."

For a moment, desire for the normal, for the status quo, overwhelmed Stephen. He had no desire to sever or even hurt his family—in fact, it hadn't even occurred to him to do so. Besides, he had a duty to earn his keep. And of course he looked forward to his marriage with Alis, as any young man would. His father talked on while he turned these things in his mind, and Stephen's heart grew warm within him.

"...and you can more easily pursue your religious interests here as well," he concluded, almost as an aside.

"Father, the Christ has come. What has happened… it…cannot be spoken of as mere religious curiosity," Stephen stammered, more out of respect than uncertainty. "All that is written in Moses and the Prophets is fulfilled in Jesus of Nazareth. I…we must all turn in faith to the God of our fathers in his name. I am staying in the Holy City because…because I must. The Day of the Lord is at hand."

Again, silence. His father was impassive, Arsenios was a wall, Jason was an open window.

"My son," said his father, the warmest yet, "I do not claim to know what you claim to know, nor do I deny that you might indeed possess something that is beyond me."

This was as generous as his father would get when Stephen knew in his heart he hadn't budged an inch, and rather hoped to outwait his son's momentary enthusiasm. So his son believed the Scriptures. What was wrong with that? The rest remained opaque to him, but other fathers had lived with far worse.

"We will go back to Alexandria," his father continued, "and you have things to arrange here."

"Yes, father," Stephen conceded. He had spoken his peace, and he would be praying for his family. "I ask only one thing, if you will grant it."

"My son?"

"Permit me to send a letter to Alis myself, written in my own hand. She should know my intentions directly from me."

His father stroked his beard thoughtfully for a moment, nodded in agreement, and rose to his feet.

Prayer: Lord Jesus, send Your ageless Holy Spirit upon me. Empower me, as You did Your earliest saints, with the ancient newness of divine springtime in my soul. And with that power, give me the grace to love You in the costly way that You are worthy of, and indeed command. Let all other loves, loyalties, and ambitions bow the knee to You. The Wind of God blows where He wills. Will to blow upon me, Lord, and may my will bend to You. Amen.

The Vision

Day Thirty-Eight

As Stephen now approached the Temple he thought back to the first time he had laid eyes on Alis in the synagogue. He remembered catching his breath, remembered giving her a second sidelong glance. And he remembered thinking it terribly unfair that such a lovely creature walked the earth and that someone like him could never have her. Then when he learned who she was, and one thing eventually led to another culminating in their betrothal, he also felt *that* somehow unfair—that life would be so kind to him when others could not hope for such good fortune.

Now it was unfair that he had lost her, lost her for believing the promise that he thought dwelt in the heart of every faithful Jew. It was unfair that his father seemed to blame it on him, and that though the family business went on, Stephen felt more and more like one of the cold connections they made and maintained for business. It was unfair that only Arsenios came with a servant or two and Stephen could not explain things more deeply to Jason, whom their father now never allowed to come to Jerusalem. It was also unfair that since that Pentecost—several years now—Stephen had seen less and less of his mother. And it was utterly unfair that Jesus of Nazareth had been betrayed by the kiss of a friend, and that his own disciples had abandoned him when he needed them the most, and that the very priests who taught of the Christ conspired to send him to a shameful Roman cross. Unfair. Unfair that God's Son should suffer so, and unfair that Stephen's sinful soul should be ransomed by that suffering, and unfair that he receive the gift of the Holy Spirit, the very breath of heaven, when he knew he deserved none of it. It was unfair that Stephen was born a son of Abraham, and unfair that he happened upon the apostles that fateful day, and unfair that God had granted him an ear to hear and a heart to respond when others wandered away from the fulfillment of the ages like witless hens. Unfairness seemed the very thread of which the fabric of Stephen's fortunes had been woven.

Truly, the Lord's own word about bringing not peace but a sword had come to pass for him. Yet for all the pain of loss in his heart, in those early days after his conversion Stephen's life brimmed over with fullness. Something ineffable had begun that miraculous day, when he had heard the glory of God in his own tongue from a woman he now knew for a fact spoke not a word of Greek by her own understanding. His hunger for the Scriptures redoubled, only now a wisdom and a power guided and quickened him as he read so that he knew the Spirit worked these things in him and not he himself. He could no more take credit for his burgeoning understanding of God's ways than he could the color of his eyes, and this realization only increased his joy. What would the Spirit speak to him today as he read? He spent long hours sitting at the feet of the apostles, then fairly ran to check and recheck the Prophets and the Writings. Link after link, connection after connection, ever deeper, ever more wondrously revealed, ever more unsearchable. He slaked his thirst with pure truth and yet blissfully thirsted for more. For all the miracles he witnessed, for all the spiritual ecstasies he himself experienced, the greatest was the comprehensive vision that emerged from the mists that had shrouded his previous grasp of the Scriptures. Passage after passage, once dark to him, now lit up and not only waxed clear like so many unique stars in the firmament, but rather shone as parts of a whole, constellations linked with constellations that filled the heavens with one all-encompassing story from Genesis to the last words of the Chronicler. The Seed of the Woman, the Prophet, the Son of David, the Son of Man—the Christ was everywhere Stephen looked as he studied, and even passing glances yielded his presence, binding up the story of Israel into a glorious whole. Stephen might have been Moses on Mount Nebo, taking in at a glance the panorama of the Promised Land from Dan to Beersheba to the Mediterranean—and beyond. And as he prayed—oh, what hours of prayer passed like minutes—his understanding became personal, and a hushed humility overshadowed his heart when he pondered the anointed ones of the Old Covenant and had a strong sense that he, too, incredibly, had some purpose to play in God's plan.

And for all the price he paid in solitude, his faith in Christ had also opened an entire world of brotherhood to him. He had never conceived that such unity, such mutuality of affection and oneness of purpose could exist between people. Up until that

Pentecost, he had been the very definition of a stranger to the people he now called brothers and sisters—a true family, more close, more sympathetic, more mutually understanding than he had ever conceived as possible. Naturally, he had a particular connection with other Hellenists like himself because they could communicate more freely and held so much in common. But the mystery of it all manifested when he met a newcomer to the faith who hailed from a corner of the world he had never known. Here would be a man he struggled to converse with, second language to second language, but with whom he nevertheless felt instant— even prior—kinship, and shared bread at the Lord's table as if they had known each other all their lives. It was a profound enigma and at the same time felt as natural as it could be—the very sense of what normal was in God's eyes.

Yet headiest of all for Stephen was to walk and talk with the Twelve, or anyone who had seen the Lord. He revered the apostles and their authority, but not for the sake of fawning after their status (which they did not permit anyway). No, he longed for firsthand testimony of Jesus the Christ. As opportunity presented itself, he asked personal questions of those who had known him, had conversed with him, had touched him. Stephen wanted to learn the little things, what might be the story behind the story, the parables and the miracles, the things that cannot be preached but can be chatted about—not to know anecdotes for knowing's sake, but to know the Christ himself, to see Jesus. He watched the Twelve relate between themselves while they spoke and laughed unawares, conjured in his mind what Jesus in their midst might say and do in response. Gazing at the Lord's brothers and mother, even some of their cousins, Stephen tried to catch a glimpse of Jesus in their eyes and manners, but in the end found common people who had had an uncommon relative. He spoke to those who had heard him teach in Galilee, or even in Jerusalem the week of his betrayal, and some whom the Lord himself had healed. One evening events came about in such a way that he found himself speaking with the elderly Pharisee, Joseph of Arimathea, who had witnessed the Lord's trial before the Council and had asked Pilate for the body to bury in his own tomb. Riveted, he listened to the old man's scratchy voice tell of the inquest after midnight, of the false witnesses and the foregone verdict, of the Lord Jesus' dignity and poise in the face of spittle, blows, and accusations of blasphemy which were themselves blasphemies. Stephen would mull these things in his mind as he lay down on his pallet to sleep, each time feeling he knew the Lord a little better, but each time only longing all the more to see Jesus for himself.

Prayer: *Lord Jesus, I have barely scratched the surface of what it is to know You. But I rejoice and am glad that to grant me this knowledge, which You call eternal life, You suffered the grossest of injustice. Let the fire of my desire to know You consume all of the petty grievances I may entertain, the unspoken accusations about the hardships I have suffered and the questions I cannot resolve, but cloud my view of You. Amen.*

Day Thirty-Nine

But though the Spirit seemed to hover over him in nearly perpetual comfort, the face of the Son eluded him. Stephen reasoned and ultimately rested in the melancholy truth that though his life and that of the Lord Jesus had overlapped, God had not seen fit for him to lay eyes on the Christ while he yet walked among men in the flesh. So Stephen settled himself on the hope of the resurrection, the hope born of the Lord Jesus' own glorification. One day he would see the Lord face to face. And while he lived in hope for that time, he determined, he would not seek a separate peace, he would not merely search and pray and close himself in, seeking ecstasies in the Spirit. He would give himself to this people that had become his family, the church.

Stephen's work among the poor began as a personal concern. The Kingdom was at hand, time was short, he had spare time and money, and the word of the Lord was clear. Up to that point, Stephen had treasured the gift of the Holy Spirit and had grown in his conviction that God had prepared him for the faith all his life. But business, well, that was just something that he *did*. Now, though, he began to see that all he had been given and learned by whatever means was a gift to be thankful for, and a sacrifice that might be offered up to the glory of God. So he moved to humbler lodgings, set aside his profits, and—careful of the Lord's own command to keep his left ignorant regarding the actions of his right—began helping the needier ones around him as he could. Sometimes he did it through the apostles, and sometimes he did it in other discreet ways, but he did it consistently and without fanfare. Since the church itself had organized the care of its weakest members as an expression of obedience to the gospel, he felt it would please God to participate and do the same. It was a blessed time for him.

Stephen's first disappointment with his new faith family, then, came as a surprise—a minor complaint that soon escalated into full-blown conflict. Some of his own Greek-speaking brethren noted that while the church sought to care for widows, those Hellenistic widows in their midst—Greek-speaking foreigners to the ones carrying out the daily charity—had not been receiving enough to survive on. Stephen was no firebrand, and he earnestly wished to pass off the issue for the sake of peace. But shortly it seemed that, as the dispute grew, there actually was some substance to the claim. Although part of the problem was that the church had simply outgrown its spontaneous way of handling such charity, it became clear that an invisible pecking order had factored into the situation as well. This could not be resolved by soothing words alone, and the rare atmosphere of love and unity that Stephen had found so intoxicating suffered the threat of ethnic and cultural strife—a strife that touched him deeply. All looked to the apostles for guidance, who summoned the congregation to Solomon's Colonnade. There the Twelve admitted to two things: first, inequity had indeed crept into the daily care of the widows, and second, they as apostles could not resolve this alone. Rather, they asked that the people themselves choose seven servants who would look after this issue so that the apostles could continue the work of the ministry without being hindered by these secondary but nevertheless important matters.

In the discussions that followed Stephen learned what God's servants always eventually learn: he learned that good deeds cannot be hidden, and that faithfulness at small tasks leads to being charged with much more challenging ones, and that recognition and position in the Kingdom always follows the selfless and consistent execution of ministry—and not the other way around. Before he fully realized what had happened, he had been chosen as one of the Seven. He found himself kneeling before the apostles in the presence of his fellow believers, accepting his ordination. On that first Pentecost, hands had been laid upon him after his baptism in order to impart the gift of the Spirit that he lacked; now hands were laid upon him precisely because his brothers and sisters testified that the Spirit already reigned in his heart. As Peter and John called on God, and the rest of the apostles murmured in agreement, an indescribable presence and power overshadowed Stephen. Now he understood firsthand what David received when Samuel anointed him with oil before his brothers, or how Elijah must have felt when the Spirit came upon him in power, or what Ezekiel meant when he wrote that the strong hand of the Lord rested upon him. The Holy Spirit changed him that day, once again.

Yet the work that Stephen embarked upon with the other deacons was, in essence and spirit, the very thing he had already been doing privately. But now his own concern for the needy channeled itself into an ordained role along with all the responsibilities and difficulties that went with it. He organized the purse, consulted with the others, reported to the apostles, and worked out an efficient and just way to care for the poor. He learned the ins and outs of relationships, resolved squabbles, and played the diplomat. In short, by love, tact, and hard work, he and his fellow deacons diffused the strife that had endangered the *koinonia* of the church. It was remarkably mundane, natural work, but Stephen felt a deep satisfaction in his calling and he would have been satisfied to carry on ministering funds to needy widows as long as he had breath. It occurred to him that he had all but lost his mother for the sake of Christ; now he had *dozens* of mothers, Apollonias who filled his life with their doting and false alarms and sincere thanks and useless offers to help. He had longed to see the face of the Christ; somehow in the midst of the people he ministered to—the wonderful, exasperating, ever-needy people—he perceived Jesus more than he ever had before.

****

Yes, the Stephen that stepped onto the Temple Mount that morning was a very different Stephen than the one who left Alexandria alone several years back, for what he thought would be another trade mission and festival in the Holy City. He knew it himself, but he did not recognize it as much as others around him did. Though he revered the gravity of his stewardship as a sacred trust, to himself he continued to be Stephen, a lesser disciple who needed these people as much as they needed him, always hungry for more of the Holy Spirit, still learning from the Lord's Twelve, ever-longing for the face of Christ. But other believers around him had heard him speak, and they grew increasingly astonished by his ability to unfold the holy writings in the ears of the ignorant, to answer difficult questions. His ministry to the poor took on unforeseen importance as he had the ability to instruct people in the Lord as well minister to their physical needs. And then there were the miracles. Stephen's touch had healed many, and the frequency and power of the signs and wonders that followed him grew and grew. He had, in a very short time, become one of the strongest voices in the church, powerful in presence, effective in speech, wondrous in spiritual gifts. Believers revered him and many unbelieving Hellenists became obedient to the faith as a result of his work. He was no longer surprised when fellow believers approached to greet and honor him, and to seek his blessing. Even now, walking down the colonnade towards Solomon's Portico at the southern end of the complex, several believers Stephen recognized warmly called his name.

It happened then that Stephen saw from the corner of his eye a small crowd of men walking purposefully towards him across the Court of the Gentiles. Now he heard some of them point and cry out, quickening their pace as they approached him. These men, too, were known to Stephen, at least those in the lead, and they disliked him as much as the believers loved him. Chief in their midst was a fierce-eyed, sharp-tongued young Pharisee from Cilicia.

Stephen's personal history with these men had been brief, straightforward—and hostile. They were men like him, Hellenistic Diaspora Jews all, some his age, some a bit older, and they had not taken kindly to his beliefs and his labors. Judaism in Judea was hardly monochromatic; one might be a Pharisee, or an Essene, or a Herodian, or (if you were among the elite) a Sadducee, or if not truly a member your sympathies might lie with one of them. You might even differ with others within your clique on minor matters of doctrine or practice. So it wasn't just that Stephen was different. It was *how* he was different. These Galileans were bad enough, and the priests had had to deal with them, though in the end they more or less wrote the sect off and took a watch-and-see approach. Such groups rose and fell as a matter of course—it was the way of things in Jerusalem. But Stephen represented something altogether more threatening to these young men. As a Jew and a Hellene who was successfully drawing others like him into the ranks of the Nazarenes, this Alexandrian endangered what fragile standing they felt they had in the region. Zealous to defend the traditions of their fathers, fiercely patriotic after their own fashion, their vision for the nation did not include Stephen's way of thinking and living. They viewed him as an affront to Judaism, and affront to the Temple, and an affront to them personally. He made them look bad, and they had grown weary of him and his misleading doublespeak.

Stephen saw no sense in trying to evade them, so he turned and met their eyes as they drew near. He had grown accustomed to their faces—dark with anger and hate as several of them at once had tried to best him in front of others, outflank him with superior knowledge, humiliate and discredit him. Some had enjoyed the best training the religious elite of Jerusalem had to offer, and their confidence had brought them forward, one by one, to challenge him. But the humiliation they anticipated inflicting became their own, and time and again they had departed in shame and bitter frustration while Stephen's position was strengthened in front of those who listened. But though Stephen saw the hate, there was no hint of frustration in them now. Now ugly triumph glowed in their eyes; behind them marched a detachment of the Temple Guard.

Prayer: *Lord Jesus, You call me by Your name and therefore call me to be like You. You give to all gifts as You see fit—even to me. Help me not fall into the logical lie that such power means I* *should be immune from suffering for Your name's sake. Give me the grace and courage to receive even those who would speak evil of me, mean me ill, and even harm me because I serve Jesus of Nazareth. Thank You for counting me worthy to suffer indignity for Your name. Amen.*

Day Forty

Surrounded by enemies, Stephen was summarily arrested then hustled across the courtyard. They led him into the antechambers outside the great room that served as the meeting place of the Sanhedrin. The guards held him fast, though he made no effort to resist them, while his adversaries gave him black, knowing glances; they did not speak to him, choosing rather to whisper to each other and some elders who met them there as they waited for something. Stephen prayed softly under his breath, eyes half-closed, an incomprehensible spiritual peace rising from his inner man to do battle with the anxiety that assaulted his mind.

Suddenly the doors opened, and an attendant nodded to the men. They entered the chamber with confident strides, the Temple Guard ushering Stephen in behind them. Seating him before the council, his captors sat on either side while the young Hellenists prepared to speak. The Council had convened itself and its members already sat in their places, but Stephen's case was announced as of first importance, with witnesses forthcoming.

The charge? Blasphemy and sedition.

Now men came forward, men whose faces, if pressed, Stephen might have vaguely recalled as spectators to some of his discussions with the other Hellenists. He certainly had not spoken with them before. At the prompting of the Council they began to testify, accusing Stephen of violating in speech and action everything that those sitting there held holy. They told a story of a Stephen that despised Moses, despised the Law, and despised the Temple. His words about the coming of the Kingdom through the Lord Jesus were twisted beyond recognition to fit their narrative of a young foreigner from Alexandria who had embraced the extremism of a dangerous sect, who had filled his heart with hatred for the traditions of his fathers, and who ceased to practice the standards and values that held their society together. As he listened to witness after witness spin their yarn, Stephen did not know himself. But he did recognize, in the midst of the exaggerations and the outright lies, the real story they told. It was the story of holy office corrupted by ambition, of raw power and fear and coercion, of manipulation and falsehood so pervasive that those who practiced it couldn't admit to the truth when it stared them in the face. It was the story of God's house turned citadel, of God's priests turned despots, of God's service turned into the idolatrous worship of itself. It was a story that had forgotten The Story. The unfeeling spirit behind it differed little from the wheels and ropes of the machines Herod had used to lay the great stones upon which the Temple now sat, gears that would heartlessly crush any and all who ventured into their midst. In the mouths of those witnesses lived the very spirit that had murdered the Lord Jesus himself.

"Are these things so?"

There stood the high priest himself. The witnesses had finished their harangue, and the Law required the Council to allow the accused his rebuttal. It was Stephen's turn to speak. Stephen, alone. The trap had been well-laid. He had had no time to prepare himself, no way to properly weigh a response to the accusations they had so carefully rehearsed. He had no witnesses in his favor, none of his fellow disciples or pathetic, legally disqualified widows to plead for him, and this moment only to make his defense.

Slowly and without a hint calculation, Stephen lifted his eyes and gazed into the face of the priest, then calmly around at the Council members. What was it that he discerned as they looked back at him? He could not behold himself as they did, but they saw *something* as he fearlessly met their unspoken impeachment, one by one. Was it confusion? Was it wonder? Did he even detect a hint of fear in their eyes? The witnesses, moments ago bold as lions, could not bear his countenance; silently, they quailed and lowered their once-haughty bearing.

And when they bring you before the synagogues, and the rulers, and the authorities, do not worry about how you should defend yourselves or what you should say, for the Holy Spirit will teach you in that very hour those things you ought to say.

No, the archdeacon did not mull his words. A deeper question rolled over in his soul. As it had in the confrontation with his father, years ago now, a natural longing rose within him, that old yearning for the typical. It wasn't so much a desire to have things as they were before Christ found him, as much as it was a hopeful wondering whether it might be possible for Christ to fit the life he once imagined was his. It was the passing wish that he could have it both ways: to have his Jesus, his otherworldly joy, his ministry to the widows, the power of the Spirit coursing through his heart and his hands—*and* to have the favor of the city, and a laugh in the market after pocketing a solid profit, and fellowship with his countrymen rather than debates, and no duty to speak the bitter truths as well as the sweet. True, Stephen had been ambushed. He had not had the benefit of preparing his mind or his speech as his adversaries had. But he was no fool. His thought for a common life—a wish that came as a whole emotion and not a string of arguments played out in his head—hit him in a moment and couched itself in the very earthy confidence that he could, in fact, handle this. His enemies had hollered and sweated, but their testimony was false. He had only to point out their folly and their inconsistencies, shame the more temperate consciences in the Council, and he might yet walk free. At the very least he could try. All of this passed through Stephen's heart and mind in two blinks of an eye.

My Father, if it be possible...

Just as quickly the answer arose within him. Was there really another way? The Lord Jesus had laid down his life for this truth, for the redemption of Israel, for Stephen's own reclamation. His Shepherd had shown the path forward, setting the example of life for all who would learn of him. Might Stephen improve upon it? Did the atoning blood of the Christ wash away his obligation to carry the cross? He was the Lord's disciple. Speak not of rights, my soul, nor of fairness. The Lord Christ has redefined victory itself, the very meaning of the word *strength*. No, Stephen could not return to the darkness of the womb. He could not make peace with a lie, he could not tell them one thing and mean another, only to patch it up with his God later. He could not divide his life into body and soul like the philosophers did in the Alexandrian agora, being one thing on the inside and another on the out. No, he was *one man* or he wasn't a man at all. What did it cost to kneel before the cross, to love and worship him who had loved unto death? What did it mean, verily, to live entirely for the glory of the Crucified One? Give up the air he breathed or deliver his soul—these were his choices. No middle road lay before him, that much he saw most clearly. Though they had indeed plotted against him, the Lord was he who had truly given his servant this moment; he daren't squander it. He must open his mouth and let the Spirit speak—on God's terms, to his ends—or renounce his witness entirely and become worse than his accusers had made him out to be. They had told a story; he would tell The Story.

...let this cup pass from me...

"Men—brothers and fathers—hear me..."

Thus began Stephen's defense. Through it, the Spirit within him set ablaze every word of truth he had ever learned, from his earliest recollection of teaching in the synagogue to his most intimate searching of the Scriptures by lamplight. He recounted the great epic of their people, but in truth it was the epic of his God. It spoke of longsuffering faithfulness, of miraculous deliverance, of promises made and promises kept. It told of salvation. But woven into the saga of God's love wound the threads of human failure, of rejection, of capricious and inexplicable betrayal. Their own fathers had rejected and mistreated the very patriarchs they loved to boast in.

If Stephen had been concerned for his own welfare, if he had been speaking to convince the elders to reject the accusations and believe the best of him, he might have noticed the growing astonishment on their faces. Here before them spoke a wisdom and a depth of understanding in the holy writings rare among those even twice his age. But Stephen was lost within the song, his heart hot within him now, and he rolled on.

Were these abuses dark anomalies? No, emphatically not. They were mere dress rehearsals for the ultimate betrayal. They matched the pattern of idolatry and misuse of God's house that were all too familiar, with the worship of human thoughts and human stratagems. His voice deepened in holy anger, all the more fierce and cutting because it was not his own, an onslaught of righteous wrath that he channeled but that coursed above and not through his flesh. His opportunity to turn his soliloquy into a means of escape was fading fast.

...yet not my will, but Your will be done.

"You stiff-necked men, uncircumcised in heart and ears! You continually resist the Holy Spirit—as your fathers did, so do you. Which of the prophets did your forefathers not persecute? They even killed those who foretold the coming of the Righteous One, whose murderers and betrayers you have now become, you who received the law ordained by angels but did not keep it!"

Shock struck the Council, like a slap to the face. This turn they had not expected. Now their ugly voices rose in unified, cacophonous rejection of this word, though the accused had not finished his defense. Fury twisted their features. But Stephen paid no attention. He directed his enraptured gaze upward, his eyes filled with his life's longing.

"Look there, I see the heavens opened and the Son of Man standing at the right hand of God."

Now they screamed to drown out his blasphemy, yelling with their fingers in their ears, rushing forward as one, the fiery young Cilician Pharisee in the lead. No further questions, no deliberation, no verdict, no adjournment. The accused had spent his moment; he had passed judgment on himself. As they dragged him from the Sanhedrin, he could hear the shouts in the chamber continue behind him, demanding injustice in the name of justice.

What thoughts coursed through Stephen's heart and mind just then as they half-carried, half-dragged him off the Temple Mount and out the gates of the Holy City? His ears were filled with the rage of his mortal enemies, but his eyes fairly wept, not for his plight, but for the glory of the vision. He had seen that the Son of Man had seen him; by making his throne known the One who sat on it revealed that he knew Stephen. What else mattered now? And how could Stephen speak of protections or petty vindications? What claims might be made upon him who died to lay claim to *him*? Truly, he lived by God's mercy, and the promise of life eternal had rendered moot all the questions that mortals put to the Almighty. The lesson of his Lord's sacrifice flowed like a river of living water through his spirit: control is ever an illusion; surrender to God's will on *his* terms—with no preconditions of our own—is the closest we come to having control, the closest we come to achieving the sublime.

The mob rid themselves of their burden, and began to pick up others. Stephen did not shield himself, he did not crouch down to make himself a smaller target for the rocks they threw.

Unless the seed falls to the ground and dies, it remains alone; but if it dies...

"Lord Jesus, receive my spirit."

He could stand no longer; the stones, hurled with the strength of hate, accomplished their end. The holy music sounded its irresistible strains within him. Stephen went to his knees.

I will gladly spend and be expended...for these light and momentary troubles are achieving for us an eternal glory far beyond compare...we are as sheep for the slaughter, but nay, nay, we exceedingly conquer all through him who loved us...for it has been gifted you not only to believe on Christ, but also...the fellowship of his sufferings, becoming conformed to his death, and so, somehow, to attain to the resurrection from the dead.

"Lord, do not hold this sin against them!"

The false witnesses completed their pitiless work, the last stones were thrown. But in their zeal to eradicate this perceived threat, now lying dead in the dust before them, they blinded themselves to the perilous glory they now released in their midst with every stone they had cast.

For they laid their cloaks at the feet of a young man named Saul.

Prayer: Lord Jesus, hear my heart's cry—that I aspire to be like You, and like those who sought hardest to be like You. Your perfect love casts out my fear, the fear that tries to tell me I can be Your disciple and yet somehow be greater than You, my Master, and escape these hard things. Put steel in my soul that I might never even attempt discipleship on the cheap. Precious in Your sight is the death of Your saints. Bring resurrection, which is ever a surprising miracle, as I lay down my life for You, and may others reap the blessing as a result. Amen.

Blessed Fool

While passing by an alcove dim
I saw upon a table placed,
A solitary candle, slim
And tall. Fey and sturdy it, grim,
Fearless; darkness and gloom it faced.

Bemused, I gaze, I wonder, I
Pause to ponder. What hides the wick?
What secrets in its wax do lie?
How face the fact it's made to die?
If granted voice what end would pick?

Quick from pocket a box I draw,
Hesitate, then strike the match now.
With ugly stench flares out Hell's claw,
For bid waits not but lights the straw;
Drops flow down the lonely tallow.

Bow I and blink in newborn light,
Find a chair, then draw in closer.
How wondrous is the glow so bright.
It warms me with its gentle might,
Fills my heart with hope not known there.

Hear shadows scream; they run, they hide.
The pow'r of the flame does smite them.
Its brilliance they cannot abide,
It strikes them like a rising tide,
Fills them with a fear and mayhem.

I beam and pull in nearer still;
The candle is a joy to me.
No better way the time to kill;
Stay here longer I think I will.
I close one eye and then I see...

The candle, fixed upon its task—
It spends its substance all too fast!
Though in its goodness I do bask,
The candle forces me to ask,
"How long do you expect to last?"

Undaunted by this question stern,
The wax my nod does not await
But keeps on with its noble burn
Unwilling from its call to turn
And plods on toward its evil fate.

I screw my brow, I shake my head;
I ask myself how this can be.
I cannot see through flaming red,
I do not grasp though light it shed
The answer to this mystery.

It gives its all, it asks no help,
And for itself it seeks no bliss.
The candle does not dwell on self.
No matter how I try to delve
I cannot plumb the depths of this.

Is there now some judgment new?
A twist of jurisprudence rule
Or law to grant the smallest clue?
Why candles yield without a rue
Themselves, a luminescent jewel?

Real spark, the true revelation—
It hits me hard and shifts my view.
I, with irony, elation,
See at last, realize the station—
The candle melting in my lieu.

Did we think another way was?
Could we really live and die for
"Me" alone? The peace we seek as
We live lives if our time we pass
Not to hoard, but in giving more.

Otherworldly praise I write here
Since with the wick I've lost my duel.
I now rethink what I hold dear,
And with conviction must declare
That, O, the candle is no fool.

AFTERWORD

In writing *The Candle Is a Fool*, I intended to create a story of devotional and biblical fiction set within the context of the ancient world in which the earliest Christians lived and told the story of the New Testament. Doing this required that I appeal to a combination of sources, including of course the Bible itself, ancient historical records, church tradition, various modern scholarly writings, and my own imagination. The purpose of this afterword is to help you, the reader, sort through which elements in the story are "Gospel Truth," which are history, which are matters of debate, which are reasonable possibilities, and which are whole-cloth fiction.

Broadly speaking, the entire story depends to a degree upon a "harmonizing" of the Gospels. In other words, I combine elements from each of the four Gospels—Matthew, Mark, Luke, and John—in an attempt to create a fluid and unified whole; to some extent this is applied to the narrative from Acts as well. Though scholars (myself included) agree that the Gospels were written at different times and places, opinions differ widely on how they relate to each other. I will not subject you to that discussion here, but will simply note that in this story I am more interested in narrative flow than the idiosyncrasies of that debate, and I took liberties even with my own scholarly position on the matter. In other words, in writing the story as I do I purposefully move past the realm of static, debated positions and conflicting opinions (a realm some are perfectly happy to remain in), and into the realm of conclusion so that a human story can be coherently told and identified with. Consequently (for example), the dream of Pilate's wife (which is mentioned only in Matthew, for whom dreams and visions to righteous Gentiles are a thing) is unapologetically woven together with the story of the so-called "Good Thief" (which is found only in Luke, who cares greatly for the socially marginalized). My goal here is good and plausible storytelling for lovers and inquirers of the gospel, not purism. I would also note that while each of the first six episodes (Mary, Judas, Procula, Petronius, Demas, and Peter) begins with its corresponding headings from one or more of the four canonical Gospels (Matthew, Mark, Luke, and John) my intention is not to indicate that that sub-story is drawn exclusively from one Gospel or passage, as the case may be. Each of these broader chapters in the whole pulls from *all* the Gospels. (As I will explain below, the story of Stephen from the Book of Acts is in a class by itself, for several reasons.)

Regarding each episode, the mixture of the elements I refer to above varies.

Mary of Bethany

In respect to Mary of Bethany, fully understanding her story as I have told it (and as far as I am concerned, very likely understanding it at all) has to do with grasping her identity. This will entail understanding her *village*, her *own name and person*, and her *household name*, all in close relation to each other.

Matthew, Mark, and John all name Bethany as the village in which a woman anoints Jesus in the week leading up to His Passion. Recent research strongly suggests that the Jewish sect known as the Essenes (who are most commonly associated with the Qumran/Dead Sea Scroll community) founded this village near Jerusalem as a refuge for the poor and ceremonially unclean, but not so near to the sanctuary as to violate strict Jewish purity laws (about which no group felt more passionately than the Essenes themselves). *Bethany*, therefore, very likely means "House of Affliction" or "Poor House." It would have been, simultaneously, a refuge for Jerusalem-bound pilgrims coming up the Jericho Road who had descended from Galilee via the Jordan River valley (i.e., avoiding Samaria), such as Jesus and His disciples. The Gospels further testify that Jesus used Bethany as a staging area of sorts during His visits to Jerusalem, spending the night there rather than in the Holy City itself. It was from Bethany that He embarked on His famous and fateful Triumphal Entry. One need only pause and consider the Lord choosing a place with this name and these kinds of residents to be impacted once again by His character.

At the same time, John's Gospel specifically identifies Bethany as the home of Mary, Martha, and Lazarus (John 11-12). Luke further mentions Mary and Martha as sisters who welcome Him into their home in Luke 10, perhaps not coincidentally just after Jesus told a parable prominently featuring the Jericho Road (the "Good Samaritan"). Thus the collective testimony across the entire Gospel witness is that sisters named Mary and Martha, with their brother Lazarus, lived in Bethany, a village near Jerusalem, and that Jesus frequented their home. It seems, in fact, that Jesus had actually adopted their household as His place to stay while in that village. Earlier in the selfsame chapter in which Jesus' (first?) visit to Mary and Martha's home is described, Jesus had already given instructions to His followers regarding the acceptance of hospitality: when someone in a given village receives you, do not move about from house to house (Luke 10:5-7). The common sense reason for this is that, although the practice appears to "play favorites," in fact it does the very opposite—it shows contentment and the refusal to compare one household's hospitality to another, and thus avoids dividing the community. We may conclude, therefore, that when Jesus came to Bethany, He stayed at Mary, Martha, and Lazarus' home *habitually*, that is, each time He came. This is almost certainly the reason for the special bond between them, developed over the course of numerous pilgrimages.

As for Mary herself, it is first important for us to realize that many women in the Gospels bear this name (I will discuss this in more detail, below). It is vital that we do not confuse one Mary with another Mary, or conflate two women who do similar things. In the case of Mary of Bethany, tradition has a long and sorry history of committing both of these errors. For starters, Mary of Bethany is *not* Mary Magdalene. Magdala was a town on the north shore of the Sea of Galilee—just down the road, as it were, from Capernaum, Jesus' adopted home town. In other words, Mary Magdalene was a *Galilean woman from the north*, like most of Jesus' (male) disciples. Mary of Bethany is a *Judean woman of the south*, a stone's throw from Jerusalem. Two different towns, two different regions, two different women. Furthermore, I am convinced that Mary of Bethany is *not* the "sinful woman" described at the end of Luke 7. That circumstance parallels the events of John 12 only in that a woman anoints Jesus' feet while He eats dinner in a private home (*Simon* is also extremely common, with Jesus' brother, two of

His disciples, and at least one of His disciples' fathers having the name). The setting, the timing, the motive for the anointing, the identity of the woman's critic(s), and Jesus' response to her critics(s) and to the woman herself are all very different. People will fuss and argue about similarities, and that cannot be helped; for some the matter will likely never be resolved. But while I am willing to admit there are some sticky parallels between the Gospels, I do not believe this is one of them. (I would also add that the woman of Luke 7 is *not* Mary Magdalene either, and that the oft-quoted fable that Magdalene was a "woman of the night" is pure salacious fantasy with zero basis in Scripture, but that is another matter altogether.) So, who is Mary of Bethany? She is as she is described, and that description goes far beyond what we have for many others in the Gospels (including many of the Twelve), nothing more, nothing less.

The last issue is the identity of Mary, Martha, and Lazarus' household. Broadly speaking, there are essentially two different theories regarding this family. One is that they were wealthy elites—better described as Jerusalemites—who lived in Bethany in part to support the Essene poor house there. This theory explains how they had the wherewithal to host Jesus and His disciples and (ultimately, through Mary) to bestow upon Jesus such an extravagant gift as a pound of spikenard. The other possibility (which I have taken) is that they lived in Bethany because of the town's nature as a haven for the indigent and unclean, and Mary's gift was an heirloom of sorts—an anomalous exception to the family's economic situation rather than a reflection of great wealth. I adopt this second option because in Matthew and Mark, the event of Jesus' anointing during Passion Week is described as happening while He dined in "the house of Simon the Leper." Some have conjectured that Simon the Leper was an otherwise unknown man, and since the events of John 12 (i.e., Lazarus at table with Jesus, Martha serving, and Mary performing her dramatic sacrifice) match Matthew and Mark's accounts, it must mean Simon (whoever he was) invited those siblings to dine there, too, and that's how the narratives match. However, given Jesus' own teaching about not moving around from house to house within a village, that seems unlikely. More likely (as at least one scholar has suggested as a possibility) is that the "House of Simon the Leper" *means* the family of Mary, Martha, and Lazarus. "House" can mean dwelling, and it can mean family line, both—and in this case, it very possibly (and I consider probably) *is* both. When we consider that this is the only reference to this "Simon," and elsewhere Martha is always described as dominant ("her home" per Luke 10, usually taking the lead in conversations, and serving at table), and toss in the previous information about Bethany, a scenario emerges as quite nearly a self-telling story.

One Simon, who once had standing and wealth (hence his daughter's later access to the spikenard flask), is afflicted with leprosy. ("Leprosy," as many know, would not have been what is called leprosy now, but was likely something like psoriasis.) He must leave Jerusalem, but stays as near as he can—in the paupers' village of Bethany. At some point he passes away, and wife as well (if she had not already). His children are left in the same village, which has become their home, but they are still known collectively as the "House of Simon the Leper." Martha is eldest, likely Lazarus is the middle, and carefree Mary the youngest. One day a young Galilean rabbi visits, a bond is formed and they take Him into their home. The bond turns into a lasting friendship, and each time He comes to Jerusalem, He stays with them. Tragedy, then the miraculous, occur, leading up to the events described in this story. This scenario, in my view, is a sensible possibility, strains the text of Scripture hardly at all (perhaps not *at* all), fits the history of Bethany as we have come to know it, and explains several details in the narrative very satisfactorily.

Mary's actions, the nature of her sacrifice, and how people in a village of the poor came to possess something worth a year's wages that could fit in your palm, I have already described. The question is, *exactly what was that flask to Mary, herself?* There is no knowing for sure. But we can conjecture in an educated fashion. First, I believe that Mary acted alone, apart from her siblings, and very likely surprised them as well as everyone else in the room when she poured out the oil on the Lord. My justification for this is that in each and every account, the Lord Jesus *praises her and her only.* If she were merely the agent for the household, the sibling chosen to offer a gift that was really from them all, then I see Jesus noticing that and His exultation would be for the entire household. But He is rather pointed in that the gift was from *her,* and that *she* would be honored perpetually for having given it. This means that in some very special way, that oil was hers, particularly, and hers alone to give or not give as she wished. Now, that Bethany was a paupers' village explains why John describes Judas (or several unnamed disciples, in Matthew and Mark) as invoking the poor; one who lives in the midst of their sufferings shouldn't be so casual with such wanton expenditures. That they have a point *is* the point. We are supposed to see the sense in their words so we can see the heroism in Mary's actions as a contrast. This should lead us to ask, why did Mary, in such a poor place and likely in a (at least relatively) poor situation herself, still have this precious thing? Why had she not already "liquidated" it for cash to better her family's situation? As far as I know, my guess that the nard is actually her *dowry* is not proposed by any scholar. But it makes perfect sense to me. A dowry would have been guarded as sacred against all but the most extreme need. It was the key to a young woman's future, and, in fact, was an heirloom for the household itself because it gave them power to unburden themselves of a costly dependent—not just for one year, but for all time.

So, we see what is happening here, especially in light of the Jewish brother's role in helping to secure a husband for his sister. As I paint it (according to what I consider most likely), Simon is dead and Lazarus is now the only living male left to Mary and Martha by which they might be properly married off. Lazarus dies, and their hope for marriage essentially dies with him. Jesus restores their brother to life, and with him, his sisters' futures. Mary, in a breathtaking show of faith, responds by sacrificing her dowry—a treasure that embodies that same hope, and hers alone in the midst of crushing poverty—to show her gratitude and devotion to Christ. Thus, in my view, Mary anointing Jesus in Lazarus' presence in John 12 depends on our understanding of events in John 11 in a very specific way. Similarly, Mary's actions prefigure Jesus' own greater work of washing His disciples' feet in John 13. She must surely be regarded as one of the most remarkable characters in all of Scripture once we fully weigh her deed, as Jesus' unique recognition of her seems to indicate.

I will make a final remark about timing. As I will explain later in this afterword, the days and times of the Passion Week are a complicated question, made more complicated by the fact that the Jewish day began at sundown, that partial days can be counted as whole days, and that biblical writers often count days inclusively (i.e., "four days later" would probably be *three* days later if counted by us moderns), among other things. Since I will discuss this later, I will restrict my remarks to the nature of the dinner described in the Mary episode.

Some have surmised that since Martha was *serving*, this supper could not have been a Sabbath's eve meal (meaning, Friday night). In other words, we might reason that since work is disallowed on the Sabbath, and Martha was working, *ergo* it must have taken place on some other night. The dinner, described as "six days before the Passover" (John 12:1), is thus used as another detail to date the events of Passion Week. Most following this line of reasoning settle that it must be the meal *after* the Sabbath, that is, *Saturday* night. But this poses problems of its own, because that very day is indicated as a day of travel for the Lord—which would not be allowed on the Sabbath either. (Travelers would have left Jericho in the morning and made Bethany by nightfall—one does not sleep on the steep and dangerous Jericho Road.) Furthermore, the kind of dinner that is given seems to fit the formality associated with the (most ancient) Sabbath's eve meal. The quandary was resolved for me by an orthodox Jewish rabbi, a friend of mine, who, upon hearing my repetition of prevailing wisdom about Martha "working on the Sabbath" promptly shot the entire thing down. "Somebody's got to serve," he said bluntly about his favorite meal of the week. Here is where Gentile understanding of Jewish Sabbath laws founders. After I described the passage to him, he assured me that such a description could very well fit a Sabbath meal; there was no need to push it to a later day. This is why I cast the meal as I do, and why it fits with the timeline I describe later in this afterword.

Judas Iscariot

The matter of Judas Iscariot is at once far more complicated than that of Mary, and far, far shallower. At issue is his name. "Judas," of course, now might as well be used as a curse word; to call someone a Judas says it all. While this is understandable and even unavoidable (see John 14:22), Judas was an extremely common and popular name at the time. It is a Hellenized (i.e., Greek) version of *Judah* (which would have been pronounced *Yehudah* by Jesus and His disciples), a name that was quite the rage in ancient Israel not only because of the patriarch but because of the insurgent war hero Judas Maccabeus who fought to liberate Israel about 200 years before these events. Mark 6:3 describes Jesus Himself as having a brother named Judas, who is likely the author of the book known as *Jude*, though in the Greek the name in the first verse ("Ioudas") is identical to that of our villain. There were also two other disciples amongst the Twelve named Judas, namely, *Judas son of James* (Luke 6:13— almost certainly John's "other Judas"), and *Judas Thomas*, who is simply known by his more familiar nickname, *Thomas*. There was also a *Judas called Barsabbas*, a prophet prominent among the disciples of the early church (Acts 15:22, 32). In other words, "Judas" might seem rare and sinister to us, but the warning from Scripture could very well be that Judas was in many respects a typical man with a common, well-loved name.

More troublesome is "Iscariot." Theories abound regarding its true meaning, and include "red" (possibly meaning the color of his hair, the blood that spilled out when he died, or both), "liar," "hander-over," "killer," "choked" (also likely a reference to his death), "of Sicarii," and different "man of" options, including "man of Kerioth" and "man of town/towns." The difficult reality is that we cannot know for certain, and for the time being that is probably something we need to admit. But as I consider the last three options in my list the most plausible real possibilities and the most worthy of discussion (and I take less stock in the others), I will address them.

The idea that *Iscariot* might mean *of Sicarii* is more popular and pervasive than many people even realize. The Sicarii (literally, "daggermen") were more or less domestic Jewish terrorists who sought to disrupt Roman rule via murderous hit and run tactics. They knew they could not win an out-and-out conflict, so they carried out attacks that would terrorize and sow uncertainty. The phonetic similarity between *Sicarii* and *Iscariot* has led some to fashion Judas just such a man, and then interpret his betrayal in the light of his supposed revolutionary inclinations. In other words, as misguided as he might be, he is really just misinterpreting Jesus' messianic claims and appropriating them—albeit erroneously—for his own nationalistic purposes. I have two major problems with this. First, the Sicarii did not exist this early in history; they arose later on in the first century. Second, the Bible says Judas betrayed Jesus for money, not over his sense of what might be best for the nation. Nevertheless, the concept of Judas as a "revolutionary" of sorts has found lodging in the collective mindset (even bolstered by books and movies), with no solid justification for it.

The "man of" options are, in my book, stronger. By this theory, the first syllable in *Iscariot* reflects a Greek transliteration of the Hebrew/Aramaic word "ish," meaning *man*. The rest of the name refers either to a small town in Judea south of Jerusalem ("Kerioth"), or it refers to "towns/cities"— potentially even "the City," Jerusalem. I will not be dogmatic on this, lacking the solid justification for being so, but I lean toward the idea that Judas was a man of Judea, either by being from Kerioth or of "towns," quite possibly Jerusalem itself. This could very well explain (in part) why he felt the confidence he did to approach the priests, though it is hard to be too sure. In any case, that is the identity I have settled on, and why.

The rest of Judas' story reflects my fearful disdain not just for him (his story in Scripture is indeed a devastating read), but for all the ballyhoo about him as some sort of fascinating enigma worthy of tragic regard. People have personally argued with me regarding everything from Judas' good intentions, to his inability to do other than he did (and therefore should be viewed with nothing but sympathy), to his sainthood (!). I see all that not only as mistaken, but as inconsistent with Scripture which, inexplicably, many simply do not want to take at face value even when it is remarkably unambiguous about an issue (for the references, see Matthew 10:4, 26:14-16, 26:21-25, and 27:3-5; Mark 3:19, 14:10-11 and 14:18-21; Luke 6:16, 22:3-6 and 22:21-22; John 6:70-71, 13:2, and 13:21-30; and Acts 1:16-19). The hard truth is that Jesus chose Judas, Judas was good and did good things like the other apostles, Judas rose to a position of responsibility and trust among the disciples, and then Judas went bad for simple, straightforward, ugly reasons—as any number of other Old Testament characters we could name also did. Judas is a hard warning to us, the warning that we can be around Jesus and even be used by Him (in the best sense), and *still* turn from Him and become hardened by good old-fashioned self-justifying avarice. Satan (who is said to actually indwell Judas—the only case in Scripture so described) need not reach for new weaponry, not even to combat those apparently closest to God—the old tactics just keep on working. I tell the story as a descent in darkness because that's the way these things go. But again, the text tells us a great deal more than we often give it credit for. The trigger seems to be the anointing at Bethany. Judas recognizes that the priests want Jesus, else he wouldn't have gone to them. Judas expected money for his role, and got it. Then Judas follows through with his betrayal.

The only caveat to the whole Judas story appears to be his remorse and suicide, which lies outside the scope of my Judas narrative but is mentioned later, in Matthew 27:3-5. People read that passage and ask questions: Didn't Judas think of the consequences of his actions beforehand? Why the change of heart? He gave back the money; doesn't this mean he isn't such a bad guy after all? My position, in reverse order, is as follows. First, just because he is smitten with crushing regret doesn't mean he hasn't become damnably wicked; many ungodly but completely unrepentant people suffer terribly from remorse. In 2 Corinthians 7:10, the Apostle Paul calls this "worldly sorrow," telling us that such sorrow brings death—precisely as it did in this case. Second, he did not really have a redemptive change of heart so much as the fruit of his sin manifested itself; *of course* people feel badly about what they've done once that happens! And third, it is entirely possible that Judas was blinded to the real consequences of his actions, not only because he was captive to sin, but because of how the betrayal was negotiated. Thirty pieces of silver is indeed the price of a slave (Exodus 21:32). By offering that price the priests could have been preemptively allaying whatever fears they thought Judas might have—for all we know, they said as much, though Scripture obviously does not include all the specifics of Judas' negotiations with them. The point is, by paying that price they may have been deliberately implying, "We'll try Jesus and sell him into slavery"—a well-known punishment in those days. This lie would have made it easier for Judas to go through with the deed. When he saw, however, that they condemned Jesus to death, he tried to renege on the deal, but all too late. So there's another lesson here: if you cut cards with the devil, don't expect him to deal honorably with you.

Procula

"Procula" (also sometimes "Proculla" or "Procla") is the name traditional sources give for Pilate's wife; she goes unnamed in the Gospel of Matthew, the only Gospel that mentions her. Though honored as a saint in the Eastern Orthodox and Ethiopian Orthodox traditions, we really know very little about her. An apocryphal legend alleges that she had a lame son named Pilo whom Jesus healed, but this story didn't exist until centuries later and is clearly pious fabrication. For the sake of narrative color, I chose to borrow from this fable, however, the idea that Procula did bear Pilate a son because it is entirely plausible that she would have. What we *do* know from the Gospel record is that she was a Roman noblewoman who accompanied her husband not only to Judea but also to Jerusalem that fateful Passover. We may also strongly infer that she had the kind of relationship with her husband that gave her boldness to speak her mind if she felt it important, and that her husband gave some weight to her counsel. This characterization is in keeping with what we know about Roman women of status as well as Matthew's brief testimony about her.

Perhaps more weighty in this chapter is the prominent inclusion of Aelius Sejanus. Multiple histories bear witness to the rise and violent demise of this powerful Roman and his family. Their spectacular political success, followed by their sudden and fatal fall from imperial favor, is one of the most well-known tales of the ancient Roman world; once a would-be successor to the imperial throne, within hours Sejanus was deposed and executed, and his family members were condemned to die with him. The connection between them and Pilate (and through him, his wife) is attested to by the Jewish historian Philo of Alexandria who attributes Pilate's appointment as prefect of Judea to his friendship with Sejanus. Hence, while my imagination is the source for the idea of a relationship between Procula and Sejanus' wife and children (whose names I accurately communicate in my story), Pilate's historical connection to Sejanus lifts that idea from the level of mere fancy to that of plausible conjecture. Taking all these things as a whole, therefore, the reader should understand that though the tenderness I describe Procula as feeling for Junilla is likely just fiction, the nightmarish account of Junilla's final pleadings followed by her violation and murder is, tragically, broadly attested to by multiple ancient witnesses. (And so that you, the reader, understand, and do not presume the inclusion of her story to be gratuitous, I must sadly relate this: Roman historians explain Junilla was raped before she was killed because Roman law contained no provision for the execution of a virgin; what actually happened, therefore, illustrates better than any fiction I could fabricate the horrific collateral price of sinful ambition.)

Given Philo's account, the larger issue regarding the subject of Sejanus' fall in relation to Pilate is a matter of scholarly debate. In the final analysis, how we read the Gospels in this respect comes down to dates. Most agree, for reasons having to do with the ancient calendar, that Jesus was probably crucified during Passover of either AD 30 or AD 33 (though in the end we cannot even be *absolutely* sure of these dates, for a variety of reasons having to do with pinpointing events in the ancient calendar). Since Sejanus and his family were deposed and executed in late A.D 31, the date we choose has a direct bearing on how we understand Pilate's actions when the priests brought Jesus to him. Obviously, if Jesus' trial took place in 33, the execution of his mentor and patron would have been relatively recent history and Pilate would have been understandably nervous about his position. The priests would have known this and exploited it to their advantage. For this reason many scholars who feel AD 33 is the proper date for Jesus' Passion comment on the passages that deal with Pilate's judgment with this in mind. On the other hand, if Jesus was tried and executed in AD 30 (or earlier), Sejanus' fall would not have taken place yet; on the contrary, he would have been at the height of his power. For a variety of reasons having to do with dating the events of the Gospels, and completely independent of the Sejanus issue, I believe that the earlier date for the death of Jesus (AD 30, or earlier) is the best one. Other ancient sources tell us that completely apart from the fall of Sejanus (i.e., whether it had happened at that point or not) Pilate had every reason to fear imperial displeasure. At least once, and perhaps even twice by this point in time he had been rebuked for stirring political trouble by his insensitivity toward Jewish faith and practice. In other words, all by himself Pilate had badly misjudged how to rule in Judea, and another mistake could mean disaster for his career.

In the end, there is obviously no knowing what Pilate's wife dreamed, though people have guessed at it for generations. For my part, I have cast the nightmare as a prophetic premonition combining Christ's death, the bloody fallout from Sejanus' fall (symbolized by Junilla's death, which history tells us was a direct result of it), and, ultimately, Pilate's suicide. The sources for these ideas are Gospel witness, well-known ancient history, and early church tradition, in that order.

Petronius

"Petronius" is the name the non-canonical *Gospel of Peter* gives to the centurion who oversaw Jesus' execution and burial. While it may have been the name of the man, my choosing it is not intended as an expression of belief in that apocryphal book. Unlike Pilate's wife, the centurion is mentioned in all the Synoptic Gospels (Matthew, Mark, and Luke—though not in John), but like her he goes unnamed. "Petronius" is both plausible and as good a name as any in a story like this.

The most significant historical aspect of this chapter is the setting for the trial and scourging of Jesus. By means of my narrative I have agreed with recent scholarship that places the initial encounter between Pilate and the priests who arrested Jesus at the fortified palace of Herod the Great (not to be confused with Herod Antipas, his son, who is also a character in the Bible account). Herod's palace, rather than the Fortress of Antonia adjacent to the Temple, is a more likely official residence for Pilate (and the location of the Praetorian Guard) while he was in Jerusalem for the Passover. Since this residence is located in the wealthy Upper City of ancient Jerusalem, a guard such as Petronius who formed part of the permanent garrison in the Tower of Antonia would have had to march there to witness and participate in those events. Though we cannot be sure, it is entirely plausible that regular troops most familiar with Jerusalem (rather than the elite Praetorians that came and went with Pilate as his personal bodyguard) would have finally executed Jesus.

Additionally, I have drawn extensively from the Gospel of John in my retelling of the story in respect to setting, dialogue, and the order of events. John's narrative, in my view, fits well with the idea that the initial stages of the trial took place in Pilate's palatial residence, and includes quite a few "private audiences" between Pilate and Jesus while the priests waited outside. John also specifically indicates that Pilate scourged Jesus at some sort of a midway point in the proceedings (sometime around the offer to release Him or Barabbas) as part of a last ditch effort to set Him free. This contrasts with the Synoptics, which give the impression through scanter detail that Pilate had Jesus scourged only once things were beyond the point of no return (though Luke 22:16-22 does tell us Pilate attempted to use the offer of a scourging as a compromise, but to no avail). The way I read the Gospel of John, Pilate was attempting to appease the Jewish leaders by punishing Jesus severely in the hopes of not having to execute Him; Pilate was trying to have his cake and eat it too. My story reflects my conviction on this point. My reading and (I believe) a plausible conclusion is that only after this ploy failed did the trial move to the Gabbatha (Greek

Lithostrotos, meaning "Pavement"), the place of public judgment, where the crowd got more involved, Pilate washed his hands, and the final sentence was pronounced. I recognize this has issues and will be unsatisfactory to some. But when drawing from multiple Gospel accounts in an attempt to speak with one voice the story has to be told one way or another, and better storytellers than I have been criticized for less. It is important to keep in mind that the Gospel accounts, while invaluable historical sources in themselves, were written as faith documents and their writers were not interested in giving us all the details that we might wish to know.

As for the specifics, the centurion's confession in various forms is found in all of the Synoptics, but is most specific in Mark. For the sake of my story, I have obviously fictionalized the matter of Petronius' letter to accentuate the contrast between his ambition and Christ's selflessness, and that has to play out at the end. While it is certainly possible under the circumstances that several officers could have been on hand for extra security, there is no specific evidence for such an assertion in the biblical text, one way or the other. In any case, I deliberately paint Petronius' angst over his location in Judea as a historical irony: Forty years later the Legion of Judea was powerful enough to impose its will on the rest of the Roman Empire in the form of a new ruler and a new dynasty, the Emperor Vespasian of the Flavian line. As always, selfish ambition blinds us to larger truths.

Demas

"Demas" is a fictitious name I ascribed to that biblical persona commonly called the "Good," or, "Penitent Thief." This moniker is consistent with sacred tradition from the 4th century that bestowed upon him the name "Dismas," which is almost certainly a later fabrication (and by its etymology clearly associated with the darkness of that day). Not only are there variations on this name (not only "Demas" but also "Dysmas" and "Dimas"), but there are other names used for him in various religious traditions that bear no resemblance to this name or each other. None of these are really plausible for the kind of first century Jew that I describe below, and the simple truth is that there is no knowing his name. In the end I chose the variant "Demas" as a nod to tradition and also because it is a Hellenistic name found elsewhere in the New Testament (Colossians 4:14, Philemon 24, 2 Timothy 4:10), though obviously not in any way meant to be identified with that personality associated with the Apostle Paul's ministry.

The primary issue surrounding his character is not his name but rather his true identity, his associations, and the crime for which the Romans crucified him. It is fairly clear from the vocabulary used to describe him and others (the Greek term *lestes*, plural *lestai*) that this man was not a common thief at all, but rather a revolutionary or insurrectionist who engaged in brigandage of a kind for religious reasons. In modern parlance ones such as this might be called domestic terrorists, but they would have called themselves "zealots." Matthew and Mark use the term *lestes/lestai* to identify those condemned with Jesus; John uses *lestes* to describe Barabbas. Once we properly interpret this term in this context (some modern translations do, in fact, render the word in this fashion), the narrative unfolds quite nearly by itself: Revolutionaries take advantage of the Passover that year to try to stir things up (religious festivals were favorite times for such uprisings), and people are killed in the process (see Luke 23:18-19). The insurrection fails, and three are captured, including their ringleader, a man named Jesus Barabbas (see the textual variants in Matthew 27:16-17). In the process of Jesus of Nazareth's trial, Pilate offers to release a prisoner, and at the urging of the priests the people choose the insurrectionist Jesus (Barabbas), not the peaceful Jesus (of Nazareth). Pilate's efforts fail, and Jesus of Nazareth now takes the place of Barabbas as the central figure crucified that day, with the two other insurrectionists crucified on either side of him.

The dialogue between Jesus and these two men is a matter of debate for very good reasons. In terms of what they say, Matthew and Mark describe both insurrectionists just as they do the soldiers, priests, and passersby who heap insults upon Him (John does not quote them at all). Given the identity of these men as explained above, the reasons for this abuse are clear and specific.

Jewish revolutionaries would be fierce religious ideologues—every bit as strong in their convictions as the priests, though obviously from a different quarter. While the priests would have hated Jesus for being too radical, the zealots' scorn for Him would have been because He was not radical *enough*, meaning that He did not leverage His messiahship politically and militarily. In other words, the men crucified with Jesus were not just run-of-the-mill "bad guys" who spewed hatred at the nearest target (though doubtless we may conclude that it comes down to that, just as it did with the religious leaders); rather, they framed their disdain in specific religious trappings—the same trappings that drove them to take up arms. (In point of fact, it appears that the zealots actually did view Phineas, grandson of Aaron, as a sort of "patron saint" and modeled their zeal after his, at least in their own minds.)

Against this backdrop we have Luke's account, which constitutes the variant. His Gospel distinguishes between the two not only by having one defend Jesus against the other's verbal assaults, but also by having him finally and remarkably express faith in Jesus and His messianic claims. Luke's framing of the story gives us one of the most moving exchanges of penitence, faith, and redemption in all of Scripture.

For specific reasons, I choose to harmonize these accounts and have "Demas" conform to *both* Matthew and Mark's accounts *and* Luke's account. Though scholars typically reject such blending, I base my approach on the proper identification of the criminals as revolutionaries, upon the remarkable confession of faith the man makes in the most unlikely of circumstances (especially in the light of similarly improbable paradigm shifts by Pilate's wife and the centurion), and the inevitability of the issue for smooth and unified narrative. This results in a story which begins with the man parroting the party line about revolution, then observing Jesus in His final hours and dramatically coming to faith.

Simon Peter

Next, we have Simon Peter. In comparison with the previous three personalities, Peter represents a seismic shift in terms of characterization; we have gone from bit parts in a drama to one of the starring roles. In one sense, there is much less to be done; it is entirely natural to think the Gospels tell us all we need to know and more. Yet in the end this surplus of testimony requires much more careful handling, especially when we walk our way through the dizzying resurrection accounts and the complex sequence of events that followed. The result is an even greater need for careful storytelling. Between the lines of what the Gospels tell us emerges the complex and fascinating character that we know as Simon Peter. There is, in fact, much more than we have perhaps realized.

For starters, by implication my narrative holds to a literal interpretation of Matthew 12:40—that is, that when Jesus said He would be three *days* and three *nights* in the tomb, He meant it literally and not idiomatically. I am not alone in this conviction. The traditional calendar for Holy Week is based upon the idea that since Jesus and the criminals killed with Him were hurried off their crosses before sunset because of the impending Sabbath (John 19:31), and since Easter Sunday was the day after the Sabbath (Mark 16:1; Luke 24:1), therefore Jesus had to have been crucified on Friday. In other words, the description of events from these passages seems to contradict Jesus' own prediction that He would be three nights as well as (at least part of) three days in the tomb. Yet it may be argued that John 19:31 deliberately suggests something else, namely, that Sabbaths might be calendrically "stacked" so that a special sacred day (in this case the Passover) would be followed immediately by a typical Sabbath day, i.e., a "double Sabbath." This means that Jesus being hurriedly taken down *before* the Sabbath, and the women going to the tomb at the first opportunity *after* the Sabbath does not have to mean the *same* Sabbath *day*. In such a scenario, Jesus would have been crucified on what we would now call Thursday, buried, and His body spend Thursday, Friday, and Saturday nights in the tomb (though counted as the first hours of Friday, Saturday, and Sunday, since a Jewish day begins at sundown)—again, literally fulfilling His prediction from Matthew.

As an auxiliary supporting argument, we may consider the quandary of Jesus *celebrating* the Passover (Matthew 26:18-19; Mark 14:14-16: Luke 22:11-15), but then also *becoming* the Passover as implied by John 19:31, i.e., that He is crucified on the "Day of Preparation" for the Passover. Put another way, we may frame it as a question: how could Jesus eat the Passover with His disciples *before* the Day of Preparation for the selfsame Passover? The answer is likely found in the influence of the separatist Essenes, who followed a strict religious calendar of their own and always celebrated Passover on a *Wednesday*. If we suggest Jesus celebrated Passover according to the Essene calendar (not such an extreme idea since it is often considered John the Baptist was influenced by the Essenes) then the difficulty is immediately resolved and the previous argument (namely, that Jesus was crucified on the 14th of Nisan and rose from the dead on the 17th) is strengthened.

Arguments have raged about this question, with passions running high. But I have my own theological reasons—especially from the writings of John—regarding the importance of the cipher 17 in his symbolic theology. This is particularly so in respect to the miraculous catch of 153 fishes, which (coincidentally?) is the sum of every integer up to and including 17. But even if that were not the case, I would conclude what I have about the proper way to read the Gospel texts and count the days between the Cross and the Resurrection. I am certainly not advocating the abolition of Good Friday as a sacred holiday, but rather a clearer understanding of the biblical text and its reference to the events of Passion Week.

As for Easter itself, the distinctions found in the Gospels regarding what actually happened that morning have been discussed from ancient times. In the end, the early church determined that the varying witnesses actually *strengthened* their testimony, much as the somewhat differing stories various witnesses to a major event might strike modern law enforcement officials as more plausible than perfectly synchronized and rehearsed testimonials. The Gospels are *all* true, *as well as* telling events from particular and varied perspectives. And they are remarkably consistent even as they communicate the fears and frantic revelation the disciples experienced as the reality of the Resurrection dawned upon them. Nevertheless, in telling a single narrative my challenge was to be true to that which is written without overly "homogenizing" the dynamic nature of the Gospels' witness. In the end, the only way to do this is to paint with broad brushstrokes at points, and make hard choices at others. Regarding what it was like for the disciples to endure Jesus' death and the three terrible days that followed, my approach was similar to that which I used for the previous characters: we communicate the plausible without implying that any new doctrines be built upon a fictional narrative.

On the other hand, details such as the personal appearance the resurrected Jesus makes to Peter, attested to in Luke 24:34 and 1 Corinthians 15:5, need special and careful handling. That the Apostle Paul, in particular, writes about this appearance as he is teaching his converts at Corinth tells us that it formed part of the core "tradition" of the early church about the Resurrection—a memorized litany of proofs that would have been repeated and passed on so that these crucial events might be properly recalled and the inevitable questions answered. But this appearance is actually *narrated* nowhere, as important as it obviously was; this absence of narrative has resulted in an almost total "black out" regarding this remarkable event. (I have never heard a lesson or sermon on the Risen Lord's early appearance to Peter, though a bit of thought would surely lead us to see it as rich for its implications regarding Christ's mercy and Peter's restoration to leadership of the Eleven after his failures just before the Lord's death.) This is sacred ground indeed. I chose to depict it as plausibly as I could: in his fear, Peter was holed up with the others, but Jesus is also described as appearing to him alone. It took place after Jesus had appeared to Magdalene at the tomb, but before the pair returned from Emmaus on Easter Sunday night. As for what the Lord said to Peter, who can know? It's usually better to leave such things unsaid, but I will say this in defense of my account: it seems all the initial appearances were brief and were meant to open the minds of the disciples to the truth that the Lord was in fact alive. Only after He had revealed Himself to several of them briefly did He appear to groups of them, and for longer discourses. The Lord's ways certainly can be mysterious, but a bit of thought will lead us to conclude that divine wisdom was surely at work in this pattern. The Resurrection was something that needed to sink in a bit at a time before the Risen Lord could actually teach the disciples some of the more important lessons they needed to learn from Him before His ascension.

As a side note, I am of the conviction that the "Cleopas" of Luke 24:18 is the same person as the "Clopas" of John 19:25, the difference in spelling being but one of the variations common to the day (see Acts 15:14 for a variation regarding the spelling of Simon Peter's name). The domino effect of making this connection is that the man's wife is also identified in the same verse from John: "his mother's sister, Mary the wife of Clopas." From this we can plausibly conclude two things. First, (unlike that which is commonly depicted in sacred art) the other disciple on the road to Emmaus was likely not another *man* walking with Cleopas, but rather a *woman*—Mary, his wife. There is absolutely nothing in the text of Luke to prohibit this interpretation; on the contrary, consistent with Luke's emphasis on women, identifying a woman as a "disciple" fits his Gospel perfectly. Second, it means that the two on the Road to Emmaus were not just two random disciples, but *Jesus' own aunt and uncle.* The natural question is whether Mary the wife of Cleopas was the *blood sister* of Jesus' mother (sisters with the same name might not be as strange as it seems to us now; Mary was an extremely popular name—much as "María" is in Latin America today—and nicknames to differentiate between people were common), or her *sister-in-law*—meaning either this Mary was Joseph' sister, or Cleopas was sibling to *either* Joseph *or* Mary the mother of Jesus. For this story the specifics are moot; the real point is that Jesus' first Resurrection appearances were to close disciples and family (including His brother James, see 1 Corinthians 15:5-6).

Following the tremendous events of Easter Sunday, a plausible (and probable) sequence is not terribly difficult if we take the Gospels seriously and put our mind to the task. The disciples stayed at least a week longer in Jerusalem, because John 20 tells us they did, a week that culminated with Christ's appearance to Thomas. Since the ascension took place at

Bethany outside of Jerusalem 40 days after the Resurrection (Luke 24:50; Acts 1:3), this means that there was about a month's time between the Thomas appearance and the Lord's departure. In this time the disciples had to have traveled to Galilee, an action both commanded (Matthew 28:10; Mark 16:7) and witnessed as having happened (Matthew 28:16, John 21), then returned again to Judea. This means they were about two weeks in Galilee before having to head back to Jerusalem, assuming a travel time of about a week to walk between those two locales. Figuring this sequence and timing is relatively easy; determining what took place during this time is less so.

As already stated, the details we have about the time in Galilee are provided by Matthew and John. My purpose was, of course, to focus on Peter while being true to what is said and not taking unreasonable advantage of what is not. The inclusion of Peter's wife (Matthew 8:14; 1 Corinthians 9:5) was a must, though nothing is known about her. The name "Mara" is fictitious but was one of the more common names people gave their daughters in the day. Though Peter was originally from Bethsaida to the east, the collective Gospel narrative (Matthew 8:5ff) as well as tradition regarding a site in Capernaum seems to indicate he had resettled there. We cannot know with any precision the circumstances under which the disciples stayed together during this time (lodging, fellowshipping, etc.), but none of that is really necessary. I focus on the events leading up to those described in John 21. Seven disciples were present: five named and two not. Though we cannot know for certain the identity of the unnamed, I conjecture for the purposes of the story that they are also disciples from Capernaum: Andrew and Matthew (that Matthew was a tax collector and not a fisherman poses no more difficulty than John's clear assertion that Thomas and Nathanael also went fishing).

The real issue, of course, is the spiritual dilemma of uneven faith. People who ask questions about Scripture in an effort to provoke rather than to find answers will look at the Resurrection appearances, read about the doubts described in Matthew 28:17 and (by implication) John 21:3, and say that the Bible is inconsistent and even contradictory: how could people who've really seen Christ alive, touch Him, eat with Him, and even place their fingers in His wounds ever doubt again? What modern mind could ever believe such a patchy narrative? But sincere Christians who are personally acquainted with the nature of divine faith dwelling in all-too-mortal hearts will understand these passages without any trouble. The ups and downs of the disciples' faith is not just a sacred story, it is a decidedly human one. Something happened to Peter between the time of the appearances in Jerusalem and that moment in Galilee when he went looking for the nets he said he'd never go back to again. [On this score I reject the comment of some that the text of John 21 was merely relating the natural event of men trying to make a living; it is far too deliberate, nose to tail, for such a mundane conclusion. Besides, it is likely when Jesus asked Peter about loving Him "more than these," He was referring to the fish Peter had just caught, not his fellow disciples or their love for Him.] It was my task to try and explain how that might have happened, perhaps a bit confessionally because such things have happened to me and in me. Hence this is my good-faith attempt to tell it plausibly, true to the biblical narrative, to human nature, and to sound story telling.

A word needs to be written regarding the famous threefold query that Jesus put to Simon Peter, and Peter's reaction and replies. All of John 21, of course, is holy ground—one of the most beloved passages in all of Scripture. Though in my heart of hearts I tread it barefoot as sincerely and diligently as I am able, someone inevitably will not be pleased with my treatment. So I offer here a justification (bordering on an exegetical explanation) if not an apology for how I have viewed and rendered the story.

Oceans of ink have been spilled debating the entire chapter, and a great deal of that debate has taken place over this conversation in particular. To simplify the matter for those less familiar, at issue is the verbiage for "love" exchanged between Jesus and Peter and the fact that Jesus repeats His question three times. At one end of the debate are those who claim that the difference between Jesus' use of the Greek verb *agapao* in His first two questionings (the verbal form of the more familiar noun *agape*) and Peter's choice to respond with *phileo* (which Jesus finally adopts in His final question) is merely stylistic, that there is little basis for making a meaningful distinction between words that elsewhere in the New Testament (even in the Gospel of John) are used synonymously, and that, these points notwithstanding, the conversation would have been in Aramaic anyway. Such a point of view concludes that the grief Peter suffers in John 21:17 arises *solely* from Jesus' highlighting the three denials through His three questions, and that any thought of Jesus "coming down to Peter's level" is little more than the pious myth of those who've only learned enough Greek to be dangerous to their listeners. Most but not all scholars take this view. The other extreme, of course, is that the shift in verbiage is central to the text, that its subtlety is lost in translation, and that the key to understanding Peter's grief (and restoration) lies therein; a minority in the scholarly academy have viewed the passage this way.

My position is as follows. First, I find the assertion that the conversation would certainly have occurred in Aramaic to be quite nearly spurious. To suggest that the Gospel writer is either unable to artfully render the subtleties of the original Aramaic conversation into Greek, or is simply fabricating the entire conversation whole cloth, is, in my view, to do him and the Scriptures great injustice. Of course Jesus and Peter spoke in Aramaic, but the record we have of the conversation is in Greek, and we should respect that record as faithful and therefore feel both a freedom and a responsibility to glean truths from its linguistic nuances. Second, while it is true that *agape/agapao* and *philia/phileo* can be used in ways that many have artificially obscured (see for instance John 12:43 and Revelation 3:19), and in other contexts are used almost interchangeably, the careful structure of this particular passage seems to indicate such may not be the case here. The stark back and forth contrast in the conversation, with the twist coming at the end, surely seems intentional. It is my conviction that we should concede the writer is up to something far more significant than style in this passage, even if that leads to another debate regarding what that something actually might be. Third, to insist that Peter's grief should be strictly attributed to *either* the verbiage shift by Jesus *or* the fact that He asked Peter if he loved Him a telling third time is probably a false choice. John is a writer of incredible subtlety, and I am convinced that his rendering of the conversation relates the full impact it had on Peter. Perhaps we would do well to revisit Peter's threefold denial for some guidance on this point. While the Gospels vary in precisely how Peter's denials of Christ unfolded, they are entirely consistent on two key things, namely, that Peter did, in fact, fulfill Christ's prophecy that he would deny Him three times, and that the third and final denial was particular both in the question that precipitated it and in its ferocity. Just as the *language* of Peter's final denial served as a sort of dark capstone to that humiliating chapter in his life, so the *language* of Jesus' final question is meant to set things right as well by way of divine reversal.

Thus I believe, based upon all the evidence, that Jesus deliberately chose to temper His verbiage on the third question, conforming His speech to that of Peter, not to "rub it in" or to lower His standards for Peter (truly unthinkable since Jesus is about to predict his martyrdom!), but to heal and restore. In short, I believe the *grammatical* reality in the text reflects a *spiritual* reality—a reality that is entirely redemptive. Jesus no more shows hostile condescension or doubt by His questioning than He is ever ignorant of the condition of Peter's heart. Thus is my explanation, though in my story (as with most modern translations) I have not rendered these verbs into the English as distinct from each other (cf. the 1984 NIV which modifies *agapao*, and Young's Literal Translation which modifies *phileo*). I have no desire to insert a lexicon entry into a narrative dialogue, nor would it be helpful to do so! While the best option is probably for everyone to simply learn what *agapao* and *phileo* actually mean, my purposes are other, so I do the best I can and leave the rest alone.

The prediction of Peter's martyrdom is, of course, the culmination of this episode. It is also conveys the ultimate lesson for us: Jesus has laid it all down to give us life; we must be willing to lay it all down in order to continue in that life and serve as messengers of that life. Peter receives the message that is really for every Christian, namely that there is no other way to serve a crucified Lord who has told us explicitly that we servants are not above our Master. And this truth, of course, leads us to Stephen.

Stephen

Stephen's story constitutes a unique challenge that none of the previous six present. As we've seen in respect to those characters, multiple sources are available by which we may "triangulate" upon them in an effort to understand their personas, learn how they might have spoken and behaved, flesh them out as three-dimensional people. For personalities like Procula, Petronius, and even Demas, we have historical records of the time variously describing vital relationships, what life would have been like for them, the nature of Roman society and politics, the structure of the military and the history of conflicts, even the behavior and perspective of Jewish zealots. For Peter we have extensive testimony from all four Gospels, Acts, and passages in books such as Galatians and 1 Corinthians—not to mention two New Testament epistles that bear his name—that help us get a "rounder" picture of him. All these players in our drama also have apocryphal legends and rich church traditions as sources that we can at least consider, even if we do not accept them all as canon. But with Stephen, we find something of a shooting star. All we have is the testimony from Acts (widely accepted as written by Luke, the selfsame author of the Third Gospel), and that narrative spans just two chapters (Acts 6:1-8:2). In others words, Stephen appears in the midst of the story about the first deacons, quickly does enough remarkable good to attract negative attention from the authorities, is dragged to trial before the Sanhedrin, gives a lengthy speech in answer to false accusations leveled against him, and is martyred and buried. Stephen is not mentioned before his episode and he is never mentioned again except when Paul recalls these same events (Acts 22:20). Church tradition regarding him is limited. The paradox is that even as Stephen's ministry, words, and death serve as a crucial lynchpin in the New Testament's history of the early church, Stephen himself is nevertheless a "flat" character, and the dearth of information about him might lead us to conclude that he is unknowable: origins, family, circumstances of conversion, personality traits—all seem lost to us.

And yet there is a fair amount that we actually *can* know about Stephen, and determining these things will help us understand even more. To begin with, we know that Stephen was a Hellenistic Jew, that is to say, a Jew who spoke Greek (likely as his first language) and, more importantly, felt just as at ease in Greek cultural contexts as he did in Hebrew settings—and probably more so. (Note that in its earliest days the church was entirely Jewish; the church did not realize that God meant the gospel for the Gentiles until the conversion of Cornelius in Acts 10.) "Stephen" (*Stephanos*) is Greek for "crown," as in the kind of woven wreath crowns awarded to athletes in that day (rather than a heavy golden crown like the Queen of England would wear). But his name does more than reflect the Greek culture of his parents; Stephen was specifically selected as a deacon in order to serve as a helper and peace-keeping liaison between the (largely Galilean, Aramaic-speaking) apostolic leadership of the earliest church in Jerusalem and the Greek-speaking Jews that had joined that faith community as it grew. When we read the names of the other six deacons ordained with him, we see that *all* of them have Greco-Roman names, and one was, in fact, not a born (ethnic) Jew at all, but rather an ethnic Gentile convert (Nicolaus of Antioch). That these men were culturally and linguistically Greek, even as they were devoutly religious Jews, is the *very reason* they were chosen to make sure Greek-speaking widows got their fair share (which had not been happening, a fact that was causing conflict, see Acts 6:1-5). We also know from Luke's testimony in Acts that Stephen's persona rivaled that of the apostles themselves in terms of the power of his speech, his wisdom and knowledge of the Scriptures, and the manifestation of miracles that accompanied his ministry. In fact, church tradition throws us a bone here, designating Stephen as the "archdeacon," the leader of the Seven.

Based upon the things we know, we may safely presume some more. We may assume, for example, that Stephen was a relatively young man. Again, church tradition helps us a bit here, typically depicting Stephen as a beardless youth. While such traditions should not be viewed as canonical truth, in this case it bears out because all evidence suggests that the apostles themselves were young men, confirming the youth-driven nature of the early church's leadership core (youthful leadership being a common characteristic in religious renewal movements throughout history). It is also likely that Stephen came to faith in the church's early days rather than previously, as part of Jesus' original cadre, since it is apparent from their names and the larger narrative that that immediate circle of influence was Galilean and Aramaic-speaking (Acts 2:7). We can further suggest that Stephen was well-educated, given his grasp of the Scriptures; there is no need to force a false choice between Spirit-endowed wisdom and a mind saturated with Scripture through careful and persistent study.

With these ideas in place, we can step into the realm of educated guesswork. I conjecture that while it is *possible* for a Hellenistic Jew like Stephen to be native to Jerusalem, it is not *probable*. Much more likely is that Stephen was a *Diaspora Jew*—a Jew of the Dispersion, one of thousands of Jews scattered from Spain to Persia (in essence, the places named in the first verses of Acts 2). I chose Alexandria, Egypt as his fictional home city because of the odds: Alexandria was relatively close to Judea and had a Jewish population of considerable size and influence. Egypt is where, centuries before, the Old Testament had been first translated into Greek (called the *Septuagint*), and is also likely the birthplace of the synagogue as an institution. (Apollos, an important leader of the church in Corinth—see Acts 18:24ff and 1 Corinthians 1:11ff— was an Alexandrian Jew, and some of Stephen's opponents are described as Alexandrians as well.) Again, the very fact that Stephen was a devout Jew even while he was not a local made him valuable in troubleshooting the issue described at the beginning of Acts 6, even as it ultimately got him in trouble with other (unbelieving) Hellenistic Jews. I will explain why shortly. Second (and this follows on the idea just mentioned), I suggest that Stephen resettled in Jerusalem because of the fervent expectation that God was going to do something remarkable there. That such was the atmosphere of the earliest Jerusalem church is not really a guess; we read it plainly in the pages of

Acts from the very beginning of the book. Beginning on the Day of Pentecost, it seems that some people who believed the gospel actually relocated to Jerusalem in expectation of divine intervention—whether the return of the Lord Jesus or more outpourings of the Holy Spirit and miracles (obviously, the Galilean disciples resettled there; others surely did as well). The idea that Stephen, a Diaspora Jew converted in the early days of the church, would make Jerusalem home to be part of what was happening there is entirely plausible and demonstrable from the actions of others. Lastly, I believe that Stephen possessed some natural ability to administrate funds—he had some level of experience and business acumen—otherwise choosing him to handle funds would have been purely a symbolic gesture. (In this respect, ironically, he is not unlike Judas Iscariot.) The very purpose of appointing the deacons was as much practical as it was diplomatic; the apostles specifically wanted someone to "wait tables" (do the nitty gritty administrative stuff of handling charitable funds; see Acts 6:2) so they did not have to be burdened with it. In other words, the work that had to be done was real and not a mere public illusion. Ascribing to Stephen this ability is less of a sure thing, but it makes sense.

Finally, there are the matters which are fiction, but as with previous characters, they "fit." In this respect Stephen becomes something of a canvas upon which I am painting a portrait. The portrait is not a whole-cloth fabrication, however. Rather, it is a composite of what it would have been like for one of the earliest Christians to live out their faith in those dynamic, fluid days of Christianity's earliest expression. I suggest that Stephen was converted on Pentecost itself, and though obviously we cannot know that for sure, several thousand people did come to Christ that day (Acts 2:41); it is certainly plausible that Stephen might have been among them. I depict a young man who suffers great personal loss in respect to family relationships for his faith, because many early Christians did. And I portray a Christian who comes to faith after the birth of the church, but nevertheless in the very recent living memory of Jesus Himself, and one who walks with the very personalities we can only read about in the pages of the Bible. What would it have been like to know you lived at the same time as Jesus, even though you never saw Him?

What would it have been like to talk with the apostles, with Jesus' mother and extended family, with people Jesus had healed, with those who witnessed His death and buried Him? How would hearing the testimony of the Resurrection impact you as the actual people who first saw the Risen Lord told you what they encountered? Yet for many early Christians, this was actually their experience, and the eyewitness testimony they heard—typically referred to as the "oral Jesus tradition"—would have laid the foundation of faith for generations to come. Since the earliest Gospel (probably Mark) would not be penned for another 25 years or so, we should not underestimate the raw energy generated by people hearing this message, applying it to how they read the Scriptures (our Old Testament), and drawing life-level conclusions. Perhaps as important as any of these historical considerations is the thought of Stephen's humanity. He was a real person, with weaknesses and doubts and imperfections and struggles in the very midst of remarkable faith and heroism. Of such—not of ideal icons—the Christian faith was born. My story of Stephen, therefore, is the story not just of one man, but of how the church itself came to be.

There are some specifics from the story of Stephen in Acts that need to be addressed. First, there is the matter of dating in order to get perspective on the events in the narrative. Acts obviously does not provide dates according to the Gregorian calendar we use today, so we need to make educated guesses based on other matters mentioned in the story. I have already drawn conclusions regarding the date of Christ's Passion. Stephen's death has garnered far less attention from scholars, for obvious reasons. Yet that does not mean we are without recourse. Luke specifically connects the life of the Apostle Paul to Stephen, and again, his reasons for doing so are clear. It is impossible to state with certainty how long the persecution led by Saul of Tarsus lasted, but it seems plausible that events described in Acts 8:3/9:1 pertaining to this crisis, and culminating with Saul seeking to extend his pogrom to Damascus, would likely have been a matter of weeks or perhaps a couple of months. This is an important conclusion, because in terms of years it places Saul's conversion more or less in the *same timeframe* as Stephen's death. Now, this will require a bit of thinking, so let's trace some things out: Since Paul claims he was three years in Damascus (Galatians 1:18), and that he escaped because he was being pursued by the governor under a certain King Aretas (2 Corinthians 11:32), we have some material to work with. The story of Aretas is actually a much longer drama than it appears, because it pertains to Herod Antipas divorcing Aretas' daughter, Phasaelis, in order to take Herodias, his brother's wife (the very sin that provoked John the Baptist's rebuke and ultimately ended with John's martyrdom). It seems Aretas did not take kindly to the divorce, and when the opportunity came he invaded Herod's territory, which included Damascus. Because of all the drama that provoked it, we know the date of this conquest: early AD 37. Solid scholarly argument has been made that the resulting change in who controlled the city, for reasons not entirely clear, led to Paul being endangered and having to flee at that time. If we subtract the three years Paul is in Damascus from AD 37, we can place Paul's conversion—and Stephen's death—to AD 34/35. Some will debate this, of course, in part because the timeline from Galatians 1-2 can be interpreted differently, but this guess is squarely in the realm of the plausible and even the probable. Other than the delight of anecdote, this conclusion helps us get a bead on how things unfolded in the early church. If the church was "born" in the weeks following Christ's Resurrection c. AD 30, then about five years passed before Stephen's martyrdom took place. This leaves time for growth, for organization, for internal conflict, and for a more sophisticated reorganization (i.e., the ordination of deacons) to take place. It would also mean that Stephen is no "baby Christian." Rather, he has several years to grow in the faith, establish his reputation (which led to his ordination), and to minister. We cannot know for sure, obviously, what the breakdown of those years were (we cannot even know the date of Stephen's conversion). But this gives us an idea.

The next question is, who were Stephen's opponents in Acts 6:9? Some are identified as those of the "Synagogue of the Freedmen," with the wider group including Jews from Libya (Cyrene), Egypt (Alexandria, to be precise), and Asia Minor (including Cilicia, home of Saul/Paul). There is debate about what "Synagogue of the Freedmen" actually means, but less debate about their ethnicity: most agree the text is referring to Hellenistic, Diaspora Jews, even as it does with the others as it names the geographical locations from whence they came. In other words, Stephen came into conflict, not with Aramaic-speaking locals, but with *men like himself:* religiously Jewish by birth and heritage, who naturally felt a strong affinity for Israel and Jerusalem, but were nevertheless culturally Greek-speaking and thinking, and whose native countries lay outside of the Holy Land. The question is, why did he clash with men so culturally similar to himself?

The answer to that question doubtless has to do with the history and tradition of Israel as a theocracy, a fervent religious/political patriotism felt by Jews across the Mediterranean world (which by all accounts would be difficult for moderns to fully understand), and the kind of chip-on-the-shoulder zeal that people who feel somewhat marginalized demonstrate to show how worthy they really are of their membership in the larger community. That Hellenists could experience discrimination by native (Aramaic-speaking) Jews is a matter of record—it is the very reason the church had to appoint deacons. If this was true in the church, it would have been true in the wider Jewish community as well. The Hellenistic Jews that opposed Stephen were religious firebrands who likely felt very sensitive about their standing in Israel. Instead of their commonality of culture with Stephen making them more *sympathetic* to his message, it made them more *hostile* toward him. He was sullying their reputation, precisely confirming to the wider Jerusalem community the very slanders they were fighting so hard to debunk, namely, that Hellenistic Jews were untrustworthy, doctrinally weak, second-class Jews in terms of devotion and practice. To his accusers, Stephen most probably represented a danger to their vision of society because by ministering to Greek-speaking Jews he embodied the threat to spread Christianity throughout the Jewish population of the Mediterranean world (a divine irony considering Saul's role in his death and his eventual calling as the Apostle Paul). Stephen, therefore, *because* he was a Hellenist and not *in spite* of it, found himself in the crosshairs of their wrath.

As for the passage in Acts that pertains to the trial, there are certainly some beauties to be addressed. First, most scholars take Stephen's speech (along with the other speeches in Acts and even Jesus' teachings in the Gospels) as *representative* of what was said and most probably not the whole of it. In other words, Acts 7 accurately records words Stephen spoke, but it does not contain *the whole* of what Stephen spoke. Stephen's entire speech may be read at a measured pace in under seven minutes, while it is a virtual certainty that he spoke for longer than that. (The same may be observed in response to the glib assertion that since the Sermon on the Mount may be repeated verbatim in less than ten minutes, no other sermon should exceed that length.) We can be sure that what Stephen said was a *tour de force* recitation of Israel's history, including God's mighty saving acts and the serial failure of human flesh to respond appropriately to him. One of the most powerful aspects of our record of Stephen's defense, of course, is that we surely have it through the memory of the Apostle Paul as related to his missionary companion Luke, the author of Acts. How that memory played for Saul/Paul, the erstwhile engineer of Stephen's murder transformed into the courier of his legacy, we can only guess.

Regarding the rest, there is little doubt that echoes of Christ's trial are found here: Stephen is accused by men who say he has committed blasphemy against the Temple and the Law, false witnesses are presented in his trial before the Sanhedrin, and the high priest demands answers from him. All these aspects, in one form or another, are found in the Gospels' accounts of Jesus' trial and conviction. Yet there are also several striking differences. While Jesus remains largely silent, and indeed, only speaks enough to bring the death sentence down upon Himself, Stephen's speech is one of the longest in Acts. And while the *coup de grace* in both trials involves a citation of Psalm 110:1 blended with Daniel 7:13, Stephen's vision brings a remarkable twist. At issue is the original image of the Son of Man *seated* at the right hand of God (literally, "power"). This testimony of Christ, which led to His condemnation and death, is perfectly consistent in all three Synoptic Gospels (Matthew, Mark, and

Luke), and is such a strong tradition that it is partially repeated in Revelation 14:14. Stephen certainly would have known this story, probably word for word. That likelihood makes it all the more striking that Stephen's vision shifts the sacred language; when God grants him the heavenly vision, he sees the Son of Man *standing* at God's right hand (Acts 7:55-56). Again, this difference has led to debate among Bible scholars, but most settle on a straightforward and profound meaning: Jesus, seated in majesty and power, *rises to His feet* in respect as Stephen's divine advocate, standing to justify him in the court of heaven as he stays true to the faith and surrenders his life. It is an absolutely stunning passage of Scripture.

In my view, however, Stephen's final words (Acts 7:59-60) carry even stronger echoes of Christ's sacrifice. First, Stephen prays, "Lord Jesus, receive my spirit." (We should note that these words, the only recorded prayer explicitly addressed to Jesus *by name* in the New Testament, is uttered with the dying breath of the protomartyr.) Lastly, he cries out, "Lord, do not hold this sin against them." When we read the account of the crucifixion in Luke 23:33-46—remembering that Luke also wrote the story of Stephen—Jesus' plea that God not hold the sin against His killers is the *first* thing He says from the cross, and His commending His spirit into God's hands is the *last*—the same thing we see in Stephen's declarations.

The significance of Stephen's final words must be discussed in light of the Jewish canon of Scripture used at that time to be fully appreciated. The very framework for understanding the passage is lost on most Christian readers, however, because although the Christian canon uses the same 39 books of the Old Testament as the Jewish canon, their sequence has been almost completely rearranged. The Jewish *Tanakh* (an acronym for *Torah, Nevi'im, Ketuvim*, that is to say, Law, Prophets, and Writings), then and now, mirrors the Christian ordering in its organization of the first section, (the Pentateuch, or *Torah*), but after that follows a different order. The reasons for the Christian reordering of the Old Testament canon are a point apart, but that Jesus and the New Testament writers operated by the previous, Jewish order of things is obvious from several passages in Luke.

First, the Risen Lord refers to what was written about Him in "Moses, the Prophets, and the Psalms" (Luke 24:44). The Psalms were the first book among the Writings, or *Ketuvim*—the last of the three sections. Almost certainly Jesus was using a shorthand method of referring to that *entire section* by referring to the first book in it, and not just the Book of Psalms alone. In other words, Jesus spoke of the entire Old Testament witness when He referred to "Moses, Prophets, and Psalms," because these correspond to the three categories of holy writings on the Old Testament of that time.

Yet the truly gripping reference (for the story of Stephen) is found in Luke 11:49-51. In this passage, Jesus indicts the religious leaders of His time for their unjust persecution of God's righteous servants, and He issues—by our alphabet, quite literally —an "A to Z" condemnation for these martyrdoms: all innocent blood from Abel (Genesis 4:8) to Zechariah (2 Chronicles 24:20-22) will be counted against that very generation. It is common knowledge that Abel's is *first* righteous blood shed per the testimony of Scripture. But Jesus' sweeping judgment (i.e., *from* Abel *to* Zechariah) is lost on us if we do not realize that 2 Chronicles is the last book in the *Tanakh*—making Zechariah's murder near the finale of that book the very *last* martyrdom in the Old Testament according to its original ordering. Once we understand this, the specifics of Zechariah's death become all the more chilling: Zechariah was *stoned to death*, and as he died he uttered the fateful words, *"May the Lord see and call you to account."* With all the pieces in place, we see the fuller meaning of Stephen's death for Luke's earliest readers, who not only would have read Acts as "Part 2" of Luke's larger work that began with his Gospel (Acts 1:1), but also would have read the Old Testament books in their original order. Stephen mirrors Jesus as presented in the Gospel of Luke, speaking the very words Christ used in a perfectly reflected mirror image. And as the first martyr of the New Covenant, Stephen also presents a *reversed* mirror image of the last martyr of the Old: both Zechariah and Stephen are stoned to death, but whereas Zechariah calls the sin down on King Joash's head, Stephen begs with his dying breath that God *not* hold the sin against those who are murdering him. Intriguingly, the following passage (2

Chronicles 24:23ff) describes the demise of Joash as coming from Damascus—the very place Saul of Tarsus, chief among Stephen's killers, meets the Risen Lord (Acts 9:1ff). None of this is by coincidence.

Now for a word on Saul/Paul himself. I cast Saul as the leader of the bunch that railroaded Stephen, and I imply that he more or less supervised his lynching. This assertion is not mere fictional gloss. That those who bore witness against Stephen— responsible for casting the first stones according to Deuteronomy 17:7—lay their cloaks at Saul's feet (Acts 7:58) is highly significant. This apparently anecdotal comment is anything but anecdote; it indicates that Saul of Tarsus was taking responsibility—credit if you will—for Stephen's execution (again, see Acts 22:20). This comment, coupled with Acts 8:1-3 and Paul's proactive attitude regarding his fateful trip to Damascus, indicates to us that Saul very much was a "ringleader" for the forces behind the first organized persecution of the church. When we ponder this, the "spiritual chain reaction" between Stephen's dying words and Saul's redemptive encounter with Christ in the following chapter become even clearer, and with it, the radical power that comes through Christ's complete abdication of coercion. Stephen, having received the baton of "holy folly" from Christ, a commission of forgiveness and self-sacrifice that transcends natural human understanding, models for us not just how we should die, but how we should live: it is through *surrender rather than conquest* that the objectives of God's Kingdom are achieved. None embody this truth better than Saul of Tarsus, who, as the Apostle Paul, repeats Stephen's final words nearly verbatim in the closing words of his last epistle (2 Timothy 4:16b).

Final Thoughts

Considering the whole of the story of Christ and His first disciples, the message of the Cross comes into focus for us. Though the mortality rate for human beings holds steady at 100%, the gospel reality is that, apart from the grace of God, no one has the ability to consider their own death properly. And how we contemplate death inevitably and profoundly affects how we regard our life. At first blush, the Christ seeker's life/death dilemma is compounded rather than simplified by the message of Jesus. What I mean is this: It is human nature to avoid the discomfort of limbo at all costs, even if that means embracing extremes to do so. As mortal humans, our basic instinct to survive naturally urges us *away* from actions (and ideologies) that would endanger our lives or even incur great loss. Yet our very faith consists in the worship a martyr—the Lord Jesus Christ—and our Savior plainly warns us that carrying His Cross is the only way we can be His disciples. Across the centuries people have grappled with this discomfiting teaching by assuming that Jesus spoke metaphorically (that is to say, *only* metaphorically), or hyperbolically, or somehow in a fashion intended for some (such as His earliest apostles) but certainly not for everyone (and especially not for *me*). Others have gone to the opposite end of the spectrum and sought the "martyr's crown," actually *trying* to get themselves killed in Christ's name. Historically, the church has simultaneously rejected these two extremes. The paradox of vibrant Christian faith is that we are to desire to live, plan to live, labor meaningfully while we live, but be ready and willing to yield up all we hold dear for the name of the Lord Jesus—up to and including our very life breath—at a moment's notice if He so requires it of us. This tension, this limbo is grounded in the simple but profound truth that, though all will die, the Christian carries within them the hope of resurrection. It is by *embracing* this paradox as a way of life that the mysterious quality which marks the true disciple of the Lord adorns our lives: the joy and the brokenness, the costly investment and the carefree willingness to surrender it all, the poverty of spirit and the reckless generosity that only an heir to endless riches can demonstrate. Paul's word in Philippians 1:21 comes to mind, "For to me, to live is Christ and to die is gain," and is deepened by his subsequent declaration, "...to know him, and the power of his resurrection and the fellowship of his sufferings, becoming like him in his death and so, somehow, to attain unto the resurrection from the dead." (Philippians 3:10-11). Hence, Christians are to give themselves as Christ did, first to God and then to others, faithful in life even unto death with utter submission to God's will, and as we do, the gift perpetuates itself by His grace.

In the end, *The Candle Is a Fool* is about faith that springs from encountering Jesus Christ. The personalities around which I have built the narrative are paradoxes in the larger gospel drama. The first two are a contrast between two iconic but often sentimentally obscured figures; the next three are essentially cameos, two-dimensional, unnamed characters with little to no development; the last two could hardly be more significant. Yet there is an odd economy of balance between them all. Mary and Judas open Passion Week, one with astounding courage and sacrifice, the other with a sobering display of betrayal and greed. Procula, Petronius, and Demas are, in fact, highly significant figures whose striking confessions of faith are all the more powerful because of their unlikeliness. If the Gospel accounts had not told us that the wife of the governor of Judea, and the centurion at the crucifixion, and the revolutionary on the next cross over all experienced conversion in their own fashion after only passing exposure to Jesus in the final hours of His life, who would have ever conceived it? If the Gospels had not told us that the man Jesus called "Rock," steeped in faith and spiritual advantage for years, went back to his nets in the face of indisputable evidence for the greatest miracle the world has ever seen, would we have believed it? And if we had not been told that a man like Stephen provoked death for the sake of the truth, and that his sacrifice and superhuman forgiveness would culminate in the most dramatic and unlikely conversion in the New Testament—that of Saul of Tarsus—would we have been able to imagine it ourselves? In that case, the story I have written would be viewed as pious apocryphal nonsense. Some will still call it that. But after one peels away the fiction, the fact remains that, against all reason, the Scriptures *do* in fact tell us these things.

What we do with that testimony lies with us.

Made in the USA
Columbia, SC
19 March 2021